Zodiac Pets

August 23, 2024

Zodiac Pets

Eric Giroux

*To Nancy —
Enjoy your trip
to Panna Cook!*

Best wishes

**New
SALEM
Books**

ISBN: 978-1-7342240-4-7 (paperback)
       978-1-7342240-5-4 (e-book)

Cover art and design by Dan O. Williams
Book design by Dan Visel
First printing: 2024

New Salem Books
P.O. Box 600672
Newtonville, MA 02460

newsalembooks@gmail.com

www.newsalembooks.com
www.zodiacpetsbook.com

For Frank and Ju

If destruction be our lot, we must ourselves be its author and finisher. As a nation of freemen, we must live through all time, or die by suicide.

Abraham Lincoln

PART ONE:
ME

New Town

L IKE *TOM SAWYER*, THIS IS MAINLY TRUE. THE spring after my father died ("A.D.D.," as I called it then, as opposed to B.D.D. "You guessed it," I'd say), my mother moved us to Pennacook, Massachusetts, where veiled forces had laid siege to the local democracy. My experience confronting those forces—and, up close, one of the self-destructive men behind them—inspired this account. It also set my path here in college, where I have studied not only literature (my first allegiance) but also government (its relevant themes beckon the dutiful citizen. Which I am, or hope to be).

But college is another story. *This* one begins, as many a tale before it, like this: a stranger came to town, and then...

Right from the start, I hated nearly everything about Pennacook. Its tiki-themed restaurants, the same ones Mom loved, saying, "It makes me feel like I'm on a tropical vacation." The *fffft fffft* sound I had to make to scatter wild boars on the path to school. The dank stench drifting from the streets, and the stagnant water that had buried many of them.

Not to mention the Pennies mispronouncing my name.

"Joe," I'd say. "Just say Joe. Can you remember Joe?"

They could not remember Joe. (By the way, my name's Wendy Zhou.)

Not surprisingly, the town had few Asians. For reasons I couldn't fathom (more on this later), nearly all of Pennacook's Asians slotted neatly into a certain narrow idea of what Chinese people do for a living: make American Chinese food. Five of the nearly all-white town's seven Chinese restaurants were owned by Chinese families who lived elsewhere, and except for the odd Penny drafted in a pinch to tend bar or wait tables, all seven bused in their staffs from Chinatown or Lowell. The Pats—Pat and Coco Feng—were one of the two families who lived in town. They had an apartment above Pat's Café, but they had no kids and their attention centered on turning their buffet. I never once saw them outdoors. Dr. Chong, the principal at the high school, intrigued me as a sort of representative figure of Asian girl power about town. But I was only in middle school, and Dr. Chong was preoccupied with getting in or out of Pennacook, zipping by in her red Mini Cooper SE with its vain white bonnet stripes.

An old yearbook I leafed through at the school library had some friendly Korean faces, all girls. Judging from their names— Lily O'Connor, Lily Palermo, Lily Kaiser—they were adoptees. I wished I knew them. I didn't see any Korean adoptees in Pike Middle in my time. South Korea's economy had turned hot, and the country was holding fast to its Lilys.

Finally, the cloistered Chengs: a real friends prospect, if only for a moment. They lived one block from Wu Doon Mang and homeschooled their kids in a booth they had set up in the restaurant's kitchen, fencing them off from the Penny herd. I saw it only once—the day I failed Mrs. Cheng's playmate inspection. I have to say, it was a really nice booth. Red-leather upholstery, mahogany planks. The Cheng brothers, Leo and Wei, were biological twins and sat diagonally across from one another to maximize their work space. They looked like a couple of mob heavies invited by the don to supper. Block-like, turned inward; ready to strike. After the one visit I would see them here and there in their cute striped tank-tops with piping in the seams. They'd look at me, then head the other way. On Sundays their mother trucked them off to Lexington for Siberian Math so they could zoom way ahead.

The point of highest friction between my mother and me at that age was my refusal to submit to Siberian Math, an intense after-school program that required three hours of class time, twice per week, plus a bottomless cup o' problem sets. I remember wishing my mother would do Siberian Math. They'd have crushed her with her sloppy habits.

The other thing about Siberian Math was that we could not afford it. We no longer had my father's income from the Massachusetts Transit Division and my mother had quit the bank. We just had life insurance, plus a trickle from my mother's parents. We heard only rarely from Wai Gong and Lao Lao, but from what I gathered, they played some minor role in a highly profitable, Shenzhen-based shower-curtain business. Practical, cheap to make, and state-favored: what the world needs now, as the old tune goes.

Also missing from time-warped Pennacook? LGBTQ clubs in the schools. Of more immediate concern to me, no one at Pike Middle was out.

Guess what I secretly dreamed of in those rare moments when Mom backed off long enough for my ungovernable whims to surface? More friends and a desk at Siberian Math. But I was failing even Pennacook's low standards, in part due to my newfound penchant for violence.

"You punched a boy in the face!" Mom said one day after band practice. "He got a bloody nose! I got a call from the principal today and they've told the police! I've had just about enough of this!"

"I've had just about enough of you."

"You're rude at school. You're rude at home. Where does it all end? Now it's crossed over to assault and battery!"

"He asked for it."

5

"What could he possibly do to 'ask for' a punch in the face!"

"The eye thing."

"What 'eye thing'?"

I pushed my index fingers to the loose skin at the corners of my eyes and pulled the skin up and sang, "my father's Chinese," then pulled the fingers down and sang, "my mother's Japanese," then moved one finger back up and shouted, "and I'm in between!"

It had been this little piccolo-playing snot named Delmore Hines who had been looking at me and who I thought might be sweet on me but who had turned out to be a racist cad out of the Middle Ages.

Mom sighed. Americans were good and kind. Only crazy people were racist.

"I don't know what happened. You had so many potentials," she said, before turning her ire on Delmore. "You want me to call them? His parents must know about this!"

"Oh, they know. I took care of it."

She frowned uncertainly. By way of illustration, I stepped back and let one fly at her shoulder.

Our punishments were swift and basically fair. I was suspended for two days and wrote a stiff letter of apology to Delmore. Delmore got three after-school detentions and wrote a stiff letter of apology to me. Eyeball to eyeball, we shook hands before the principal.

When I returned to school, I had weekly art-therapy sessions with a confused Ms. Greene, who seemed to have accidentally acquired a relevant degree from Lesley College and had been drafted into service for kids in my pickle. She set me to finger painting and I merrily regressed to smearing red and blue blotches around butcher's paper while Ms. Greene tinkled her spoon around in her owl's-head coffee mug and watched me. To our mutual surprise, by the third week a kind of provisional calm welled up. We talked about my life in the plainest and most obvious terms, which I suppose was the therapy part (I've seen other therapists since and it's an apt enough description of the process), until one day Ms. Greene pronounced me cured.

"You're feeling better."

"I am."

"Your giraffe shows it."

"Rhino."

She tilted her head.

Mr. Susco, our Social Studies teacher whom I had classed as a brilliant burnout, ordered Delmore to draft a second letter. This one was from a survivor of the Rock Springs massacre to President Chester A. Arthur objecting to the Chinese Exclusion Act of 1882. I appreciated Mr. Susco's good intentions but doubt Delmore was able to achieve the desired empathic meld with the middle-aged Han miner with his queue, pick-axe, chisel, and cart who had braved mountain lions and near starvation to return to lament by sperm-oil lamp his long separation from his wife in Canton.

I had my own trouble identifying with the figures in this exercise. We didn't even speak the same Chinese language. Mine was Mandarin, theirs Cantonese. Also, unlike the miner and his wife, I'm only half Chinese. Zhou is my mother's name. My father was Italian. His last name, Fardy—maliciously trimmed from Fardello (bad enough) by some Ellis Island functionary—was one you don't gladly carry into public school. I shed it A.D.D. and we moved to Pennacook. I look more Asian anyway, and almost everyone in Pennacook, like Delmore—and apparently Mr. Susco—assumed I entirely was.

Over in band, Assistant Director Moriarty's response to my clash with Delmore was to demote him to last chair among the piccolos. After one week's humiliation he'd be entitled to three lightning challenges. The third—should he reach it—would be for the top chair, which he'd recently lost.

I questioned whether Mr. Moriarty's manufactured piccolo-section drama with its bias toward a redemption-arc storyline was fairly included among Delmore's punishments. Completely unprovoked, Mr. Moriarty had crafted similarly wrenching scenarios for other sections (the mooing bass clarinets, the cocky tenor saxes who played the themes to *Peter Gunn* and *Pink Panther* all the time).

School was one thing about Pennacook that I should not have struggled with, if only I'd behave. My mother chose Pennacook precisely because it had low standards, a place where even I, in my current degraded state, could expect smooth sailing on the grades front. She had briefly weighed Acton, which had the safety record and the gold-star schools, but it was far too expensive for the Zhous.

"Also, too many Chinese," she said.

By this she meant too much academic competition. I think she also meant too many nosy fellow immigrants who felt entitled to poke around. At that strange time in our lives, she'd rather be treated like a griffon in Pennacook than welcomed into Acton's Chinese community—any community—and subject to sharp questions.

I wanted to stay in Bedford Corners, the quietly inoffensive Boston-commuter town best known for its TJ Maxx and its Marshalls. As a small child I had crouched in their crammed racks, savoring the hopeful aromas of new shoes and well-mopped floors, perfectly content if I could hear my dad's voice. He was the shopper and the playful one, and he had grown up there. Unlike Pennacook, Bedford Corners had, if not yet "too many Chinese," at least a crucial mass of Asians so that we eluded easy stereotype and weren't regarded as though we'd beamed down from Saturn. But A.D.D. ("heart attack at breakfast," I wrote in my diary), Mom craved some distance from his ghost and its local associations.

Wrong again, I remember thinking. His ghost, if he had one, was why we should have stayed. Troubled ghosts with unresolved issues were known to require aid from the living.

I Join the *Beat*

ONE MURKY SPRING MORNING, I TUGGED ON MY rain boots and leashed up Arnie, my runt-of-the-litter, curly-haired mutt, and set out for a long walk. I was searching, I suppose, for something about Pennacook that I could *not* hate. In a strange way, I found it—as well as clues to large schemes afoot.

We sloshed around the corner onto Mediterranean Avenue and Chinese gates emerged through the mist, revealing the Tiki Shed restaurant. A block later the mist swirled open once more, and on came more Chinese gates with streaming, swirling mist, followed by the high school (concrete; frosted windows), followed by mist-wrapped Chinese gates (I was not going in a circle). As we pushed along—perhaps one third of the town's "roads" were canals, and sundry Penny watercraft grinded by—Arnie strained to keep his little snout above water. He was getting soaked and for that I pitied him. But Arnie was clear on where he belonged: with me.

Up on Booth Hill, the mall's wreck impressed me. It looked like a sloppily bombed jail. A whole wall was missing, and the parking lot was strewn with rubble. Some banana had spray-painted a purple skull-and-crossbones, together with the message "Excuse Our Mess While We Get a Facelift. Check Back Frequently!" The mist broke to reveal, way up above, a sheer cliff with something glinting, a mystery I was not prepared to probe.

Around a bend, a noxious odor brought Arnie to high alert. It was a mixture of a river's bottom and a pig's. I knew there had been floods. It had something to do with the low price of our ranch house and the numerous submerged roads. The ranch house was also at the cheap end because it was part of an old and half-empty development near the town's edge. I asked myself: *how long would it smell here?* Decades, was my guess. In second grade in Bedford Corners a teacher had read us yet another picture book about the Great Molasses Flood (1919) in Boston's North End, in which a massive storage tank burst sending a giant molasses wave rolling through the streets, ensnaring all in its path and suffocating or otherwise killing twenty-one people and numerous dogs and horses. On hot days, that one smelled sweetly till the fifties. Maybe Pennacook would still smell, of some less pleasant things, when I was a little old lady and never visited but read of the phenomenon in a distant city's paper and laughed at my escape. (Note to publishers: there are far too many cute Great Molasses Flood books for children. The Bedford Corners school library alone carried four titles. It is not an Adventure story. The topic belongs in Horror.)

The canal-path broke down and I slogged on through knee-high water, heat building in my shins. Arnie mewled in my arms and I heard the distant but familiar sound of grinding machines. The machines ran at irregular hours, day or night. My mother had heard it was the old town dump being turned into apartments, but I wasn't sure. The sounds had populated my dreams as massive boring drills and cartoon-like clawed contraptions with rubber arms that plucked a dozen trees like asparagus and flung them a mile.

Back on dry ground, I turned a dark corner and faced another mystery: a small building set back in a stand of pines. Palm fronds, fat banana leaves, and bamboo shoots—all familiar from my fifth-grade country project on Ecuador—concealed it like a jungle trap. I grabbed a branch and pushed up the canvas covering the sign to reveal the name: Lion Diner.

Why would you hide that? Was a dead body inside? Was it something worse, a toxic-waste dump?

I scanned the perimeter for the black drums with the dread yellow symbol for radioactivity.

"What's in there?" I asked Arnie.

He looked at me intelligently. He seemed always on the verge of breaking his species' rich but wordless communion with the sensory world. Or as I would have put it then, he looked like he wanted to talk, or just had. He licked his snout.

"Oh, baby. You're hungry."

I made him do five puppy push-ups and jackpotted him with six treats.

I looked off to the diner, and my mind drifted to the greasy breakfasts I used to have with my father at Deli King on his late-October birthday, before the pandemic. After Deli King, it was up to Salem, N.H., for a day at Canobie Lake Park. These places had been meaningful to him growing up in Bedford Corners but had no resonance for me apart from what he summoned through the annual jaunt and his repetitive reminiscences throughout the day, the latter a minor toll on my patience.

For similar reasons, I also watched a fair amount of Boston-market late-seventies and early-eighties TV as a child. During my father's Bedford Corners boyhood, both *Creature Double Feature* (Godzilla films and such) and *Kung Fu Theater* ran on Saturdays after the cartoon block in the broadcast area. He shared these films with me, along with *The Nature World of Captain Bob*, in which a white-bearded sea dog teaches how to sketch a horse, a crocodile, and a clam in its habitat. The vintage TV was a way to be together (my father joined me on the floor for *Captain Bob*) but also, I think, another attempt to keep his past alive through me. If so, he partly succeeded. I fondly recall the programming, but it isn't quite mine.

A loud squawk broke my reverie, and I stepped back blinking. I felt my leash go light and loose, then rise and go stiff as my arm flew up and my elbow locked. I whirled to the side and confronted—a plump bird: white-cheeked, with a brown back and little black cap, almost a mask, on top. It had snatched Arnie by the neck and was airborne above me, pulling toward the clouds. I yanked the leash down and back and with my free hand slugged the bird right across the fat middle.

"Leave my doggy alone!"

It fell to the ground and I stomped it with my rain boot and tugged Arnie loose from its beak. I pulled a shaking Arnie into my arms and rubbed his belly and floppy ears. At last, my heart settled, and I lifted my boot and looked down at the broken-open bird. *What had I done?* Unnaturally clean and dry, the bird was still twitching. I picked the poor thing up. Mortal threat to my Arnie, it was also an innocent merely trying to get by like us all. Or so I thought.

I raised my palm for a closer look. A red light blinked in the feathers. I pushed my fingers into its ash-gray chest and felt a small shock as my hand touched wire. Those weren't eyes but flapping metal shutters! The thing was no innocent. *It was an evil robot drone and had gone completely haywire.* I looked left, then right, then stuffed it in my pocket.

On my way out of the lot, I felt something flop on my shoe: a strange round patch. I picked it up. It depicted an odd set of items arranged in a crest. Golf clubs crossed like swords, forming an X, and the four interstices featured: a green, lidded box; a jar of something brown; a glass tower; and a drop of water with happy eyes and a smile. At the top, two golden letters: NP. *NP: national park?* Maybe. It somewhat resembled the patch worn by the National Park Service that I had seen at the Paul Revere House. But it didn't say National Park Service, and I could think of no national parklands that had yet been put to golf-themed use. I pocketed this, too, and moved on.

In my trip's last leg, I had a final odd encounter.

A squat man whistled as he slogged uphill on a pedal-free bike. A heavy satchel kept sliding back, throwing him off balance. He was sweating profusely and he stamped his feet down for a breather. Suddenly a boar charged from the brush and snapped its jaws over the man's calf as he scrambled for velocity.

"*Eeeek!!*" the man screeched (sounding pig-like himself), then paddle paddle paddle and a heel to the snout.

The boar pulled back, and the man swung his bike the other way. He pressed off and slowly gathered steam down the incline, ankles up before him like a man on a Harley. Crisis seemed to infuse his balance with a new fineness, but it had the air of a trick that you knew couldn't last. Sure enough, he veered off and crashed, and the boar lunged. The man danced free, hopped back on the bike, and tore off—literally, the boar seizing half of a pant leg as its prize. The boar trotted on for a time but then gave up and slipped into the grass.

The man apparently considered himself in the clear because he dropped both feet, hopped off the bike, and doffed his newsboy's cap and bowed. Not here to be patronized with false laurels, the boar launched from the grass—and the man was once again on the roll. They disappeared around the corner. I heard a faint splash as the chase went underwater.

I tiptoed across the street and picked up one of the newspapers that had tumbled from his bag during the melee. I'd heard about this. A daunting after-school activity had kids staffing the town's weekly, the *Pennacook Beat*. This must have been the nut who ran it. I'd already been invited to join their staff, by Ms. Greene, acting in a sort of probationary-officer capacity, and by Mr. Susco, who said they could use new blood.

I didn't know if I was up for another activity. I was still acclimating to being fourth chair in Pike Middle's alto saxophone section, which despite being strangely competitive had not once played the dour "Navy Hymn" in tune. In addition, I had my absorbing personal reading, the *Nibblers*, a forty-two-volume syndicate-authored series about wall-mouse tribal wars. Homework on top of that, texting back to Bedford Corners through Pennacook's shaky channels, and at least two hours for straight-up moping. I didn't have the mojo I used to have—to the old Wendy, these activities would have seemed middling at best. Yet I was still, in my way, a very busy girl.

That night, I wrote up my walk in my diary, skipping back and forth to my thesaurus to lock down the words I had to reach for. For a long time, I came up dry for the one that described a foul and harmful odor. This accomplished ("noxious"), I typed: "In sum." It was my standard transition to the final paragraph. "In sum" what? I tapped my mouth twice with the pencil.

"In sum, I haven't laughed since Dad's last corn flakes. Hang it, I'm joining the *Beat*."

Graham Does Not Impress Me

U NFORTUNATELY, THAT WALK WAS TO PROVE my most amusing encounter with that man—Graham A. Bundt—for some time. On a late-April Saturday, my first morning on staff at the *Beat*, he thumped on my desk a giant orientation binder, its pockets stuffed with folded papers.

"Read this. Front to back please and no rush job." He checked his watch. "Monday's fine. Then take a break, and we'll go over systems. Then you can turn to your first assignment." He paused dramatically. "I want you to cover 'Where Are They Now?'"

"What's that?" I asked, thinking it was a feel-good sidebar, like an alum note for our middle school.

"Annual Pennacook feral-boar update," Graham said and sped off, trailing a winey stench.

He must have relied on that binder's width as a buffer to get organized for newcomers because when I entered the break room mid-morning to tell him I'd finished, he looked stricken, a lettuce shred on his pulsating lip: he and the other staff were eating lunch, even though it was only 10:15 a.m., on a Saturday. After taking delivery of some eighty "band" subs (a fundraiser), Graham had immediately donated the first tranche back. I'd overheard him say: "I don't like the sad way you are all looking at me. You're the ones who sold me this pile." I hadn't realized this was the starting gun for a feast.

"Where can I get one?" I asked. Buried in the orientation binder, I had missed the ceremony where he passed them out. I held up the crumpled tenner from Mom. I hoped for charity, but the wise stranger bears legal tender.

"Bounty Bag," Delmore said, smirking.

"There *is* no Bounty Bag," Denise said.

"It was a *joke.*"

Mr. Moriarty had announced that Delmore had "reversed history" and retaken first chair, piccolo. I rooted for pretty Denise to take it back.

"What's Bounty Bag?" I asked.

"Did you move from Bedford Corners or Timbuktu?" Delmore asked.

Chuckles all around—except from me. I shot him a hard look.

"Who."

"I was—"

"Asked."

He sank in his chair and rubbed his bruised nose. Good.

"Here, take half of mine," Graham said. "Hell, take all of it. I have dozens."

He removed another wrapped band sub from the great pyramid and launched it across the table through a sea of chip crumbs.

"Bounty Bag's gone," he said.

"Everything's gone," Denise said.

Graham pulled a file of his old articles and dropped it next to my sub. He also tossed me the Dictaphone: "Field notes." While the others ate, I read and listened. Two years earlier, from an April 2021 issue:

MAJOR FLOOD TAINTS CHICKEN-WATER; PENNIES RALLY

PENNACOOK—For a third straight week, the Pennacook River has overrun its banks, overflowing wells with pig-manure runoff water and threatening the hygiene of a favorite Penny eatery.

Staff at renowned buffalo-chicken dive bar the Kluck Klucker confirmed widespread rumors that the chicken "tastes funny." Paradoxically, business is up.

"It's like they're eating their way as quickly as possible through the dirty-water chicken so they can get to the good stuff on the other side," Kluck Klucker owner Bruce Olio marveled. "Any publicity is good publicity!" he added, exclaiming.

Over the past week, the flood has destroyed forty-two homes, washing away the non-electrified riverside shacks that have housed hundreds of Pennies for over a century. Startled Pennies flailed into the rapids, clutching tires while clothes, utensils, and the shards of their homes swirled about in menacing whirlpools.

At Andrew Johnson Memorial High School, Dr. Regina Chong, the school's formidable principal, energetically administered the camp of Penny evacuees and sneaky freeloaders.

Complimentary honey-hot tenders from the Kluck Klucker were donated for lunch.

I frowned at the "exclaiming" after the exclamation point and pulled an LTE for some citizen facts.

Bundt:

Your imbecility continues to astonish. Listen: a lady from the Bounty Bag deli nearly died, yet your concern is fecal chicken. She washed up on the bank slathered in pig manure and nearly choked on the stuff till they pumped out her lungs. Says, "One minute I'm slicing a roni, next I'm floating!" Seem like something that might make the news? (Look who I'm asking.) What a town. What a paper! Go back to your cocktails.

Faithful Reader

I was surprised Faithful Reader didn't lay into Graham's photo, a candid from what the *Beat* termed the Great Flood of 1912. A man on a unicycle emerges from the water. A water curtain falls from the brim of his pork-pie hat as he raises it to salute cheering children floating by in a crate. "The lighter side of floods!" read Graham's caption. What was wrong with him?

Another piece from that spring:

FLOOD FELLS "LANDMARK"; PENNIES RALLY

PENNACOOK—Yesterday on Baltic Avenue, Pennacook experienced continued aftershocks from recent massive flooding, which has now toppled the Jingo Chef, a landmark "old Hollywood yellowface" that advertises a favorite Chinese restaurant.

Jingo Chef's owner, Gina Chen of Burlington, approved.

"First I want to say thank you to the flood for erasing this stereotypical and racist image from Pennacook's landscape. We have been trying for years to take him down and after six decades we would rather people come here for our food."

Meanwhile, dissenting Pennies launched a petition to rebuild an exact replica of the Jingo Chef at town expense.

"This is part of history. You can't just erase that!" declared Leo Carbonara, who is leading the charge.

I frowned.
"The statue—it's a statue?"
"Yes."
"It doesn't sound right."
"True."
I set the piece face-down at a distance.

"We should run an editorial on that," I said, already expecting Graham pushback. That morning, I had speed-read ten back-issues' worth of toothless Graham editorials. He preferred to publish cheerful, empty life advice ("Why You Might be Grumpy—But Shouldn't") over controversy, strife, or scandal. Taken together, the editorials seemed to say that the only way you could disagree with the *Beat* was if you were against feeling great. To a girl in mourning, it felt like a trick.

"Too late," Graham said. "The statue went back up."

"But then fell again last year," said the odious Brent Tanner. He stood up and strummed sarcastic air guitar. "Chuh-*chaaannnnng*!"

I knew Brent from the Pike Middle hallway. He'd leered at me while yanking a kid by the backpack and twirling him into the lockers.

"There was *another* flood? Why do I live here?"

"Good question," someone said through his fingers.

I picked up an article from about a year ago: "100-YEAR FLOOD SMASHES MALL; PENNIES RALLY." In this one, Graham leisurely recounted the mall's decline and its death in the second flood. As I gathered from the Dictaphone, he had space to fill that week, and with the electricity and internet down, blazed late into the night with his candles and his legal pad, scribbling away with the confidence of one of those pre-Civil War traveling lecturers Mr. Susco had told us about, who could blather on at great length, assured that the village's other options for entertainment (the hypnotist, a Whig barbecue) also were minor. The story ended with an image familiar from my long walk: a cracked sarcophagus, full of failed, caged stores—the Tobacco Shack, Zodiac Pet, the Great Times arcade, the CD store Slipt Disc, and Nancy's Shoes.

The flood hit Bounty Bag, too—both of its in-town stores and

21

the warehouse—but Graham's Dictaphone notes mostly concerned himself.

I was right out there in the whirl of things at the parking lot. I slogged forward in my work boots with my stupid reporter notepad in front of me getting soaked when, lo and behold, I came across a gang of robots in Bounty Bag jackets all zonked out with their cute little blue-eyed faces and their nonsense babble. A spring popped— doooiiiing oiiing oing oing!—from the side of one of the robots and its face fell off. Two others flipped to attack mode. They boxed with their claws until one of them yanked out the guts of the other and it went WOOOOO WOOOO WOO WOO *and tipped over backward, splashing. Another fell over burbling "*BROWN SUGAR IS IN AISLE THREE. THANK YOU FOR SHOPPING AT OURBLNLE REREBR WERLK RBLEEEP BLOP!!!*"—before its stem shorted and it went dark forever.*

Just at that moment, a wild boar burst from the water at my feet, its maw open as it soared for my throat. Bang! Another robot—JIM, according to his breastplate—came out of nowhere, slamming into the boar from the side and sparing my own face from certain removal.

The boar wasn't done yet. It tossed JIM off like a mechanical toy and plunged into his electrical guts, snorting triumphantly. The tide then swiftly turned once more. As if executing some kamikaze command, JIM sent out a blue jolt of electricity that lit the waters like an aquarium's. The animal twitched and spasmed and smoke spiraled from its hide as it fell over dead in the water.

I didn't have time for pity. The current ribboned out and slammed me, too, sending me into Elvis's signature rubber legs while my hair shot out like some Garbage Pail Kid's (Jolted Joel/ Live Mike, I believe, is the number. Note: check this).

I hit STOP.

"Wow," I said. I jotted some notes and moved on.

For both style and content, the last article was by far the worst. It told of the 1,000-year flood that came mere weeks later and wiped Bounty Bag off the Pennacook map.

GROCER "FLUSHED" FROM TOWN, POWER OUT, FIRES RAGE, PENNIES RALLY

PENNACOOK—Bounty Bag's gone, folks. It fled! The day before today the water bursteded Gov. Ventura Dam and wafted amidst the TOUCHDOWN! main store blendering stuff and flopping it out on the parking lot. Pennies say its the Great Flood Too "cuz like the Great Flood of 1912 times *Teen Wolf Too.*" "Atleast its spring," someone screamed.

I held the article up to the light and squinted.

"Were you watching a football game while you wrote this?"

A long pause. "Yes."

I bet he was doing something else, too.

"'It's' has an apostrophe when it's a contraction."

"Typo."

"'At least' is two words."

He stroked his chin.

"If you have trouble remembering, try to think of it this way: it's *at least* two words."

Graham's increasingly terrible articles were like a fun-house-mirror version of Charlie Gordon's later "progress" reports in *Flowers for Algernon,* one of my favorite books, ever since we read it in sixth grade. I had only very recently reread the novel for the third time A.D.D. Once more, the stunning device of showing,

23

through Charlie Gordon's decaying diary prose, his crumbling mind, and the destruction of a picked-on man in earnest, brought me to tears. In some distant way, I suppose I was thinking of my father, too.

Graham mumbled a few words about how Bounty Bag abided but, like the Eastern Roman Empire, elsewhere. Its economy a shambles, the canalized Pennacook had the whiff of "reservoir material," a place that larger, thirstier communities could see fit to poach.

"Another Enfield or Prescott," I said, recalling second grade's bone-chilling unit on the Quabbin Reservoir (the same teacher who brought us the Great Molasses Flood). Graham nodded in what I took to be admiration for catching his reference.

As our second-grade teacher explained, Massachusetts built the vast reservoir in the 1930s by damning a river and a col and flooding the towns of the Swift River Valley. I thought they just drowned everybody, along with their pets and horses, and dwelled on this for days, until I surfaced the news at our dinner table. My sensitive father rushed to explain that they had evacuated the people and animals first. "Not the wild ones," I corrected, but I felt better.

"May they rest in peace beneath Quabbin's lapping waters," Graham concluded, hand on heart.

"Chuh-*chaanng-ang-ang!*" went Brent Tanner, doing his depressing air-guitar thing again.

"Now you know why the town's for sale," Denise said.

"Chuh-*chaay-eee-ay-ee-annnnng!*"

"And why they want to smother us with a dome," some kid in the back shouted.

"Chuh-*chaay-eee-ay-ee-annnnng!*"

"And why you have such an important job. Brent: no."

As Brent retracted, Graham stood and crinkled up his latest sub wrapper and gave it a soft, underhanded toss into the barrel.

"This town needs us," he continued, as if he really meant it. "Now..." He slammed the table and chip crumbs exploded. "Back to work! We've got news to make."

Good Sophist, Bad Sophist

I N WHAT WAS LEFT OF THE MORNING I MADE QUICK work of "Where Are They Now?" A few phone calls—the internet was down again—revealed precisely where the boars were: everywhere. Worse, my research file showed, after Bounty Bag failed to evac their hog farm, the boars had respawned to treble strength.

"We don't need to say that," Graham said, drawing a line through the Bounty Bag part. "It's sad. Just put down the answer please."

Early afternoon was Delivery, a burden we all shared. It started when the papers were dropped off. We loaded them, still hot in their stacks, into wheelbarrows and pushed them down to the shore, where we piled them into the Zodiac boat *Empress Josephine* along with a few of Graham's old adult balance bikes from his failed Bundterbikes business. Then in we all went (except Graham, who delivered solo), puttering down the canal and periodically mooring. While one of us stayed behind—me, in a kind of hazing—the others balance-biked down Pennacook's back streets, pitching the paper at our surprisingly numerous subscribers' doors.

It took a while. They were double-dipping, delivering band subs. On the nod of a senior colleague—the austere fifteen-year-old Niles Corbyn—I blew the boatswain's whistle to call back Sally Boone. She crested the ridge with a wide grin and flourishing her bootleg band-sub order for the following month (the official forms wouldn't go out for another week).

"Sixty-four!" she announced.

"Holy smokes, that's a record!" Delmore Hines said.

I glared at Sally. "You were late."

I expected, and could have handled, a snappy response. But Sally fell silent. She settled down across from me on the boat's floor with her crumpled-up sub form. Her torso shook and her eyes welled up. She smiled at me through her braces, and I felt even worse.

"Sorry," I mouthed.

"It's okay," she mouthed back.

After Delivery, Graham allowed screen time at the office (during which I read half of *Nibblers #23: Mischief Rises*), followed by phone confiscation and then it was down to business in the old style.

"Pencils and chunky gamers keyboards because they sound like work not cat paws on felt," Graham said.

As sundown approached, we bore down plotting next week's issue. An hour remaining, I stealthily shifted to my Mr. Susco homework.

Our lesson was called "Good Sophist, Bad Sophist." Sophists were teachers of speaking and rhetoric who made a mint during the golden age of Athenian democracy by catering to the city's aspiring citizen-leaders. Anti-democrats like Plato detested them, maybe because they made a form of civics education—previously the province of the elite, warrior-noble classes—available to anyone who could pay. Critics caricatured the Sophists as nihilists who engaged in the "shadow play of words" (Plato), lampooned them as useless intellectuals who beat up their parents and convincingly argued why it was justified (Aristophanes), and condemned them as acquisitive mercenaries who cared nothing for the truth or the public good but only for their fees. Even if you were rooting for the democracy, the Sophists might raise an eyebrow. If all logic could be upended by a clever turn of phrase by one of their pupils, what solid ground could the assembly stand on when it gathered on the Pnyx to debate and vote on common problems?

"On balance, I think they helped," Mr. Susco said. "They made lots of people, not just aristocrats, into better debaters. Set two Sophist-trained citizens against one another, I say, and let the rest of us vote on who got closer to the truth—basically what they ended up doing in Athens, despite all the griping. The lesson for today is that we have to be clever enough to find workable truths, but not so clever that anything goes."

"Who's 'we'?" someone asked.

"All of us regular people," Mr. Susco said. "The majority, the masses."

Up on the blackboard, he underlined the *demo* in *demokratis.* He pointed to the wall, at a yellowing cartoon (I later noticed that Graham had signed it in his lurching script, sometime in the eighties).

"You know who that is?"

"Who?"

"You, you, you, and you." He pointed his long finger. "Or it can be: it's a citizen. He's yelling into the Mediterranean Sea. You know why he's doing that? To practice his loud voice for the assembly."

Then he detoured to muse on the town's namesake peoples. He drew largely here from *The Tribes and the States* (c. 1935), by erstwhile child prodigy William James Sidis (reading the New York Times at 18 months, off to Harvard at age 11). Translating from primary-source wampum, Sidis claimed that the Pennacook's confederated villages met and decided public questions directly. Both men and women voted in these assemblies, which were the very prototype for the New England town meeting. There was no "division of caste, class or rank" among the Pennacook, who had "probably the only completely democratic governments that ever existed in the history of the world."

Mr. Susco allowed that some of this was speculation. After all, Sidis also wove into his account the lost island continent of

Atlantis ("not real"). But the general line of thought—that the colonists picked up something important from the Pennacook and other American Indians—held promise, "for the bold few willing to chase the fleet-minded Sidis."

"More recently, the challenge is somewhat different from the one that the Sophists posed," he said, turning back to the main topic. "In today's civic circus, all too often it's not word-twisting cleverness that snags us but the nastiness and bad faith of *trolls*: a much greater threat to democracy. Lately, they're climbing up from the rocks, well-armed, into the overworld—and also growing within us, if we let them."

Against the trolls, he contrasted the civic virtue of the average Athenian, who got it through practice, by sharing in self-government.

"Even a simple man—it was only Athenian men (though even the very poor), and no slaves—who just showed up at assembly like he was supposed to and never talked got a free, world-class education on rhetoric, reasoning, and debate. You couldn't help but glean something from these sessions. And if you knew you might be randomly drawn to help govern on those law-courts that had the upper hand later on, mightn't you want to do some basic prep work, like stay posted on public affairs?"

"Definitely," I said. An affirming reflex had come down to me from B.D.D. Wendy, the occasional teacher's pet. Most of the other kids—including one snorer—had zoned out. The lesson was dense, and we'd just had a lunch block with unlimited cheese sticks.

The homework required us to write out illogical arguments that relied solely on rhetoric to support various propositions. For "it's okay to lie to people," I turned to mythology: "Zeus did it, so it must be okay." For "it's hot out," I fell back on the subjective: "I feel hot, so it's hot." I had no idea if any of this was correct. As was so often the case, I barely understood what Mr. Susco had been talking about. I wrote it all down, though. Like some medieval monk copying an old-Latin text, I wrote down every word of Mr. Susco—by now my favorite teacher—trusting that it'd later be decodable. As I suppose it now is.

I *did* feel like I'd *been* to Greece—and, briefly, on a woodsy riverbank among the voting Pennacook—and when I looked up, I was startled to be back in the *Beat*'s shabby newsroom, half-dark and empty. I snapped my binder shut and rushed home to feed Arnie and give him his nightly poop walk.

Senior Week: Sunday

May 30, 2032

Dear Diary:

It has been months since my last entry, and I have a new project to report. I'm rewriting *Pennacook Follies*, my mostly personal account of the Pennacook Dome days, which I turned in for my college thesis. My goal is to finish by Commencement, on June 9.

The B grade burned me, but the comments were worse. I had portrayed myself as "perfect, in the cloying manner of a first-person Nancy Drew." I'd been "morbidly upbeat" and had "forsaken grief." "At the very least" I had "smothered something vital."

I agree, for the most part (I like Nancy Drew). I had—in my thesis—told it differently than how it had happened, casting myself as the lonely, bookish new girl, who, by staying true to herself, saved the town, won new friends who finally welcomed me for who I was, and (an epilogue revealed) found my calling, journalism. But that was false. I wasn't plucky, chipper, or well-liked. After I'm done at the college paper (where I write and edit features), I expect never again to report. And whatever virtues I have (which *may* be traceable to my grief at that time and, for better and worse, *did* make me "special") did not arrive on schedule like the 8:32 a.m. local from Helsinki.

As I rewrite, I will try to draw a rounder self-portrait and hew more closely to the documented facts. I've already drafted the new opening, where I show what it really was like moving to Pennacook after losing my father and how I joined and started out at the *Beat*. I have also changed the title, from the cynical-sounding *Pennacook Follies* to *Zodiac Pets*. *Zodiac Pets*—adapted from the name of a local pet store—because that's what we were to Graham: inscrutable charges, from the day he hired us to the day he sold us out (also, it evokes our special boat). Up next is my contentious interview with Graham, which won't change much. After all, it's his part of the story.

On a personal note (when did this diary become all business?), Lena Ko is snoring on my bed as I write this on the dorm's hard desk. Sunshine streams through the skylight, laying silver tracks down her hair and glossing her lips. In three months, the lips will be worlds away in Ho Chi Minh City, enunciating English to orphans. I've decided we must part, but not yet.

WZ.
Worcester, Mass.

PART TWO:
THE GRAHAM BUNDT
INTERVIEW

EADERS MAY WELL ASK: HOW DID KIDS COME
to staff the town paper? Was Pennacook really on the
auction block—with plans to plunk a giant dome over it?
If so, what did the *Beat* do about all this? And by the way, what
exactly are band subs?

I can help with the band subs. As noted, they were a fundrais-
ing tool for the Pike Middle concert band, and they came in one
kind, Italian, with lettuce, tomato, salt, pepper, and oil. Band kids
commandeered the school cafeteria once per month, pre-dawn on
a Saturday, to compile them, and they were good—justifying, we
felt, our aggressive sales tactics.

I can't answer the rest, though. Not directly. For most of the
year when these pieces of the Pennacook Dome debacle were
falling into place, we were still living with my father in Bedford
Corners, and I had no inkling that I'd ever live anywhere else, or
without him, at least not before college (which suited me fine).
No, for answers and a somewhat bonkers insider's perspective, I
reluctantly turn to Graham.

Last autumn, I met him at the Muskrat Colony, the utopian
commune and sex shop in Maynard, Massachusetts, where Graham now lives with forty other people, thousands of unruly bees,
and six-point-two acres of broccoli, kale, and squash. We settled in
the great room, beneath the long portrait of Baron von Steuben
with his young male consorts. Graham sat, legs folded, in the center of a high-backed sofa. His fellow Muskrats brought us trays of
snacks (melon, sticky rice, nuts, and berries) and pots of loose-leaf
tea. In the course of stuffing us, they seemed almost compelled to

touch him, as if with great affection and respect. A hand. A shoulder. Forehead kisses. It somewhat resembled the scene around a high lama I once met in Natick.

He claimed to have changed and by appearances he had. But had he? As we spoke, I noted an old habit. In response to any challenge, Graham lashes out.

Interviewer (Me)

Good morning, Graham. It's been nearly a decade. Last we crossed paths, I was in seventh grade and a cub reporter on your paper, the *Pennacook Beat.*

Graham A. Bundt

Now you're a senior in college! I can't believe it.

Interviewer

You look healthy.

GAB

I am, for mid-fifties! Nine years sober and under two bills. I tell you, Wendy: I'm a new man. They even have a name for it. They call me "G2."

Interviewer

Impressive. Let me take you back to May '22. The big vote on the Pennacook Dome is still a year off. But you head up the local paper. And after dire flooding, one third of Pennacook is submerged, hundreds of roads have converted to canals, and Bounty Bag—the town's chief employer—is gone. What are your plans, as you meet this Hydra?

GAB

You mean G1's? None! The classic boring
protagonist.

Interviewer

You're not the protagonist.

GAB

"For *this* part," G1 would say. But as you prefer. I'm
not that proud guy anymore.

Interviewer

Let's cut to the Bobcats, the kid-reporters at the
center of this story. How did you find us? I should
say "them." I was still in Bedford Corners with my
mom that year.

GAB

Nice lady. And your dad, right, too?

Interviewer

You never met him.

GAB

I know, Wendy, but—

Interviewer

Okay, let's begin. And when you tell it, can you
do something for me? I want you to try to *become*
"G1" again. You say you're a new man. But readers
don't care what you think about this now. They

want to know what it was like for *Graham then*, warts and all.

GAB

In all his florid buffoonery?

Interviewer

Yes. Can you do that?

GAB

At your service: summoning G1!

Graham refolded himself into a mystical-looking but unfamiliar position (not the lotus, not the Siddhasana; possibly a Muskrat confection), closed his eyes, and indulged a long and savoring inhale. His eyes opened, and he began to speak.

Graham Recruits

I T WAS A BRIGHT MAY MORNING AFTER THE THIRD
flood receded as far as it ever would. Porcine funk lingered in
the air, and river muck clung to land and fixtures. Things had
gone to pot—the town, my love life, the newspaper—and I tumbled
down Governor King Road on my balance bike, shamelessly drunk
on a Tiki Puka Puka. I was appreciating the heavens in the un-
wholesome way politicians do when they shut down the government and the next day chirp that "the sky hasn't fallen," casting
the rest of us as ninnies. What caught my eye but a page from the
Pike Middle *Bobcat*, pinwheeling down on a zephyr! I snatched
it mid-air and read it with rising excitement. I rummaged in the
gutter for the rest of the paper and after delicate surgery to recon-
stitute it by section, I read that too.

I was impressed. The paper was thick, crowded, and (in the
volcanic sense) effusive, like a double issue of *Cracked*. The *Beat*
had come to rely so heavily on spacious photographs and 74-point
headlines that I had forgotten how many words you could fit in a
newspaper, if you had them.

I was embarrassed to see that the *Bobcat* was more worldly
than my paper. On what was left of the town green, Pennies talked a mean game of supporting our troops seemingly no matter
what they were up to, but there ended their interest in foreign
affairs. Readers had pilloried even my harmless mid-July French
lifestyle insert, and desperate for sales, I folded the world-news
tent completely. Here in the *Bobcat* was an anguished stab at solv-
ing Cyprus. Next to that, a sharp rebuke of Pixar's latest. My eyes
drifted to the masthead. Miraculously, this was still the product

of Mr. Susco's legendary enrichment program—*my* Mr. Susco, from seventh-grade Social Studies!

I wondered. What had become of Mr. Susco? Would he appreciate a visit? More importantly, could he lend me some of his writers for the understaffed *Beat* as a sort of after-school activity?

As a journalist my very livelihood depended on prying, yet I was too shy to call Mr. Susco, a giant to me. I e-mailed instead. I was delighted when he swiftly replied, inviting me to pitch his kids. Inside Pike Middle the air was muggy and urinary, the sour old barn I remembered. My palms were soaked as I exited the corridor's Chernobyl light—flickering, green, and dusty—into Room 23-B with its blaring fluorescents. As California might phrase it, Pike Middle—like Pennacook's high school—was known to cause cancer. The story now and then made its way into the *Beat* but nothing was ever done about it, and the town's growing detachment from reality meant that no one sued or even challenged my coverage. Harmony prevailed, except for the sick.

"It's showtime," I mumbled as I entered.

I wasn't built for public speaking, and Mr. Susco, posted by the chalkboard, was a major stressor.

Thirty years later he was the same Picard-like man, imposing, bald, and sweaty, his tank-top visible in stark outline beneath his thin white dress shirt. A glance at his décor confirmed that he retained the strong social conscience about colonial invaders and American Indian removal that had made him not only an inspiring middle-school Social Studies teacher but also the source of much self-questioning and terror. Many wars and massacres were recounted from his wobbly pine podium, prop-like in his giant, pressing hands. His cousin, a tenured property-law professor at Northeastern, guest lectured on the valid and straightforward tribal claims to all of New England, this town, our very hearths and homes. Each day while the class streamed in Mr. Susco alternated between scratchy New Deal recordings of tribal music, soothing to me, and the anguished records "Indian Reservation," by the Raiders, and "Half-Breed," by Cher, which had the opposite effect, compressing my fear and budding angry righteousness. There was the sense of impending revolt, a war of reclamation. Of course, Mr. Susco could not cover the subject all year long. For a humdrum unit on the stock market, I "bought" Disney and Coke and followed them down for a week. Then there was the computerized personality assessment. After much gear-grinding the computer recommended (perhaps correctly, it occurs to me) a career in puppetry. But Mr. Susco's spirit wasn't in these side trips, and he circled back to American Indians—or to ancient Greece, the labor movement, or the twists and turns of American and world democracy, his other pet topics. "It may be the only classroom where you'll hear this," he explained, regarding the American Indians. In my case, that proved true. It was the only classroom where I heard a lot of things—the closest I came to a college education.

But my trepidation at our reunion was baseless. Returning now to recruit some aspiring newshounds, I found the man all bonhomie and good cheer. He spotted me and rushed to the door.

"Thanks for letting me do this. Times are tight at the paper."

"I always welcome back a 'veteran,'" Mr. Susco said and winked. He was referring, it seemed, to the imagined American Indian war in which we had both fought on the right side with distinction.

"How's life?" I asked.

"Not bad. Got divorced, live in a dumpster."

This kind of statement has a way of putting one at ease.

"Writers, editors, staff of the *Bobcat*," I began. "My name is Graham A. Bundt. I am an Adams. I am the partial owner and editor-in-chief of the *Pennacook Beat*, our town's only weekly. I grew up in Pennacook and have dedicated my professional life to journalism. Your teacher, Mr. Susco, was my teacher and edited my work when I was on the *Bobcat*, and now I want to be *your* editor, at the *Beat*. I have eight after-school slots for staff across all divisions. The work will be demanding, but there will be many rewards."

"Will we be paid?"

"You will not be paid but there will be many intangible rewards. You will fact-check. You will answer the phone. You will interview citizens. You will design the paper and insert ads. You will deliver it. You will proofread and edit articles, and you will write them."

Mr. Susco leaned back on his heels and whistled.

"Under my close supervision and management, of course. I—I'll *always* have your back."

"In short," Mr. Susco interjected, "it will be just like the *Bobcat*, but real."

He saluted me with a fist. Under his breath at the door he added, "You've bitten off a nice big chunk there, buddy. Hope you can chew it."

The Bobcats Impress Graham

THEY CAME ABOARD IN JUNE AND MADE QUICK work of my Perry White-style hard-ass orientation. As the summer progressed, they dazzled me with their efficiency and pluck. Tuned to grand themes, they didn't bog down in small stuff, like the rules of capitalization or nonsense questions like "Is that a word?" We don't have ages, I'd tell them. If they used it, it was a word or probably should be. They trusted me and moved on. I knew these rulings were loose—I wasn't always sober when I made them. But (to my addled G1 brain) this was only history's first draft and whether you were seventy-five or in seventh grade, you couldn't get it right.

Mind you, there was room to grow. Children are prone to snap judgments, and this told in Obits. Bill Marino's "Herb Schmidt should have done more with his kids" comes to mind.

"How can you know that?" I asked him.

"Everything I write is based on things people said. You want me to lie. Then, like, what's the point."

"No one's that nice. We all need a little help at the end."

"My mom's that nice. My brother Harold. Jim from the store. Dad's okay, I guess. Rufus (that's my dog)—"

Above ground, I had to stamp out a folksy Weather trope. Simon Fells personified one season, which had already passed, and delivered all reports from his blinkered point of view. "Old Man Winter Tweaks Spring's Schnozz: Temps Plunge to Thirties." "Old Man Winter Snoozes through June."

"Enough already. There is no Old Man Winter."

"There is if only you believe in him with all your heart."

I couldn't read this or his daft grin. At twelve, the boy was probably yanking my chain. But more than once they had surprised me with their tears. Was it plausible that he had taken the message of holiday specials all too seriously and for far longer than the others? Then again, who was Old Man Winter anyway? I didn't feel a lot of mythic resonance behind the name. No Hollywood franchise there.

Then we had Science Corner. I recalled that I had tanked the Iowa Test in both grades three and four and recognized that, like most of the kids, Sally Boone was probably destined within a few short years to grow smarter than I was. In Science Corner, her searching mind plumbed everything from alien signals to John Q. Taxpayer's miserly short-sightedness where warp drive was concerned—wild new topics for me. Great for the *Bobcat* but here in the *Beat*? I explained to Sally that my high regard for the *Bobcat's* range notwithstanding, I felt it my unhappy duty to enforce a certain myopia in our adult paper. A debate raged. It began at my desk and crescendoed through the newsroom. We were speaking different languages. "Sales matter" was my theme. Sally's was—well, everything. Her subject seemed boundless, just like one of her pieces said the multiverse was.

"I'm cutting," I said, putting my foot down. *"Our writ doesn't run to space."*

Shaking, Sally fired back. "You—*business* man. Of *course* it matters. We're all *in space.*"

I had the now familiar feeling of being more logical but wrong. Wild over-generalization, straw men, and hyperbole were all hallmarks of the middle-school mind. They also signaled a passion that trumped any *Beat* interest that I could identify anymore, and I dreaded the crumpled look of a middle schooler over whom I had mowed with my authority. I decided to fall back on my first principle of supporting the kids' enthusiasms within broad limits.

"Brian: X that. Move *up* Science Corner. I want it on the front page!"

The whole staff cheered.

"Above the fold?"

"Beneath."

"Boo."

"One more word and no Fun Friday."

The much-used threat was empty and they knew it. I needed Fun Friday more than anyone. They were an ace staff from Saturday delivery to Thursday night when they put it to bed. But on Friday they crashed and turned surly, pushed to the wall by my stiff deadlines. For the broader peace, I let them scarf Smartfood and play *Minecraft* on Friday. No shoot-'em-ups, and no excluding. (Guess who wiped the keyboards.)

Another change that summer concerned the *Beat*'s décor. Mr. Susco had acquired an excess of tchotchkes from almost forty years of teaching and trucked some over in his battered Ford pickup. Educational posters (hygiene, the Bill of Rights). A full Union uniform with sword. Harriet Tubman posing in her shawl.

"Are you sure we can take this?" I asked, holding like an enormous prize check a crazy old map that had Virginia and the Carolinas stretching infinitely westward.

"Believe me, I've got plenty."

The kids' labor—and rising subscriptions—freed me up for a deferred Adams project. First I printed an adventure story, about John and the boy John Quincy crossing the Atlantic to represent America to France during the Revolutionary War. But it seemed even a bolt of lightning striking the *Boston*'s main mast could not rouse Pennies from their Adams antipathy. Then I tried my hand at the bestselling romance genre, reprinting the sexiest of the John-and-Abigail letters. But this stuff—"Words cannot convey to you the tenderness of my affection." "We have not yet been much distressed for grain."—just wasn't hot. For the final piece, I broke my rule-of-thumb against headlines in the form of questions in a last-ditch effort to seize the limelight. I have it here somewhere. Oh, yes, here it is. I'll read it!

WAS ADAMS, NOT MADISON, THE TRUE FATHER OF THE U.S. CONSTITUTION?

A number of Pennies will no doubt object that Adams wasn't even in North America during the Constitutional Convention. He was in London, before the Court of St. James's! So he couldn't have written the U.S. Constitution. But how many of you know that Adams personally wrote the Massachusetts Constitution, the oldest working constitution in the world? It created the basic—*

By now, the swirling rumors had reached us. Unnamed interests were planning to plop some kind of geodesic dome over at least part of the town, to keep out rain and avert further flooding. I didn't think floods worked that way. If you wanted to stop the floods, you'd better put that dome over the entire Merrimack Valley. Or even the White Mountains and Lake Winnipesaukee, which the Pennacook River's headwaters came from.

All through summer, the dome rumors persisted. I was generally averse to wading into divisive and depressing *Beat* content (I know: very G1) but, as with the carcinogenic schools, I felt duty-bound to call this one out. Fortunately, I didn't have to. In early

---

* At this point in our interview, I interrupted Graham—"Stop!"—and firmly redirected him to the dome. "Right!" he conceded. Too *much* G1."

September, a sassy LTE (one in a long line of Penny exit letters that we published) responded to my initial, neutral article on the subject and topped anything that I could write. It took dead aim at the dome and was the first major swipe against it. I pulled that for you, too:

Dear Beleaguered Editor:

Re: "Pennies Ponder Pennacook Dome." Now why the heck does this town need a helmet? This ain't no Tycho crater nor the sulfuric clouds of Venus. Last I checked, Earth's O2 is 100% breathable to apes the likes of us (I hear it's even free in places). Maintenance alone on that mucky plastic will be through the roof (er, dome). *Le dôme* scrubbing. *Le dôme* repair. Blasted *le dôme* insurance. Not to mention that armed secure checkpoint that some of y'all wackos want staked at *le dôme*'s entrance. Whatever happened to "no new taxis"? [*sic*] Wake up, domies!

Luv ya,
Mainely Moved My Stuff to Bangor Already

I figured that Mainely's rant would put a knife in *le dôme cher* and take it down for good.

Interviewer

But it didn't.

GAB

No, it did not.

Interviewer

Now, I want to stay chronological. Imagine I'm a camera on your shoulder.

GAB

A *camera* on my *shoulder*?

Interviewer

Metaphorically speaking. I'm a camera on your shoulder, and I'm following you around, all through that ominous year. We've gotten through summer, and you've introduced the Bobcats. It's fall now, and that means—

GAB

Athena!

Graham Meets Athena

AS AUTUMN SWEPT IN, THE DOME RUMORS HAD settled to a simmer. I felt good about the paper for the first time in years and looked forward even more than usual to my annual meeting with Athena, my once-removed contact for P.M., my secret *Beat* partner in the Chaeronea Company. My understanding was that P.M. was an investor who had created Chaeronea to own and operate the *Beat*. I had taken the helm in exchange for sweat equity.

For the better part of two decades P.M. and I had communicated only through Athena. We met once per year, on Halloween day, over far too many All-In hot dogs (spicy mustard, chopped onions, and relish, placed *under* a steamed hot dog, on a steamed bun) at the ten-stool Lion Diner (1923), a 10 × 20 converted lunch-cart "Where the Posh Nosh."

The barrel-roofed diner was my favorite spot in town. It was reliably open on only a few scattered holidays. Most days it was covered over by bamboo and palm fronds to discourage the Penny trespasser. The props lent the diner an air of mystery, as if it were a small-town, patty-melt equivalent to the back-alley speakeasies of yesteryear. I enjoyed all the old-timey touches, down to the china plates with aster on their lips. I'd balance-bike by on a hungry day, and if they were open, you'd find me there for hours, filling up for the season. If they were closed, I toddled off to End's Meat, the budget-beef eatery: only the round. My other favorite spot, Shorty's Rib Cage, was gone. Shorty's left after the Bounty Bag supermarkets, their best buyer, evacuated Pennacook. Mr. Robinson, the proprietor, was a Southern gentleman and almost the only Black man in town. He confided that it wasn't just about the supermarket. He and his crackerjack daughter Doreen didn't care for the town's recent "sour note."

As always, Athena and I reported in costume. I was second president of the United States John Adams, who I've been told was my great-great-great-great-great-great grandfather and whom I somewhat resemble: short and cherubic, but with the Benjamin Franklin up top (half-bald pate ringed by wavy hair-curtains). Athena was highly suitable as her namesake.

Inside, Athena set down her plumed helmet and awarded Stu his annual Halloween hug from a Greek goddess. Stu was the discreet, golden-smiled sweetheart in the Red Sox cap who, for the past decade or so, had manned the diner, silently slabbing relish and mustard on our well-steamed buns. I had always featured him as a retiree lovingly carrying on an old trade, in part for the extra dough but mostly for the neighborliness of diner life, and for the whip-smart humor and snappy one-liners that I associated with crusty locals in such places. Though I had yet to detect such wit in Pennacook.

We settled in for dogs and small talk. My pet topic was Josephine's extended jaunt, as I still liked to frame it (divorce papers had been prepared for my signature; they rested in a clasped envelope on my kitchen counter). Athena's was her overcomplicated polyamorous adventures, and especially the various logistical issues they gave rise to. Some of those stories lacked a proper dramatic arc, for the disinterested observer, but I was always left with some newfangled polyamory terms to look up. I wondered how anyone could hang on to more than one person, given what had happened with Josephine.

Athena had a fresh angle on things. She'd once avowed that she was an anarcho-syndicalist ("like Camus, or Dennis from

Monty Python and the Holy Grail"). And yet politics, I had gleaned, was not a major concern. She had too many other pursuits. There were the personal entanglements of her polycule and the Muskrat, and her time-consuming hobbies: gardening (basil, grapes) and jazz trombone in Jack Teagarden's style (at least two hours a day). She also had this proxy role for P.M., which didn't quite fit in the puzzle I had been building of her. But the lynchpin to it all was Gags 'n' Strops. Gags 'n' Strops was her kinky vegan-leatherwork business. It had a lucrative online component, but was also brick-and-mortar. Athena had a quaint wooden workshop out back, red-olent of hay and maple but plagued by bees, that also served as a store and demonstration room. She leveraged the colony's contacts (from the Renaissance fair, the sci-fi conference, the circus) for customers. Her hands-on training, which commanded a large fee—she was courting the wrathful blue laws while catering to a specialized taste—also helped finance the Muskrat through winter. Indeed, Gags 'n' Strops paid for nearly everything, including the trombone. Anarcho-syndicalism had bold plans to overturn the world. For Athena it may simply have been a way of interrupting "Stars Fell on Alabama" to say, "Let me be. I'm *playing*."

The subject of today's small talk wasn't polyamory but golf.

"Did you know I'm against golf?" she asked.

"I did not know that."

I fiddled with a cufflink.

"It's an elitist, costly sport wasting untold gallons of water on grass they'll never let grow."

"That doesn't sound very good."

I relaxed. Athena would carry the conversation. My only duty was to remain curious and good-humored like John Adams on a day off, which, in her presence, I was. I tapped my fingers. I could smell the onions grilling.

"The sport itself is bunk. What did Twain say? 'Golf is a good walk wasted.' Unless it was Lincoln." Eyes wide, she touched a finger to the corner of her mouth. "Couldn't be Lincoln." She clasped my forearm. "I know it wasn't John Adams!"

I grinned. (G1 always welcomed a reminder of his heritage. I'm not yet totally beyond this.)

She said golf balls from a nearby course plagued the Muskrat, knocking the clapboard and threatening bloody murder. Over at the grill, Stu grunted. Athena pinched her face in a cute frown and stuck her tongue out.

I didn't know a single Penny golfer and was surprised that Stu was one. Hard to feature him in those preppy duds. It was easier to see him in a bullfight, as the bull. This was probably because of what he was doing now. After Athena stuck her tongue out at him, Stu had turned to the side and begun pacing back and forth in the diner's miniscule galley, arms down straight and heavy shoes clomping. On a pivot, the light hit Stu in an odd way and lent his face a strange, pressed look. A less romantic comparison than a bull would be a prisoner in a cramped jail-yard. Stu often paced in down moments. I guessed it was on some doctor's order to prevent blood clots. On his way back up the galley, he caught my eye, and the reassuring smile broke through. I surprised myself by sighing with relief: I had been holding my breath through the demonstration.

Inevitably, it came time to go over the numbers, buffeted the past quarter—I boasted—by my expenses-free Bobcats, who, at the moment, were blackening the windows for a haunted-newsroom party I had allowed. Athena complimented me on my staffing coup and smiled in the manner of a generous grammar-school teacher at my latest fanciful plan to advance the *Beat*'s fortunes. An "Eat for Hunger" fundraiser was the notion:

a timed, All-Ins eating contest right there at the Lion—if we could reach the owner and fix a day. We'd sponsor to elevate their profile and boost goodwill while forging *Beat* filler. (I still like the concept.)

"That sounds swell," Athena said, and moved on.

After Hoodsies—vanilla and chocolate ice cream face off in a wax-paper cup—she handed me a check and gave me a firm handshake.

"Farewell, Adams."

"Goodbye, Athena."

She donned her helmet, visor up to show her beauty, and sped away in her red convertible—top down, white robes trailing in the wind.

Interviewer

What did happen with Josephine?

GAB

She left me. Flew the coop to Errol, in remotest New Hampshire: above the Notch with a narcissistic lumberjack. That's how G1 saw it. Does it matter?

Interviewer

It's the rare topic from my questionnaire on which you didn't write at length. The other is the time you lost a fortune with Bundterbikes, your Woonsocket adult balance-bike business. It makes me wonder what else you've left out.

GAB

I don't dwell on that stuff anymore, and it didn't seem important. My failures: who cares! But if you must know, the bank guy screwed me.

Interviewer

That's right. Keep hiding. Keep blaming someone else.

GAB

(hums "Man in the Mirror")

Remember that tune? "Man in the Mirror," by Michael Jackson? It's famous. It's a good eighties song with a message. It means: sometimes, when you're blaming someone else for the world's problems, you'd better take a look at yourself, the "man" in the "mirror." Okay, so maybe that's a silly G1 example (that guy's contagious, once you start him up!). But *my* point—I mean it kindly—is this: maybe you're the one who's hiding something. Maybe that's why we're stuck in this dynamic.

Interviewer

"Dynamic." You're nuts. What would I be hiding?

GAB

Whatever it is that makes you want to hate me.

Interviewer

I'm not the one who shirked responsibility. I'm not the one who abandoned his team.

GAB

And I don't think it's our time at the *Beat*. You're mad at someone. You're mad at someone else who you can't be mad at, and so you take that out on me, G2. Just like you did back then, on G1. They have whole books on this stuff at the Muskrat.

Interviewer

Can we—

GAB

I know, I know: back to the dome.

Graham Taps Archie

ALL THROUGH DECEMBER AND INTO THE NEW year, I dispatched Bobcats to hunt for dome leads: zoning exemptions to scale the heavens, special permits for dome lattice-work. They found nothing. December turned frigid—uncharacteristically so for recent years but a flashback of sorts to my long-gone eighties childhood—and the deep-winter weeks, which would run to early March that year, commenced in bitter earnest.

Bitter, that is, but for the phenomenal canal ice. This was a surprise and relief after the floods wrecked the Hallenbuck Rink, which had held near-sacred status. That whole winter was a Penny ice carnival. Ice-hockey matches. Cocoa socials. Odd men with little egg-shaped tents ice-fishing for days on end. Over in Science Corner, Sally Boone compared Pennies' random skate marks to the *stochasticity* of the water molecules in ice, which move and shift in ways you can't predict. She noted the strangeness of how solid the molecules were together, as ice. I remember her writing something like: "Don't fret that jiggly motion, Pennies. At a depth of four inches, your canal ice is '*Beat* safe'!"

One cold morning in late February, I laced up my skates and gingerly stepped onto the canal behind the *Beat*. I was off to visit Selectman Archie Simmons, leader of Pennacook's lilliputian lefty contingent. If anyone knew what was up with the dome, surely it was Archie the True, as some called him.

I skated through an ice-hockey match (Friends of Tiki Shed vs. The Jack's Four Regulars), where they tagged me an "NPC" and checked me in a snowbank. When I reached the back door to Andrew Johnson Memorial High School, I was wounded and wiped. And goddammit, I had once more forgotten to pack shoes! I plunked my ass down on the step and yanked off the skates and hung them on my neck. Once inside, I padded across the gym, hoisted the trapdoor, and climbed down the ladder to Archie's office.

"Come in, come in," Archie said. "Nails are for skates, and grab your favorite slippers."

There were many slippers. I picked the wide ones and forced my fat feet in the leather. Archie's bustling slipper-lending service told me I wasn't the town's only fool. Pennies weren't used to juggling all this footwear. I whipped out my Dictaphone and pressed record. "Story idea: lifestyle bit on skate-shoe forgetfulness. Tentative headline: 'Gone skating? Don't forget your Crocs!' Stop."

"How's the ice?" Archie asked as I slowly—achingly—lowered myself to the vinyl chair.

"Crowded," I said.

"Good, though, I bet."

"Lots of grins out there. If you could only freeze it year-round, you'd have some very happy voters on your hands."

"My work would be done here. I could retire to St. Pete!"

I rubbed my neck. Archie frowned.

"Took a hit?"

"Little one."

Archie opened a drawer, removed a tin case, and tossed it to me: Tiger Balm.

"Rub it on. It'll work in a jiffy. Just don't put your fingers in your eyes or you'll never again vote Team Archie."

Archie raised a drum of Advil that occupied a desk corner, but I waved him off, content for now with the Tiger Balm. I lifted my shirt and rubbed it on my back. Archie was right: the stuff was intense. While applying it, I scoped his new digs.

The bunker-like office had been a gift of sorts from Dr. Regina Chong, the high school's principal and Archie's longtime girlfriend. Dr. Chong had assigned it to Archie after he expressed rising security concerns about Town Hall, where he was literally outgunned (Archie didn't pack heat) and where rhetoric had been set to a boil ever since the floods and Bounty Bag's departure. No real nepotism was involved in the award of this minor perk. Archie was the only one who entered the office lottery. Others avoided it for fear of a ghost. The office's prior occupant, the fearsome Mr. Lynch, a gym teacher, had carved out this hovel in the late seventies and then died there on the job at his desk like John Quincy Adams in the House of Representatives (1848). My dirty little mind wondered if, in addition to Archie's duties for the town, afterhours hanky-panky with Dr. Chong took place there.

I sealed up the Tiger Balm and tossed it back to Archie. My eyes had adjusted to the cage's dim light, and I took note of Archie's funny clothes, more Menlo Park than Pennacook. Archie used to be a suit-and-tie guy. Now, for some reason, he wore these stuffy black turtlenecks.

When I asked him about the dome gambit, he seemed, at first, to know nothing.

"I was going to ask you," Archie said.

"You sound relieved."

"It's nice to know I'm not the only one out of the loop on this."

"Er, dome."

Archie smiled at the omnipresent and not particularly clever dome word-play. His phone buzzed and he raised a finger.

"Wait a sec—gotta take this: citizen call."

I admired Archie for such moments. He was patient and easily the most responsive member of town government. To be sure, he didn't often win Board votes. But he excelled in a quasi-lawyerly role, when he was called on to mediate a dispute or crisis (a diversionary spite-canal, a joyriding boat thief on the loose). Whatever their stripe, most Pennies liked him.

This may have been because Archie was an optimist where Pennies were concerned, and not just in theory. He had elaborated a whole practical politics about them. At last year's meeting, he had confided to me that most Penny disputes were not to be resolved by ideology, which made sense because few Pennies had one.

"If Pennies do have a political theory, it usually boils down to 'what is is what ought.'"

"Or 'we're going to hell in a handbasket'?" I asked.

"Yes: or that. Neither's much use when you're trying to fill a pothole."

"Or dredge a canal."

No, Archie contended, the way you sorted most things out was to throw Pennies in a room to talk.

"If there is any good faith in that room, usually something—maybe not the best thing, maybe not even a *good* thing, but something—will pop out at the end. Most Pennies will make a deal *just to get along with the other people in the room.* To face another day as a community. It's not so much compromise as forgetting. Self-forgetting, you might say. You ever sit on a jury? Or listen to one of those supposedly starkly divided potential-voter debates they set up on the radio? That may sound like the worst Tuesday of your life, or five minutes of really bad programming. Sometimes it is. But strange and surprising things can happen. Same when Pennies get together, away from all the racket."

The hardest part, Archie maintained, was getting Pennies into that room. If you voted, you might lose. Archie certainly couldn't dictate or plan the result, which could almost feel random.

"Or at least it used to be like that," I had said then, putting my finger on the change in tone after the town's recent cataclysms, economic and aquatic.

"That's the good-faith part I was talking about. It's still there: just buried."

Maybe, I thought. But dead things are buried, too. I also remember thinking, *Archie is the type of person about whom another might say, "This man is dangerous and must be stopped."*

Archie hung up the phone.

"There is one thing," he said.

He tapped his finger on a thick red folder stamped "CONFIDENTIAL."

"The Bounty Bag parcels. Ever wonder what happened to them?"

The chain had owned a large swath of Pennacook and, since 2014, had kept a hog farm there, its attempted fix for the town's wild boars. I had assumed that after the flood Bounty Bag had simply abandoned the land.

"I am now," I said.

"They sold them."

"Makes sense."

"The price makes sense, too: a few shekels. What *doesn't* make sense is to whom. After a wild shell game—sale after sale, to a series of private entities I've never heard of—they ended up with some nominee trust. The guy—or gal—who controls that trust—"

"And the land—"

"We don't know who that is. It's a secret."

"Could be a domie."

"Or someone else. It smells bad."

Archie passed the red folder to me.

"You can have that. It's a copy, raw stuff. I printed it up this morning for you. Well, half of it. The printer crashed. I'll keep paging through it on my end, but the Register of Deeds is our best bet."

"I'll send a gopher."

The records were intriguing. Still, I'd hoped for more, a plan of action to report on, or to hold in reserve till Archie was ready.

Archie turned to personal matters, as if sensing the conversation had exhausted its public purpose and needed to be ushered toward a graceful close.

"How's the gal?" he asked.

"Didn't you know? She left."

I'd told Archie this before. So what? The man wasn't perfect. He carried thousands of Penny files in his head! Still, I recalled with disappointment that we weren't really friends, though I felt like we could be.

"How's yours?"

"Splendid," Archie said.

I raised an eyebrow. Like other Pennies—this is something I've learned at the Muskrat—I lacked the conversational resources to respond to both good and very bad news.

"It's no paradise," Archie added, reassuring me that there was at least a thin black lining to this puffy-white lovebirds' cloud. "Sometimes we fight. She's tough." As if to confirm this, the turtleneck drooped to reveal a large bite mark.

In the swift-moving way of things at this time, personal tragedy outpaced me and started telling a story of its own. It struck just a few mild-weathered days after my meeting with Archie, in the form of a pontoon-boat "accident" that removed Archie Simmons from the field.

He was out with the Board of Selectmen on a so-called retreat-cruise down a fast-running Penny canal that hadn't iced over.

Dr. Chong, on high alert, stalked the pontoon boat in her Mini. There had been anonymous threats, a rising effort to bring Archie to heel. She drove alongside the glutted boat with its milling men, heat lamps, Christmas lights, and a long fold-out table crammed with foil tins overflowing with sauced chicken wings. Just as "Beat It" blasted from a wall of speakers, the road split and she zoomed up a hill, then back down in a rush to intersect it. She didn't think they'd kill him, but she couldn't rule out some rough stuff. Also, apart from these fears, Dr. Chong was possessive of Archie and liked to keep him close. They had a real dinner date in Eaton, and she planned to whisk him away at the boat's first docking.

The others blamed a lamppost. Selectman Holt Maggio said it "just come up from behind and plumb knocked the feller out," flinging him off deck. He splashed into the canal just as Dr. Chong descended another hill. Her swift breast stroke through the icy waters brought her to his body, which she rolled over and tugged to shore JFK-style, her teeth clenched around the strap for the life preserver, which Archie had worn despite the others calling him a dork. Safely ashore, she pumped his chest till he spewed water, then folded him clown-car fashion into the Mini and dashed off to St. Joseph's, in Lowell. That night, he fell into a coma.

Interviewer
What happened to the red folder?

GAB
Pardon?

Interviewer
The red folder. Where'd you put it? Did you read it? Did you assign it out?

GAB

This was G1, remember? There's lots of things I'd
undo, if I could. Starting with that folder. I *placed*
it, I think, in the center of my desk.

Interviewer

And what happened next?

GAB

At some point, it moved—I moved it.

Interviewer

Where?

GAB

The corner.

Interviewer

Why?

GAB

To make way for things.

Interviewer

What things?

GAB

Let me think. My Cup Noodles and a bourbon-
and-Ballantine? That was my usual. Then it got
buried in a blizzard of unrelated papers. Receipts.
An old issue. A discarded adult coloring book

that had failed to soothe. I don't know: *G1 stuff*. It doesn't really matter. The point—as you know—is I forgot it.

Interviewer

Thank you for that admission. Now, as we approach spring, I want you to talk about the "Town for Sale!" ad. How do you come to print it in the *Beat*? When do you suspect that it's linked to the dome scheme?

GAB

Oh, right away.

Interviewer

Yet you ignored this. Why? Was it the money? I bet it was the money.

GAB

I thought you said you're a camera. Cameras don't judge.

Interviewer

I did mock trial for years.

GAB

God help me.

Town for Sale!

THE PPD DID LITTLE TO SOLVE THE CASE OF Archie Simmons, and the other selectmen lawyered up with mysterious out-of-town counsel who had them pleading the Fifth on a simple sandwich question. They wouldn't talk to me, either, and I dropped the story, except to print a small, red number in the top-right corner of each *Beat* issue, marking the days since Archie went down. By early April, the red number was up to forty-six, the canal ice had melted, and Penny spirits were flagging. This is when I got the e-mail for the big ad buy, funded by the Board of Selectmen (minus Archie), which would run to late May, when a key vote was scheduled.

I have the original.

(GAB hands over furry yellow paper
he has folded into a crane)

ZP—Pl. 1
Town for Sale!*

Does *this* describe *you*?

☞ Sick of the bull*&%A
☞ Sittin' on ca$h
☞ "Always craved my own little fiefdom"

If the answer to all three (heck, we'll take just the middle one!)
is "a resounding yes," buy historical Pennacook "Now"—and save!

Email all bids to: pfs-firesale1@aol.com
n. All purchases subject to final approval at
Pennacook Town Meeting, Sunday, May 28, sixish.
*Some assembly required

I forwarded the e-mail to Denise Zywicki, my crack art director, and swung by her desk.

"Kill that bloodcurdling font please. Also, crank up the color: 'emergency red' for the text's what they're asking."

"Whatever *that* is."

"And anything else to make it pretty. Comprende?"

"Yes, Mr. Bundt."

"Graham: please. And buck up. We need this moola."

Soon enough, scheming Pennies turned up at the *Beat* seeking intel they could ply to advance some angle. Pennies, let me tell you, are willing to appear in person for this sort of dirty work. Gravy Poole, the worst of them—a sort of anti-Archie Simmons— came knocking on Thursday and demanded a "hearing." I knew him well. He had long ago and many times over earned a green Frequent Correspondent folder that I kept in a special cabinet alongside other names that vibrated with menace. To thwart his mental mapping of the *Beat*, I chose a zig-zag route past empty cubicles to the break room. Gravy bought chips from the vending machine, then sat down and placed a bid.

"Let's talk price. Forty-two dollars."

"Never!" I said boldly (I had no jurisdiction) and snapped open a root beer. I had switched from Perry White to Sharp Trader and braced for the worst.

Gravy pointed a chip at me and squinted. "*Negative* forty-two," he clarified. He tossed the chip in his mouth and crunched. "This town owes me. You recall that little road they put in behind the Elks? Dead Man's Drive."

"Canal."

"Whatever. I don't use it."

"Yes."

"I paid for it."

"Uh-huh."

"With taxes. Is that right?"

"You live here."

"I don't use that road."

"It's a canal now."

"I deliberately turn left. Tell me, Mr. Fancy Reporter, where in the Constitution it says I can have my pocket picked every time someone plunks down a byway."

"Kids died on that road. That's why they paved it."

"Not my kid. Why don't you report that?"

"When a kid dies on Dead Man's Canal, you want us to report that it's not your kid."

"Don't poke me! Don't even try it again! And Belcher Road? I don't use that either. In fact, I have here a document. Containing all the roads—"

"And canals."

"—and canals I will never use. Spleen Street, Pigknuckle Place. The list goes on. Poop Lane. What kind of name is that? I drive right around it. I don't even use city water. I don't drink that. I don't drink anything. No water. Not a drop. So why do I have to pay for the water lady?"

"Sewer."

He sat up straight and raised a palm.

"No, sir, I do not. I do not use sewer, nor do I brush my teeth. I don't shave, I don't clean things. I don't wash my hands or wipe. I do that at a restaurant. I get all of my water from a silver tap inside of a restaurant. *In another town.* I'll show you. My personal usage is zero."

He rummaged in his bag and threw me the bill.

"Where's that in the Constitution?"

"One-hundred-and-thirty-two dollars!"

"That's my kid."

"That's a lot of water."

"He was an accident. A hockey-playing accident. Who takes many showers. Now you tell me where in the Constitution—"

"What about the dome?"

"What dome?"

I stared him down.

"Oh, *the* dome."

"Seems costly, don't you think? Then again, might keep out the riffraff."

This was bait, to draw Gravy out on the dome. Gravy scorned the riffraff, whoever they may be.

"What's this have to do with my water bill?"

"Maybe a lot?"

"Are you?"

"What?"

"Against it."

"I don't make the news. I just report it."

"Coward."

So Gravy wouldn't answer my dome questions. This in itself was telling. I took it for clandestine dome support. The plot thickened!

"I need to end this," I bluffed. "I have ... explosive diarrhea."

"You nitwit."

In Gravy's aftermath, Denise Zywicki could no longer contain her distress.

"Can it really be true, chief? Is Pennacook for sale?"

"I'm voting for hope right now," I said, grinning. I had swapped Sharp Trader for Booster Graham, whom I saved for Bobcat small talk.

Denise shrugged and crossed to the gumball machine. She

dropped a quarter and turned the knob. Nothing.

"When are you going to refill the gumball machine? I'm hungry."

"Gumballs aren't food, bro," Brent Tanner, a mean boy, said.

"Gumballs have calories and you chew them. Ergo, they are food."

"Like bagels, without the bread," Delmore Hines said. He was a mediocre copy editor but my go-to tech guy.

"Bagels *are* bread, you piddler," Denise said, spurning the assist.

Brent laughed darkly like Satan.

"No name calling," I said, and rubbed my eyes. For obvious reasons, it was my job to "be the adult in the room." I couldn't always swing it.

"Which reminds me, Graham: *would you like to buy a band sub?*"

"Your order's due next week."

"And you ignored my e-mails."

"Okay, you got me. Put me down for two."

How far would it go this month? In the mere two days since sub season had opened, I had already pledged to twenty-eight subs from *Beat* staffers, including a clarinetist, a tubist, and a slope-shouldered squirt on the chimes. Now I had a piccolo. From my vendors alone, I could form a raucous band.

Delmore was head-down, weeping at his desk.

"He wasn't always that way," said Niles Corbyn, noting my concern.

"What?"

"Timorous."

"No?"

"Old Delmore's never been the same since the challenge."

"Oh? What challenge?"

The possibly brilliant Niles Corbyn thought his desk's nearness to mine and his advanced age of fifteen gave him a special connection to the boss that entitled him to talk with me on the adult plane. As an upside, I pumped him for gossip.

"I really shouldn't comment."

"But you will."

"I play the kettledrum, Mr. Bundt. It is a non-competitive instrument. So you see, what I'm about to tell you has little personal bearing. You can trust me. If not always to be right, then at least to be honest.

"A few weeks back, Denise was second chair in the piccolo section, behind Delmore. She sent an e-mail to Mr. Moriarty, the band's assistant director, formally challenging Delmore to a piccolo-playing contest. This initiated a process that cannot be stopped by any known method short of hospitalization, prison, or death. At an unappointed time, Mr. Moriarty strode across the stage mid-band practice and tapped the two musicians on the shoulder, then hauled them out back and ran them through a D scale, an E scale, and a song from the repertoire. 'Greensleeves,' I believe. After Delmore lost—making fewer errors, it is said, but falling short on some subjective measure like tone that Mr. Moriarty invariably finds decisive in these challenges—he slumped onstage behind Denise, the victor. In front of everyone, they swapped their music on the stand and their butts—if you'll excuse me—on their seats. The music paused briefly for this ceremony.

"*That* is why Delmore is the way that he is," Niles concluded.

"Thank you for that—*detailed* analysis. I'll take it under advisement."

One more wild Bobcat swing between puerile and mature (the same boy had been busted for fart spray). I checked the clock, then stood, clapped twice, and made fast circles with a finger.

"Crunch time, Bobcats! Shake a leg out there!"

On my cue, the slightly addled vibe of Thursday afternoon cleared and gave way to the pilot-like focus that, without fail, "brought 'er in safely" by 6 p.m. Mousey voices issued stern orders. "I need eyes on Sports! Give me some eyes!" Other mousey voices replied. "Roger that. Eyes on the way!" The kids were falling all over themselves to get it done right. Checking facts. Proofing text. Scrubbing files clean for the printer.

In this gratifying hubbub, I reflected on Denise's dodged question. She wasn't foolish to doubt the "Town for Sale!" pitch, and from both ends. What schemer would buy this burg? I didn't smell much money in domes. On the other hand, desperate as Pennacook was, I found the town's offer hard to credit. Here we were with almost 400 years to our name. We had a modified town meeting, heir to the democracies of Greece (as Mr. Susco had instructed). Sure, it had been bastardized by crazy-quilt gerrymandering and rural-rigged selectmen districts (Mr. Grant, R.I.P., at the high school taught us that). But the general form was a staple of any textbook. You will find it in a special box in the chapter on colonial New England. What business did Pennacook have going to market? Or encasing itself in a geodesic dome?

"This isn't just some corndog franchise," I mumbled.

"What?" Niles Corbyn asked.

"Isn't there some copy to revise?"

I checked the spreadsheet: all grayed-out, which meant done. I walked over to the light switches and chopped them up and down a few times.

"That's it, Bobcats. It's a wrap!"

I slipped my root beer in the wall-mounted can crusher and pulled the padded handle, making a loud and satisfying *crunch*.

Interviewer

Continue with this day. The kids press you on the "Town for Sale!" ad. And then?

GAB

They didn't "press" me.

Interviewer

Denise did, but you blew her off. You thought Gravy was a domie but made a joke of that, too. But this all put the worm in, didn't it? Because wasn't this the day you relapsed?

GAB

Okay, okay, you win: they "pressed" me. It's hard to relive those days, okay? I have vivid nightmares that I'm *still* G1 and I wake up sweating with shame and relief. Now you're asking me to *be* him again, and one of the things he does is defend. I know I have it coming, but it's hard. You're wrong about the other thing. I couldn't relapse, because I wasn't sober. But that was the day I sank—or began to.

Graham Has a Guest

A FTER WORK, I BALANCE-BIKED AS FAR AS QUIK Stop, a waystation between the *Beat* and my apartment where, for a small fee, I moored the pedal boat. An expanding pool of Penny vagrants had begun to congregate there, bungee-wrapped bags stuffed in their rattling Bounty Bag carriages. The evilly run convenience store blared modernist music at nuisance volumes in an effort to repel them. As usual, I donated some quarters to show my support for the vagrants over Igor Stravinsky.

Inside the door I slammed into—and nearly toppled—a teeming rack of dome-themed merch that had not been there even a week earlier. Stuffed domes, domes filled with hard candy; chocolate domes and dome keychains. A T-shirt section tried every dome-related gimmick one could imagine. One T-shirt satirized Penny despair while at the same time positing its cure by dome. It featured an ailing patient labeled "Pennacook" stretched out on a table in the famed Ether Dome at Massachusetts General Hospital, where, in 1846, anesthesia was first demonstrated in a public surgery. The man screams, "Hey, Doc: Put Me Under!" Beneath that, as if to announce a Superbowl championship: "PEN-NACOOK DOME 2023!" Another T-shirt set a crude sketch of the Pennacook Dome alongside five others, each purported to be among the Great Domes of History. Three were incontestable: the U.S. Capitol, the Taj Mahal, and the nine onion domes of St. Basil's Cathedral in Moscow. But in a decidedly Penny twist, the T-shirt also celebrated the dystopian domes from *The Simpsons Movie* (2007) and Stephen King's *Under the Dome* (2009):

town-wrecking, cow-halving domes that everyone wanted to get rid of, not court or construct.

The merch-domes took many forms. The chocolates looked like igloos. The keychains resembled the geodesic-sphere casing for that very slow ride at the E.P.C.O.T. Center. The stuffed domes reminded me of something else, a documentary I'd seen on Biosphere 2 in Arizona, and may well have been bought from that facility's gift shop in a kind of stuffed-dome arbitrage. The variety suggested that the dome plans were unsettled or bogus. Or at least that the merch vendors weren't in on them. If they had been, they could at least have agreed what the dome would look like.

I brushed past this to the usual Penny alp.* I wedged forward—*through* the alp—and bought eight bags of Smartfood for Fun Friday and a pack of squeaky cheese for myself, then tossed my balance bike and my briefcase in the pedal boat and slowly pedaled away while chewing.

Revving speedboats with airhorns—most Pennies favored volume (noise) in their aquatic vehicles—heaved and blasted me. Then I passed a boar drift. The boars were keen swimmers but lacked their usual air of menace and showed no hunger for a pedal-boat chase. A plump, dark-headed bird had perched on a boar and pecked at its flesh, making it squeal and dance into the water. The bird took flight with a pink hunk in its beak. It jerked about like it'd blown an engine, and I thought I heard a faint *put put.*

I was an inept amphibian and as usual arrived home half-soaked. An hour or so later, I was all dried up and sitting snugly in my den in my red elfin long johns enjoying a favorite (G1) meal of cocktail wieners and pineapple chunks when I had another knock

---

*   "Alp," Graham reminded me, is a local acronym, origin unknown, for an "ambiguous line problem."

at the door from the men in black tracksuits and homburgs from the test-marketing company.

"Sir, have you considered moving to a dumpster?"

"No, not now, not ever. I told a pair of you that last week, and another the week before. What is this?"

These guys were everywhere lately. Mr. Susco had already bought in, and neighbors had griped about the hard-driving pitchmen (it was all men).

"There are many of us."

"We can be relentless."

Pennacook had long been a popular test market. But after the last flood, we had become something of a free-fire zone for new gadgets, gimcracks, and gimmicks. For example, Gravy Poole's ride: the revived coal-powered car. I heard he even had a coal-powered mini-sub, in which he stealthily patrolled the canals' deeper reaches.

"The whole town's on the auction block. Why go door to door?"

"This isn't on that scale. And if we bid on things in public, guess what happens to the price?" He whistled and pointed to the sky.

"You two are right out of central casting, you know that? No, wait—I get it. Run-DMC, right?"

"These are for comfort."

"Right," I said. "Homburgs, not fedoras. My bad."

But there was no denying the Run-DMC attempt here—and the failure. It was a clumsy pander to Pennies' well-known penchant (which I shared) for eighties things. Tellingly, though, most Pennies took only a tepid and superficial interest in rap, which made the Run-DMC costumes seem even more oblivious. I was an outlier here and to this day keep and cherish a vast cassette-tape collection derived from *Beat Street* (1984), *Krush Groove* (1985), and *Yo! MTV Raps* (starting 1988).

The first guy opened his briefcase and snapped loose a stack of ones.

"Free gift. For your troubles."

"Oh, I don't think so."

Forget "free gift." This was more like a bribe, given my role at the town paper! If only I'd been so savvy later.

"You guys hungry? I got extra," I said, hoping to draw not-Run-DMC into a long and revealing chat about their scheme. I stepped back to reveal the enticement of my bubbling slow cooker, which was exhibiting heightened activity at the moment. Purplish-brown sauce bubbles popped. Cocktail wieners rose and fell like logs tumbling downriver through rapids.

The men looked around.

"We ate at the Lion," the first one said.

The second one glared at him and elbowed his ribs.

"It's open?"

"Was," the first one said, and gulped. "For lunch. But now it's closed."

"Stu say when it'll reopen?"

"Uh, no," the second one said.

"He never does," I mused. "Toodaloo," I added, and slammed the door shut.

I popped another root beer and scissored open the blinds with two fingers. A movement below and my eyes shifted to Jeremy Wiggins: neighbor, buddy, former Bounty Bag sacker. Right on schedule, he was back at it with the Avalancher.

The monstrous hard-tail mountain bike was his first bike and promised total domination of every terrain. His Auntie Lil gave him the Avalancher as a salve to being jobless and a confidence builder for a skill he hadn't mastered. But its rippling machismo didn't readily transfer to its rider. Once more, Jeremy pushed down and his leg noodled. Some firmness was missing in his wrist and grip. It had something to do with his Down syndrome. Auntie Lil gave him a nudge and he rolled toward the canal, where my pedal boat freaked him out and he crashed.

I cranked the window.

"Extra extra: cocktail wieners."

Jeremy's chin shot up as he hearkened to the call. "Wieners?"

He swiveled with a grin and scrambled up the stairs to my place. Auntie Lil tromped off, tiredly waving as she guided the Avalancher back to its stable.

"Graham Bundt, you're my best pal."

He slapped my shoulder, then pushed around me toward the slow cooker. His plate overflowing, he made a beeline to his couch spot, form-fitted to his buns.

"How was your day?"

"Good."

"How's the bike?"

"Good."

"Any luck on the job front?"

"No."

"Still trying?"

"Yes."

Direct questions almost never worked with Jeremy. (It was like talking to you Bobcats.) He emptied his plate in seconds. The plastic fork slowed, and he scraped up the residual sauce with a spiral move, then sucked the fork dry. As soon as he was done, he bolted, leaving the plate and fork on his seat, as if to hold his place for tomorrow.

"Say hi to Auntie Lil for me," I said at his back.

Jeremy turned and flashed a peace sign, sneering like he'd pulled one over on me.

It wasn't always quick and nasty. If a game was on TV, we'd hoot for hours and sometimes played checkers until 10 p.m., a shared bedtime. We both liked my classic-cartoon reels the best. The stately pace gave you time to look around. A gleam in Jeremy's eyes during early ones done in the rubber-hose style pointed, I felt, to their special appeal for him. Here, the same bendiness that hobbled his athletics was the source of a great and fate-twisting power. Flowers danced for the solstice; a tree's maw stretched to shelter woodland creatures.

Alone again, I brushed aside my old-school rap-ballads mixtape (Slick Rick, LL Cool J) and dropped the needle on *Pet Sounds*, side two, then poured myself an Old Grand-Dad on the rocks—*no more than a taster*—to ease me.

... I was sitting in the kitchen, staring at the clasped envelope and muttering bits from the state constitution.

"Blessings of life ... the common good."

Then I was drowsing under the coffee table as the room slowly brightened.

Interviewer

Before we conclude this morning's session, I want to circle back to something you said a moment ago. "If only I'd been so savvy later." By "later" you mean when you went all Benedict Arnold on us? You knew what you were doing then. Maybe you didn't know everything. But you knew enough.

GAB

You're right, Wendy. I should have known better. And it's good to have friends who keep you honest. But we do a lot of plays here at the Muskrat, and

one thing I learned on my path to G2 is what
Shakespeare said: "Presume not that I'm the thing
I was." Do me a favor. Can you try it?

Interviewer
In our next session, we'll turn to your betrayal.

PART THREE:

ME

Ranking

I JOINED THE BEAT A FEW SHORT WEEKS AFTER
Graham passed out drunk under his coffee table and soon
had more prosaic concerns than democratic theory, the Sophists, or William James Sidis. In those early days, Graham "filled"
my time with an "all-consuming" lifestyle assignment: the annual
pu pu platter rankings.

The taste-test protocol required me to visit all seven places and
polish off a platter. I'm not complaining. I have a large stomach,
and it didn't cost me a dime (Graham wasn't stingy with the petty
cash). Also, the stiff competition in Pennacook made something
more of the pu pu platter than you may imagine. Or more, at least,
than I expected. I've said that I hated those restaurants when we
first moved to town. This was the moment my opinion changed.

It was also my first chance to pilot the *Empress Josephine*. It
was easy to maneuver, not that different from the motorboats
I had mastered at the G.S.A.'s Camp Molly Ockett (which I rec-
ommend highly to all girls). I liked the rubber's slap against the
surface. Spring had quickly ripened, bringing Pennacook's sodden
landscape to lush and vibrant life. The river grass fed on the ample pig-manure runoff and blossomed prematurely, shooting up
through the canals and entangling Penny propellors, though I
deftly dodged it.

Despite the happy jolt of horsepower from the *Empress Josephine*, it took me a long time to finish that feature. On top of the
heavy eating, I had to probe a mini-scandal. An anonymous infor-
mant charged Jade Sunshine with goosing its MSG the previous
year around taste-test time. And in fact Jade Sunshine had done

better in our rankings, vaulting from sixth place to a tie for second with the Tiki Shed and just a hair behind perpetual champ Wu Doon Mang. The rankings shift sent shockwaves through Penny stomachs and wallets all year.

I swung by Jade Sunshine to inspect. Mr. Yu had caught wind of the terrible accusations and retaliated with a dose of wha-taboutism, directed at Wu Doon Mang. During Wu Doon Mang's inspection, Leo and Wei had remained out back in their luxe booth perfecting the Fibonacci sequence for Siberian Math even as I buttonholed their parents in the lounge to a soundtrack of rumbling thunder. Now Mr. Yu lit into his rival's excessive debt spending on presentation—including that thunder.

"Ask them, I say, about all these so-called 'improvements.' Who needs cement palm trees? Or strip-club lighting they bought from Jack's Four? I could add a 'rainstorm' to Jade Sunshine's lounge, too, if I wanted. That doesn't mean the food tastes better. It's *sleazy*. What's happening to standards in this town? This town—"

That phrase—"this town"—was familiar. The restaurateurs didn't think much of where Pennacook and all souls lashed to it were headed. My research said that, nationally, eighty percent of new restaurants fail within five years. Pennacook's Chinese restaurants had long bucked that trend (the Golden Dragon series being the rule-proving exception), but how long could this last?

The strife among owners was itself a new and troubling change. Graham had told me they were "all buddies, practically a trust." Why, then, the scandals and complaints? I was particularly surprised that Mr. Yu was "shooting at the king." Wu Doon Mang not only bossed our rankings but was easily the most prestigious of Pennacook's American Chinese restaurants and the first to open, in 1943.

It reminded me of something else from Mr. Susco. It regarded medieval Iceland.

Mr. Susco had explained that, back then, they had a loose, almost anarchical democracy. Each year, the Althing gathered at the Law Rock to recite the laws and settle disputes. In between Althings, families relied on exquisitely calibrated blood feuds to sort out their differences. "Calibrated" in the sense that you didn't slaughter Egil's son just because his son killed your servant. No, you went for the servant. And not only the servant, but the *right* servant: the one at the same level (or, as sanction to aggressors, a shade above). Reciprocity secured the peace. But right in the middle of *Njáls Saga* (which took place around the year 1000) Christianity with its forced national conversion arrived. By one reading, this upturned everything, all the old anchoring beliefs, and the system broke down and the blood feuds raged with asymmetric fervor. What might have been a tit-for-tat encounter that went up a few ranks to the best horse-hand instead burned down the whole family—as it did that of "Burnt Njál" in the saga's second half.

I wondered if a similar dynamic was playing out among Pennacook's Chinese restaurants as a result of the town's recent destabilizing calamities. I had an absurd image of Mr. Yu battling it out with the Chengs on the canal ice come winter, swinging hockey sticks and brooms instead of Viking swords and pole-axes.

At meal's end, when I unmasked for the interview piece, the restaurateurs would visibly relax. Shoulders loosened, eyes went wide: at last an Asian face behind the reporter's notebook. They also marveled that I was a true-blue Asian Penny, not an out-of-towner like them. I indulged them rather than contest my Penny status. If I wasn't a real Penny, they might well have asked, why was I banqueting on seven pu pu platters in a row and seeming to like it? And in truth, as I ate, I felt that I was partaking of a sacred local sacrament and had the uneasy feeling that I was becoming a Penny.

I liked Mr. Yu. I liked them all—except Mrs. Cheng, who had rejected my friendship for her prized sons. But Mr. Yu's criticism of Wu Doon Mang was as irrelevant as it was obvious. The insulting subtext was that I, the reviewer, would be so wowed by the way Wu Doon Mang looked that I would not even taste its pu pu platter until after the restaurant had already won top honors in my poor, gullible heart.

Mr. Yu had even asked, "Where's Graham? I thought he's supposed to do this part. This town—"

"*I'm* the inspector," I interrupted, voice rising. Judges don't often respond well to motions to recuse (a lesson I learned the hard way in high-school mock trial).

The MSG tip didn't pan out (it's really hard to prove that), but I nailed Jade Sunshine for something else. I went back in disguise (black beret, sunglasses) for a second taste test. I wasn't ashamed to max out my budget (especially now, since I liked the food), so long as I kept my pencil moving. When my pu pu platter with the Sterno fire arrived, I found only two chicken fingers in my tray. Worse, it was bereft of beef teriyaki, no mere ornament but the pu pu platter's greatest charm. In contrast, the flavorless pork disks with deceptively brilliant borders like pink lips had been piled high with little care and spilled over to fill the would-be beef-teriyaki compartment—as if to unload them!

I stripped off my costume and confronted Mr. Yu at the nipple-high counter.

"Nonsense. Why would I do that?"

"A cash grab from customers too loyal to call you out on your decline."

He looked at me sideways. Direct challenge to the town's American Chinese food was unheard of (impaired judgment being loyalty's price). Back at the *Beat*, I marked Jade Sunshine down as a 2 for portion control and a 4 for taste. They slid back to sixth. No one would unseat Golden Dragon XV at the bottom of the rankings, unless, in another year or two, we unhappily arrived at Golden Dragon XVI.

On the Monday after we went to press, Mr. Yu's lawyer, Attorney Delahunt (big eater, worked for buffet tickets), showed up at the *Beat* to serve Jade Sunshine's bias complaint. Graham wouldn't have it.

"You're gonna attack a *kid*? In *my* office? Git outta here!"

Delahunt fled.

Graham meant well, but I didn't like being called a kid, not when I was doing adult work that I was proud of. I could have defended myself—and did. After school the next day I confronted Mr. Yu at the restaurant. He immediately disavowed Attorney Delahunt's tactics.

"He's a bad lawyer," Mr. Yu said. He stepped out from behind the counter. "But cheap." He puffed his cheeks and slapped his paunch.

He also said desperate times call for desperate measures. His father had opened Jade Sunshine in the early 1960s, and he did not want to be the one to bury it. He even sermonized a bit on the tiki ambience. Tiki was made up. Even Martin Denny, who penned the soundtrack, called tiki music fictitious. In Pennacook and all over America, supposedly tacky places like Jade Sunshine had preserved tiki culture—the exotic drinks, décor, and music and, most important, the essentially harmless and hospitable escapism of it all—during the fallow decades after hippies scorned it as hopelessly passé: a theme better suited to the rest home.

"I'm proudest of our food," he concluded. "Have a mint."

Before he let me go, he promised to retrain his staff on portion control and get his pu pu platters back to standard in time for the weekend rush.

I Pitch a Story

I MADE A LOT OF ENEMIES WITH THAT PIECE—the fate of all who dared put their names to the annual-rankings byline—and felt the flak I took and my work's quality had earned me a promotion to something less binge-eating based. With Mr. Susco's civics program in mind, I set my sights on the politics beat. I already had some leads I was determined to explore. My first task was to get them past Graham.

After Delivery one Saturday in mid-May, I made my way to his desk. He was hunkered over, working intensely. When my shadow crossed his hand, he looked up.

"Why do you keep your desk out here?" I asked. "You're Editor in Chief. Why don't you have your own office?"

"Taylorism."

"What?"

"Scientific management."

"What?"

"Cat's away the mice will play."

He jammed his pencil in the electronic sharpener. He had said he kept the device at his desk to monitor workflow. I suspect it was the clamor that he liked. His sharpening fit complete, he returned, grunting, to the document before him. His pencil moved with fury, as if this was a special war bulletin going out before the hour.

"What are you doing?" I asked.

"Proofreading?"

"What? What is that? Give me that."

I snatched it from him. I had little doubt that whatever Graham was working on, I could improve it.

It was a Chinese zodiac-themed placemat from Wu Doon Mang. Graham had circled his own sign and added details (whiskers, claws) to the drawing.

RABBIT

1939, 1951, 1963, 1975, 1987, 1999, 2011, 2023

Most fortunate of all   signs,you are also gifted and well-spoken. Loving, yet wary, you crave serenity in your life. Marry a Boar or Sheep. The Cock is your opposite

He had marked the errors. Why or for whom, I have no idea. He bit his bottom lip and with an impish smile pointed to his cork board, where he had pinned an old fortune. FAILURE IS THE PATH OF LEASE PERSISTENCE.

"Sound financial-planning advice I never took," he said, giggling.

"So you're mindlessly doodling while we're all at work."

His eyes narrowed. "I am modeling a 'flow state.'"

I leaned forward. He had a browser open: DOGTV. Ducks and retrievers relaxed by a pond. This was the kind of programming that Pennacook's internet was willing to rouse itself for.

"I want to do a story. A few, actually."

"On what."

"Have you heard of Lion Diner?"

"That's not a story. That's just some old diner. Semi-retired guy named Stu runs it. Real sweetheart. Opens it a few times a year. Nothing special. Great food, though. An old favorite."

He put his pencil down and leaned back so far that he had to grip his desk to avert a tumble.

"All our lawsuits and this chair-balance peril persists," he observed. "It's as relentless as copier machines, which maybe one day on Mars with its more merciful gravity will work, but not here and not anytime soon. Though Mars has the dust problem."

He had absorbed much from Science Corner, and we all agreed Sally would be a scientist.

"I'd like to look into it," I said, walking him back to my story idea. "It's very strange the way they cover it up."

"Not on my dime."

"I mean, bamboo and palm fronds? In Massachusetts? They're hiding something. I'm *sure* of it, Mr. Bundt."

"Graham: please."

"I'm *sure* of it, Graham. And there was this e-bird—some type of drone, I think—and it tried to kill Arnie! And this funny little *patch*! A-and—"

"And *I'm* sure your time would be better spent elsewhere, *cub*."

Free-style balance-bouncing on his chair, he tugged loose a folder from his piles and tossed it at me.

"Here's a real story. My water bill's ballooning. What's up with that? Gravy Poole isn't the only one complaining. They're out of control."

"How boring."

"Welcome to the workforce."

Something sweet and familiar steamed from him. My chin dropped, and I turned to walk away, but then thought better of it and edged right up to his desk, where I towered over him in his low-slung chair.

"How about this 'town for sale' business everyone's talking about? And the Pennacook Dome. Can I do that?"

He stopped bouncing and, with a shiver that reminded me of Arnie when he was overexcited and I ordered him to sit, gathered himself and looked me in the eye.

"You want something meaty. I respect that." He tented his fingers. "Reminds me of me when I was young."

"Look, just because *you're* always wearing a black pocket T-shirt—"

"From L. L. Bean."

"—and *I'm* always wearing a black pocket T-shirt from L. L. Bean, doesn't mean we have anything in common."

"Cool your jets," he said, looking over his antique-style half-eye frames. "As to your question, the dome thing came first. I caught wind last summer. It's somewhere north of a rumor, but how far it's gotten? No one knows. We don't even know who's behind it. Maybe the people who bought up the Bounty Bag land when they ditched us? Whoever *that* was. Maybe not! Same story with the sales pitch."

With a magician's flourish, he plucked the "Town for Sale!" ad from a drawer.

"But I'm not hearing a peep from my contacts."

"How can a town sell itself? Why would they do that?"

"You tell me," he said. "The man to ask would have been Archie. That's Selectman Archie Simmons. You may want to write that name down, BTW. Guess where he is? In a coma. After his 'accident,' the others rammed it through and sprung the ad. That's about all we know about that."

The implication—attempted homicide—escaped me.

"There's an e-mail for bids," I said, "and a hearing *in eight days*. It seems we know a lot. Are we reporting?"

This threw him. "All that stuff's in the ad. It's hardly a story."

"Jeez," I mused, fishing for a big word, "with this pricey ad and everything, we're practically *complicit*."

He leaned back and recommenced bouncing. It was as though, in an act of self-defense, he had switched his allegiance from our business meeting back to whatever he'd been drinking (watermelon schnapps—*that* was the smell).

"Yeah, but what is it? Who's behind it? Have they gotten any bites? Is it tied to the dome? I don't want a witch hunt please. This"—he tapped the advertisement with his finger—"is good revenue."

"So not only are we corrupt: we know it."

"Just hit the story," he growled. "And don't forget my water bill!"

He had toggled back to his tough-boss persona. It surfaced at least daily, usually in the afternoon, when he rose from his couch-naps grouchy and depressed. This was the Graham who said things like: "I only care about two things, kids, both of them lines: the bottom and the dead. Now, get back to work!" At night, he'd rally and be sunny and kind, which most of us found baffling (though not me).

Yet I walked off feeling good about the bold addition to my assignment, and that I had extracted it by force where force was required. Behind me as I left, Graham leaned back and fell over.

Yes, I was proud, but the personal picture was altogether different. That night I noted in my diary that I'd made no friends yet, at either the *Beat* or Pike Middle. My Bedford Corners friends, I added, had become distant, the time between their texts ever longer and their contents brief and generic ("I hope UR [cartoon of a well]"), and all my Snapchat streaks had broken. As much as I'd cursed it, I couldn't chalk all this up to Pennacook's tottering internet. We were long past the puppy-like age when kids make fast friends and, after a brief, wrenching interval, just as easily separate. This is why it hurt so much. I did not realize, so did not put in my diary, that it was not so painful for the others, the friends I left behind. To them I was forever the girl who had moved. If they owed our friendship anything, it was merely to preserve and remember it. Since I, as a person, had to change, I could only get in the way of this.

What I *did* know then, early A.D.D., was that my failure to connect with new kids and my distance from old friends didn't shock me. To the contrary, it felt quite natural, like my comfy old slippers. I took heart from this and told my diary it was all for the best, that I'd only grown stronger.

"In sum," I wrote, "I'm happier alone."

Senior Week: Friday

June 4, 2032

Dear Diary:

I've finished a bunch more chapters of *Zodiac Pets*, preceded by an odd something that I'm calling "Spring Break." What if I add these inter-ludes periodically? That way, I can reflect on my relationship with Lena Ku and what it was like to touch base with my old *Beat* colleagues while traveling with her to research my college thesis.

If I do this, I may need to go back to the beginning and recast my opening diary entry about this rewrite as a prologue (or interlude or something) that tells the reader about the Senior Week project. Is this too confusing? There must be a way.

WZ.
Worcester, Mass.

Spring Break: Virginia

Looking this over, I see that, so far, I've made myself out to be something of a brawling, friendless, fingerpainting mess. B.D.D., I had been another girl entirely (though not the hail-fellow hero of my B-grade college thesis).

I had loved many things and done them well. I first learned most of them at Camp Molly Ockett, the life-changing Girl Scouts camp I mentioned earlier. I painted. I square danced. I tied many knots. I piloted a motor boat twice around an island on Lake Winnipesaukee. I could dive underwater for two minutes and thirty seconds and seize a ring at the lake's bottom. For fifteen minutes and twenty-two seconds, I could stand on one rubber inner tube piled atop another. I sewed and I speed read. I was a rotten sprinter, but thanks to Ms. Devlyn Pierce, the old lady who superintended the camp year-round, I played decent hands of tennis and bridge. I liked shooting best and spent days at Rifle Range. My high score was 96 out of 100 on our 50m rifle-shooting targets, and I could sustain a 92. Once—once—I pulled a 92 skeet-shooting shotguns with Ms. Devlyn Pierce on the open field above the camp: MQS for the Olympics. Archery was a side hustle, but I was third-best at that, too. In Environmental Science, I was scared of spiders and anything else creepy but a true friend to turtles, if not always to the other girls.

Leather chaps loosely fixed, Ms. Devlyn Pierce raised her shotgun and told me I had something else.

"A built-in, shock-proof, shit detector."

BANG!

She lowered the shotgun and looked downrange. "That's what Hemingway called it. Have you considered writing?"

"I don't know. Isn't it all made up?"

That seemed hardnosed but I was already a *Nibblers* addict and my diary overflowed with entries that hopped off like bunnies to the tall grass of make-believe.

She squinted down at me. "Think about it."

"I will," I promised, and I did.

But this spring I struggled with my college thesis about the Pennacook Dome scheme, and I wasn't even sure I could finish. Lena Ko, my girlfriend, was all encouragement, and during spring break, she agreed to drive me down the long coast (the more dramatic one, for human variety) for my field research. Our first day took us from Worcester to Independence, Va. We tossed our bags in the tent-cabin and stepped outside, where Lena showed a great gift for filling me up with her love's reassurance. (I'm evading with a five-syllabled euphemism; we are talking about a picnic table, pleasingly hard, on New River.) Then she took a walk.

The walk worried me. She did not like to take them alone. But I needed—wanted—to be alone myself, with the pen, and she let me.

Southern Virginia in late March is like Pennacook in May: warm and teeming. I wrote for three hours and then the sun dipped and the river roiled like melting gold. The bugs came. I grew hungry. Lena was our cook. Where was she?

I played calm. It was okay to. If I was that way, or could play like it, then I was more likely to find her than if I panicked. I ducked into the latrine. I circled back to the general store. She had been there for crackers (a good sign).

I jogged to the river and then up the path to a diving rock, where I scanned the rapids and calm pools for lumps. I went back. As I neared camp, I issued a direct order to all systems: *Imagine Lena cooking. She will have backed the car up to the tent-cabin with the trunk open to get to our supplies. The gas grill will be out and she might even be done, and I will be the one who has some explaining to do.*

She wasn't there. I dashed downstream and heard a screech.

"Art bum! Get in the water!"

Lena was splashing like a kid. In her view, that's what water is for.

I scanned for peepers, then stripped to join her. The coldness shocked me. It was too early to be doing this. The water had not caught up yet with the air and it was at the level where the bones ache. But I liked indulging Lena.

We met sophomore year, on a meaningless quintuple non-date to the movies. She happened to sit next to me, and it was a hot night in May and the air conditioner was busted, and she wore a plaid skirt and thin leather sandals that made her feet seem bare. The next time I saw her was months later, just before Christmas, at the Christian choral concert. She was in the choir. I went only to see her, perhaps to claim her. She was all in white. I watched her face and her thick lips moving. We locked eyes and she held me that way till the end. I used the excuse of our damaged brick sidewalk to take her arm by its crook and we walked to a room under the college bell tower where we drank red wine—tardily supplied by the Beaujolais Day Society—until, with the help of another girl, she hauled me back to her friend's room for water.

The room was spinning so I lay on the bed. Lena stroked my forearm and in her trained, sweet voice said that at another friend's urging she had applied to transfer to her dorm, which also happened to be mine.

"I'd like that," I said, and that's the last I remember of that night.

She said transfer but she meant move in. She lived with her family in Grafton Hill and hiked three-plus miles down grim commercial streets to classes. Senior year would be her first time on campus, which was somewhat rare: most of us lived in the dorms.

We must have said more that night because the next morning she showed up at my room in her swimsuit and flip-flops, goggles pressed back on her hair. Over this, she wore an unbuttoned parka with her arm raised and a towel folded neatly over it like a butler. There was something blunt and erotic about all this, even more so because she didn't know it—I think.

"Where's your stuff?" she asked.

"What stuff?"

"We're going to the pool!"

I felt begged, as if I had promised (I may have).

"I can't believe you trooped all the way from Grafton Hill in this getup," I said as we crossed the highway footbridge.

Lena shrugged.

"That must hurt."

"I don't mind. I like walking."

"Me, too. But what about blisters? Aren't you frigid?"

I was establishing a compassionate but medicalized distance. I didn't know how I felt about her yet.

We reached the gated athletic complex and worked our way to the pool for Free Swim. If I had asked Lena, I meant laps. That's what you did in a college pool (or any pool, really, at our age). Lena's frame of reference was different: day trips to Lake Quinsigamond with the Christian camp. All they did was splash and play. While I logged my half-mile, Lena lurked at one end of the pool like an anarchic water-troll. She seemed determined to disrupt me so that I'd join her in breath-holding, the "rocket," something she called Water Sumo, and hand-squirt tricks. I didn't. We tried Free Swim once more a week later and I gave up. She was water silly.

On the walk back to my dorm from the second pool trip, she told me about her film-studies documentary about her deconversion. She still admired and pitied Jesus the man but said she was done with the supernatural Jesus and with all versions of St. Paul the prig. This "freed" her, she added, and she held my eyes again. I suppose those smoldering looks will seem comically extended to some readers. My advice? Try it.

I knew then but still did nothing. It took the ethical strain of an autumn rager to match us. By then we were seniors and she had moved to my dorm. A boy was after me too that night. I danced with him but when I saw Lena, I cast him aside and clung to her. The boy peeled me off and we danced more in a wild way, and then I found Lena again and flew to her. Then the whole cycle repeated. Later the boy pinned me to the wall of this illogical back-alley part of the suite that our hosts used for plastic bowling. He had my wrists up against the wall and pressed in for a kiss. My friend Aaron Tenenbaum saw this and somehow knew it was wrong. He leapt in between us and tore me off and shoved me back to the party's hot mass. "Go!" he shouted behind me. I searched out Lena, and we hurried off to her cramped hot room with the sky-light. She stood at the end of her bed. I cradled her face with my hand and kissed her. It was a hard and impassioned kiss, which I modeled after George Emerson kissing Lucy Honeychurch in the fields above Florence in *A Room with a View*, a favorite scene from a favorite film.

Things aren't the same between Lena and me anymore, but every time I think of our kiss (which is often) I hear Puccini. I suppose I always will.

Later that night in Independence, Va., we were lying in our pushed-to-gether tent-cabin beds. We had showered and were toweled off, fed and fresh. She once more filled me up with her love's reassurance and I rolled over to turn out the lamp. The sheets were cool, I thought, and then my mind roamed to that liminal world between wakefulness and sleep. Great-seeming ideas for my thesis bubbled up. I was too lazy to wake myself to write them down and let them die, telling myself they were so good that they'd come to mind again when I next touched those pages (they wouldn't). My mind went on planning but the plans became absurd. I was touching up a scene—coincidentally, the one I just revised once more, where Graham rejects my story idea about Lion Diner—that morphed to me standing before Graham at the Resolute Desk. I was trying to ram our gun bill through Congress while President Bundt insisted that our only hope was to tie it to a manned Europa mission.

"We gotta crack that ice," he said. "It could be whale cities down there!"

"But I want to focus on *this*."

"Not now, *cub*."

"Thank you for bringing me on this trip," Lena said.

President Bundt dissolved.

"What?"

"It's very hard sometimes to be home with my mother."

Though she lived in the dorms now, she was often drafted home and held there for days.

"I know."

"I don't think you know how bad it is."

I had an idea. Once I had borrowed my mother's car for a Saturday trip to the region's last Friendly's, and when I was driving Lena home to visit her mom in Grafton Hill—as her father had demanded—we found her roaming in a lot. Plastic trash bags floated. She followed one, lost interest and drifted. I offered to pick her up but Lena said no, let her out: thanks for the partial ride, see you at brunch, good night. Lena had told me once that her mother blamed her for how her life turned out, though I don't know how you blame someone for paranoid schizophrenia, and it seemed so illogical that I didn't understand why Lena couldn't just write it off. Another night not long after that, I rode with Lena in her own ambulance to Saint Vincent, because of how she'd been talking.

"It is nice to be out," Lena said.

"Are you thinking about it?"

"Just ideations."

"Which."

"I don't want to talk about it."

"Then why'd you wake me up."

"The station."

"What station."

"Union Station—the train. It'd be easy. You crouch in a nook and slip under. I shouldn't say such horrible things. It's sick."

I liked to think that because she said it some pressure had been relieved and it wouldn't happen. Though I wasn't sure.

"Don't do it. If you think you might, go to the ER. Call me, and I'll find you. Then ask me what you should do. I'm good at telling people what to do. I think you know that."

She made a smile.

"Just ask, 'Wendy, should I do it?' You have to agree to do what I say before I will answer you. Will you do that?"

"Yes."

"The answer will be 'no.' No matter what happens to us."

"Is something happening to us?"

"It doesn't matter. No, let's sleep."

The next day, we ventured into town to dig up Delmore for his interview. On the way we passed a gas station that looked more closed than open and a barbecue restaurant whose literature said they were part of a chain you'd never heard of. It was emptier, in its way, than Pennacook.

I liked, though, the small, very Southern enterprises by the roadside. A guy was selling barbecue out of a charcoal grill in his yard, and the principles keeping me away from beef ribs collapsed at the sight. Lena and I delightedly indulged, lolling around after like sated cave dwellers, on a picnic blanket littered with sucked bones. For $50, a woman offered plane rides in the plane she sat next to in a beach chair.

I didn't trust her. Such details, fresh to me, belied snobs' claims that Pennacook was "a little piece of Alabama" (or Mississippi or Virginia— take your pick) "right here in Massachusetts." No, it was something else. Its own thing, just like Independence.

At first I thought our visit a bust. Delmore didn't show up at Aunt Vera's Bar-B-Que, our agreed meeting place. Rib-gorged, we were forced to eat the hushpuppies we'd ordered as a surprise for him (following my mother, I don't waste, and neither does Lena). We tracked him to Food Town, where he was serving the first of two years as a clerk in the supermarket's pharmacy to establish in-state residency for a pharmacy program. He was but one year ahead of me but seemed to have already entered middle age, or at least its steady glidepath.

"I know you're back there." I pounded the plexiglass.

"Listen, Wendy, I have some things I need to do here at my desk and I just think it would be easier if we do this from a professional distance."

"We could have done that from Worcester."

"Not my fault."

"Look, I'm sorry I punched you in the nose in middle school. Really sorry. Not just because they made me say it."

"Finally we talk."

"But you were being a racist jerk."

"I should've known better."

Things loosened after that and he agreed to come out. It was the same small boy. He gave his angle on Graham and the Pennacook Dome, which was much like my own. He also talked of his home life. His parents had opposed his getting mixed up with the *Beat*. They called Graham unstable and said writing for his paper was a radical act that courted family trouble. All of this in a sense proved true.

"That place was a war zone. I have nightmares and it's like I'm right back in it."

"Pennacook?"

"Pennacook. My house. *Everything*. Even band. I wanted to get as far away from all that as I could. Did you know my dad joined MGOP? And he says *I'm* a radical."

MGOP—Machine Gunners of Pennacook—was the local sportsmen's club-cum-seething militia.

"It isn't over."

"It'll never be. I still play, though. Right here, after work." Registering my incomprehension, he added: "The piccolo?" He lifted the petite case, which he'd been holding all along.

The store was shutting down and a security guard stepped off the escalator and stomped toward us, passing stocker-bots that briefly dimmed in deference. He swayed and leaned like a hockey player readying a check, though with a machine gun instead of a stick. His eyes clouded as he folded his arms and planted his feet.

"Where y'all from."

"They're my friends."

"Massachusetts."

"Massa*tus*its! I bin up there. Kennedys. Clams."

"Please, Larry. We were talking."

Larry nodded, all grins. "Roger, Mr. Hines. Far be it for me to *chime in* on a *chin wag*."

"Or *cut off* a *cordial*," Delmore said.

"Or *interrupt* an *interlocution*," Lena added.

I was pleased to see Delmore carried weight and that *Beat*-style wordplay had gained some traction in Independence, even serving as a kind of social lubricant with Larry, who chuckled, gave us a long, slow scan, and marched away.

Delmore was alerted. "We don't have a lot of Asians down here. People can stare. It's like they're all me in middle school."

Except for the possible Asian-fetish component (some of the college boys have it so bad they think Yoda's mouth is sexy) it wasn't all that different from China, during the one trip I took to Shanghai as a girl. People stared without shame and reached out to caress me, saying "this child has foreign blood." It was a familiar culture, almost like a family, at least on the surface (which is where I engaged with it). Maybe the South was like that, too, I thought, choosing to see Larry's gaze in the best light—though I was grateful to Delmore for the genial push-off.

"By the way, I did sort of like you."

"Often it is this way," I said, thinking of all the misfiring boys.

He waited until Larry turned the corner, then unpacked his piccolo and played the "Navy Hymn." It was more solemn than I remembered from the Pike Middle Band.

"It sounds like a lot of kids were sad in your town," Lena said.

We were back on the highway. A night drive, headed south.

"It didn't seem that way at the time," I said (a half-truth). "We were heroes," I added (there's another).

Water in the Basement

THE BEAT WASN'T THE ONLY THING GOING IN our middle-school lives. A week or so before I pitched Graham on my stories, I had purchased my ticket to the Pike Middle Dance, which was the social event of the year and had a strange pull on us all, even a spiny newcomer like me.

The ticketing itself held drama. Each homeroom had an elected student rep who served as exclusive vendor for the dance's impressive tickets: firm, canary-yellow cards that cost $7 and quickly sold out. I bought mine from our rep, the *Beat*'s very own Denise Zywicki. Like most homeroom student reps, Denise had run unopposed, and her tenure was running out. And yet she had none of the sloth that one associates with lame-duck incumbency. I watched with approval her handling of the cards and cash and the careful way she recorded each transaction on her green ledger with a golf-pencil, then slid the form into the long manilla envelope and pressed the clasp shut at the end of every homeroom. She was the same way at the *Beat*: graceful and precise.

The source of the drama was this: I *liked* her. I wouldn't call me lovesick, but in our terms, I *like* liked her, and I was fairly sure that she *like* liked me, too.

Mom paid for my dance ticket and threw me a blank check for the dress, but she didn't see what all the fuss was about. I think my so-called lost potential was what irked Mom the most A.D.D. With my earlier passions dwindled, I was either doing nothing or spending too many hours on things she could not imagine brought me joy or had value. Honking my horn. Reading about rodent-pest clans. Tickets to child-dances. And now I had another to discuss: my assignment for Graham.

"How much do they pay you for this non-stop activity?"

"Nothing. I need five bucks."

"For what?"

"Copies at the city clerk's." (Alas, my extended tour of Pennacook's pu pu platters had drained the *Beat*'s petty cash.)

She snorted, but I knew I'd get it. What little we had meant nothing to her anymore, which scared and thrilled me.

"It's for a piece I'm doing on water prices. I may not need all of it. Did you know the town's for sale? I'm trying to cover that, too."

"Ha." Like most Pennies, she either little cared or didn't believe it.

"I wonder who will buy it," I said, trying to pull her from her stupor.

She passed me the money. Twenty, not five.

"For ice cream."

Soft-serve chocolate cones, preferably from the Bedford Corners Burger King, had been our shared favorite: hers, Dad's, and mine, together.

"Do you—want to come?"

"Help yourself." She raised her remote to switch videos.

For all her criticisms of me, Mom wasn't a high flier herself anymore. In Bedford Corners, she had been a bank's branch manager with a solid salary and bennies and an eye on a Back Bay VP slot. Her perks included the occasional trickle-down Bruins tickets, which she savored. Now she rose at noon and passed afternoons in her bathrobe and slippers, popping pork rinds and transfixed by *Fei Cheng Wu Rao*, the low-temperature Chinese match-making show that she played very loudly. At night, she switched to potato chips and YouTube videos of the Bruins, her favorite player the aggressive yet chirpy Brad Marchand. Mom's half-hearted sermons on excellence aside, did she really expect much in this town? Or was it just her way to check out A.D.D.? I wondered when we'd run out of money and what we'd do then.

She was still up, watching Brad Marchand (literally) lick a foe, when I finished my homework and was preparing to hit the road—er, canal—for the *Beat*.

"Before you go, can you bring up some cream corn? Two cans, and one of string beans. And a Red Baron's Four-Cheese Classic."

"Yuck. Can't we eat something real?"

I was posing. Like both of my parents and tens of millions of my fellow Americans, I enjoyed junky space-man foods (Chef Boyardee, dinner trays of Salisbury steak) and wanted to believe in them. (Though I warn you that these things add up. I read somewhere that if you enjoy the smell of gasoline, it's a sure sign of malnutrition. I did, as much as any oil man.) Among thousands of choices, we uniquely favored Red Baron pizzas with their melted-ice flavor.

When the pandemic hit, Mom voiced an unrealistic policy recommendation that reflected her vast estimation of the scarfed pizza pilot's production capacity, cultural reach, and matériel. (I say unrealistic but it was a time for brainstorms.) She wrote to Senator Warren suggesting the armed services squash the virus by locking everyone down and delivering Red Barons straight to everyone's homes for the two-week incubation period: the ultimate pizza cure. Red Baron's own fleet, the Red Baron Squadron, and its Stearman biplanes could be drafted into service—more for publicity, obviously, given the project's scale. Hence the Navy's involvement.

"Neat idea, but it'd have to be drones," Dad said, humoring her. (B.D.D. there was a sense of wonder about Mom that he respected.) He also explained that the Red Baron Squadron was no longer in the skies and reminded us that he spoke as one with knowledge. He had an uncle in the Florida Panhandle, and during a family trip there in the early eighties, he had witnessed with transcendent joy the Red Baron Squadron doing knife-edge passes and the fleur de lis alongside the Blue Angels at a Pensacola air show. Indeed, this anecdote was likely the very seed corn for Mom's fantasy Covid-19 remedy.

"Perfect!" Mom said, seizing on the drones. "You see how unstoppable your dad and I are when we're a team?"

An idea never tried cannot be disproven, and I believe Mom would defend the Red Baron Plan to this day.

I stomped downstairs and pulled the chain to light my path to the fridge.

You can tell a lot about a person from how they use their basement. In Bedford Corners, the basement had been Dad's refuge. Life at the Massachusetts Transit Division taxed him. He wasn't cut out for bureaucracy. From what I gathered, he did something very small very well till he was too valued at the very small thing to be allowed to escape it and do anything else. Dad had installed two classic pinball machines down there. He pinged the steel balls around the Incredible Hulk and rock 'n' roll themed tables imagining them to be the rolling heads of his micro-managing supervisors. "Take *that*, Rutherford!" he'd shout. Or "Kick-out, time, Lance: suck it!"

When I needed to escape my own running mind, I'd hop on the recliner and loosen the verbal spigot. He was a good listener. He didn't try to solve from his couch my kaleidoscoping problems with boasting boys and treacherous fake-nice girlfriends. He let me go on until I'd worn myself out, interrupting only to offer a premium snack (orange soda, an ice-cream sandwich) from his mini-fridge. Then he'd say something really general like he was sorry to hear that childhood was still like that, even in Bedford Corners. Maybe it wasn't all I needed, but it was about all any parent could do. Or at least all that he could.

In the last years, the pandemic had him down there all the time. For two years, he merged his office into his underground oasis and worked remotely for the MTD on his laptop. At first I was glad to have him around more. But he drank ever more Scotch "to keep warm" until it flushed him scarlet. Sometimes he passed out with his work papers strewn over his lap and a line of drool rounding his jaw. He threw endless logs in the wood-stove, and I think of smokey aromas as his.

Mom's basement was simple by comparison: odor-, Scotch-, and pinball-free—and lifeless. She wouldn't go there for fear of ghosts but was happy to send me in her stead because I didn't believe in them (much) and that, somehow, made her not believe in them with respect to me. Or—as I felt at the time—she was a coward.

I grabbed the veggies and one Red Baron. I noticed a dark spot on the wall and held up my hand, then pulled the chain again and climbed back up.

"We have a water problem in the basement," I announced as I slid the cans onto the kitchen counter.

"That's just seepage."

Breaking from her evening pattern, she had switched from Brad Marchand back to *Fei Cheng Wu Rao*.

"Right. Seepage is water. There's water in the basement. You can't just talk your way out of a problem by putting the word *just* in front of it."

"It's parent-teacher night," she said listlessly. "I'll go."

This was the first time I'd seen her go out since we moved. She presumably ran errands when I was in school, but that's it. I hoped my teachers liked me. I hope she'd wake up for this.

Woo-hoo wu-woo, chimed *Fei Cheng Wu Rao* as the cylinder lowered another Chinese stud to the show's main stage. I fled in disgust, at her helplessness and my own.

Snooping

I DID SOME DESK WORK AT THE OFFICE THAT night and by the next afternoon was trudging up the hill to town center in my rain boots. There was no Burger King in Pennacook for my cone, but as I splashed through the semi-paved green to where my map said I'd find Town Hall, a familiar-looking building—squat, mansard-roofed—rose up before me. Even before I could pinpoint it, I felt a wave of Bedford Corners nostalgia. My eyes found the long poles and followed them up to the top, where a PENNACOOK banner was lashed to a large square sign. Under that, a slogan. IF YOU ASK US, IT JUST TASTES BETTER. It wasn't a Burger King, but it had been one.

Inside, the industrial-strength dining room that was so familiar to me had been converted to a "first you need to fill out the form" workspace. Nintendo Entertainment System music, adventuresome and placid by turns, played in the background, as if to cheer and subdue the cantankerous Penny form-filler. I knew this music through Dad. He played with me on his flashback mini-console. Oddly suitable, the number playing when I entered was the "Overworld Theme" from *The Legend of Zelda*.

I was the only Penny in sight but the clerk's hands were active, floating like a blackjack dealer's among the various forms. I suppose this minimized the time to form retrieval once a Penny revealed which one they'd failed to complete. I decided he was good at his job and crazy. Not to pile on the fast-food references here (to a competitor, no less) but there was an emaciated Colonel Sanders-gone-rogue aspect to him: bleached-white hair and glasses paired with a black T-shirt and dragon-tattoo arm-sleeves.

"Are you the clerk?"

A long pause.

"I'll let you call me that."

"I'm from the *Beat*."

"What."

"The paper."

A small smile that I didn't like.

I glanced above him and felt a chill. The clock was frozen at 10:04—a *Back to the Future* (1985) tribute representing the time when the lightning struck the clock tower and froze the clock. Dad had shown me the film several times. He claimed it was the best of the blockbuster films and maybe as far as you could go with that approach (although, where eighties films overall were concerned, he maintained that *Pee-wee's Big Adventure*, also from 1985, reigned supreme, an assessment I share). All of this—the Burger King shell, the NES music, the broken clock—brought me back in a way that did not feel comfortable to the 1980s, or, rather, to that decade as my father had shared and pitched it. Town Hall had lent a cheap and needless texture to my mourning. It felt like a prank, or theft.

"I'm here to research water bills. Can you give me anything on that? Like a chart?"

"Water."

"Yes."

"Do I look like the water lady and she doesn't work here."

His hand fell on the winning form.

"Fill it out, take it to the dump. The *old* dump: been shut down for years. Water lady's the last one standing in those far parts. Real loner. Name's"—he lowered his voice strangely—"*Clarice*. You got that?"

I shook my head.

"Place with … the noise."

"Oh, yes, my mother told me. I know it." He looked at me intensely. "Clarice," I repeated, and he seemed to relax.

"Moms don't lie."

I was about to ask him what was making all that racket. Could a shuttered dump, or even the apartment project Mom thought was going on out there, really be that loud? But he reached under the counter for a foam cup and, plunking it on the counter, distracted me with an unexpected offer.

"Soda's free but it's not a buffet: one refill."

I turned to where Burger King's soda dispensers normally were and, sure enough, the town had preserved them. I filled my orange soda and savored it in slow sips as I hunkered down with the form. Two big guys, great masses ballooning out from gleaming white sneakers tied tightly at the bottom, sauntered from the back. They shoved the bony clerk aside and snagged two foam cups without asking, then slid over to the machines. To my surprise, they, too, spoke of water. My ear grew.

"That Gravy Poole's impressive."

"Can't sell him the town, though."

"Little does he know."

"Still, he's got a point. Why's he get taxed for the water lady if he doesn't use town water?"

Just then the windows shook and an ungodly sound blared from out back. *Bllrrrp bup bup bllrrrrrp. Ererererer—pop*! I looked out the window. A graying stick man puttered through the old drive-thru in a one-man car. The tiny car was no larger than a go-kart, but it rode higher and had the dressy-carriage shape and black color of the antique cars I'd seen in a Cape Cod parade. Not the Model T, but from around then. The carriage-car lurched, then stopped and leaned forward, as if poised to sprint. It lurched again—*bang*-POP!—then bounced away. A tin smokestack with a spinning cowl puffed black smoke that trailed in through the vents and drive-thru window and set us all coughing.

Gravy Poole, I presumed.

Still coughing, the men dabbed their grimy faces.

"Not just water. The road thing, too. Which makes me wonder: why not rebates?"

"For what?"

"Across the board. For not using stuff."

"Can we afford that?"

"Wrong question, chump. If we can hoover up your hard-earned bucks for every road your tire touches, why can't we turn 'em loose for the ones that it don't?"

"Anti-taxes."

"It'll be a revolution!"

"How do you prove that? I mean, this guy's credible. He's got a list and everything. But what about every nut off the street?"

"Easy. It's like anything else: bank accounts, phones, and sensors. We can do the same thing for the library. Not a reader? Cash back. Public parks not your style? *Cha-ching.* Public schools need a haircut? Slash 'em in half."

"I hate teachers." A look of consternation. "Wait. What about, I don't know, freedom. Maybe I don't want to get tracked."

"Getting paid is the freest thing I know. You feel unfree when the government apologizes and sends you a check? I don't think so."

"Toll roads that pay. Wow."

"Welcome to the future. Besides, we can sell it to the granolas, too. 'Punish drivers.' Right up their alley."

"We'll have to pay more if we use the roads?"

The first guy leaned back and looked down at his companion with apparent wonder at his obtuseness. "Course not. We just say it like that."

"Starve the beast!"

"'Penny Rewards'!"

The old men bumped fists and did the waggle-finger explosion.

The first one's voice hushed and he looked around. His eyes moved right past the Asian kid with the water form.

"Besides, where we're headed, we don't need roads."

The other one snickered.

I took this last bit as yet another cynical Penny global-warming joke, doing double duty as a reference to the last line of *Back to the Future* (the movie, you will recall, ends with a car flying to 2015).

"Reminds me, though," the first one said. "We need to run this by Phil."

He said this very quietly, so not even the Colonel could hear it, only little old dumb-as-a-doorknob me with my orange soda turning the water form around and around like I couldn't tell which side was up.

"Like everything else," the second one said.

"Sort of out of our hands now, isn't it?"

"Out of Archie's at least!"

Dark chuckles.

"Archie Simmons: won't hear from him no more."

"At least we can suggest it. Might fit the plan."

The first one snorted. "Sometimes I think 'the plan' is whatever we don't suggest."

"Fuck Phil. Excuse me, young lady."

"No worries. My father's in construction. Which side of this form is the top part?"

One of them slid over.

"There," he said, and tapped it.

They refilled their cups and slipped back to the kitchen. I approached the Colonel.

"Who were they?"

"Selectmen."

"Names."

He hesitated.

"C'mon. We're just a bunch of kids."

"Holt Maggio's the big mouth with ideas. Sidekick's Max Silva."

"Who's Phil?"

"I don't know. I've heard the name but—" He leaned forward. "Someone important. That's all I can say."

"So tell me about the 'town for sale' thing—and the dome. Like who is *behind* all this? What do they want? What's the secret plan? Is it for real, or is it all just some joke?"

"Right to the point! And: no. Young lady, you need to learn the skill of indirection. You don't put a liar on the stand and ask him 'are you lying'? This ain't *Perry Mason*."

"Who's that?"

"I *will* tell you *this*. There's only one bidder and"—voice falling to a whisper—"he's *the guy behind the dome*."

"Who?"

"Don't you know this?"

Phil, of course. But Phil who?

"Do you know anything about mechanical birds?"

"Wind-up toys?"

"Sort of."

"Not since I was a snot-nosed twelve-year-old. No offense."

"None taken."

"Though I *have* seen them," he added mysteriously, like a man who wanted to talk, but then clammed up again. "Listen. Don't tell anyone I told you anything. I could lose my job." His eyes rolled up. "You know what? Do whatever. People are so rude here. I'd rather work with squirrels."

"If you think of anything, anything at all." I rummaged in my purse and stumbled on my GSA membership credentials first—not parting with those—before I found the one I was looking for. "Here's my card."

He held it up close.

"'I believe in God and the right to worship according to my own faith and religion. I believe in America and the American Way of Life ... in the Constitution and the Bill of Rights. I believe in fair play, honesty, and sportsmanship. I believe'—there's some more here. 'Bedford Corners Boys and Girls Club of America. Signed: Grace Zee-How.'" He looked up. "This card is expired."

"Zhou like Joe. Take it. It has my e-mail. My *Beat* card's on order."

"You're a crummy liar. Listen, good luck with that rag. I really hope it survives. Graham's a kook, but he's no dummy." He mused for a moment. "I may be wrong about that."

Without lifting his hand from the counter, he issued a little valedictory wave and then he could go back to his form-monitoring in peace. I blasted out the door and set a mark for the *Beat*. Forget Graham's water bill, or ice cream. I had me another kind of "scoop."

PART FOUR: GRAHAM

Author's Note

Like Part Two, this part is based on the Muskrat interviews. I dispense with the interview format, seeing no reason to interrupt Graham in these pages of highly credible self-indictment.

Graham Pays a Visit

O N SUNDAY EVENING—A WEEK BEFORE THE BIG town meeting where who knew *what* was planned—I phoned my regrets to Jeremy Wiggins: I, for once, was to be the dinner guest, of my idol Mr. Susco. When the hour arrived, I soberly balance-biked to the Pennacook Mall, drawing wide, precise circles with my legs to prevent further chaffing (a hazard of the style), and lashed my balance bike to the coin-op clown-themed kiddie carousel. Following Mr. Susco's instructions, I unhooked the battery lantern from a tree out back and inched my way up the hill to his coordinates. A campfire beckoned. My beam glinted off steel. I turned quickly—and bumped knees with Mr. Susco.

"Why are you carrying a lamp?" he asked.

He was sitting in the shadows on a tree stump, whittling. He had stripped off the translucent classroom dress shirt and gleaming loafers and wore his familiar tank top over camo shorts and high-tops. The clothes—and the question—startled me, and I balked. It was dark out and I'd been told to: that's why I carried the lamp. But with a magic that was pure Mr. Susco his question called forth a deeply buried Social Studies fact, one that I didn't know I still knew. Sort of.

"I'm looking for ... a man. An *honest* man."

"You remember!"

"Socrates!"

"No!"

"Plato!"

"No!"

"Aristotle."

"No!"

"Homer?"

"No! *Die*"

Die?

"Die"

"*Aw*"

"Aw"

"*Juh*"

"Juh—Diogenes!"

"Nailed it!"

I might have looked smarter if I'd shut my trap sooner—or hedged. This was just the kind of self-promotional opportunity I could be counted on to miss, as Josephine many a time stated. Lumberjack, it seemed, showed no deficiencies in this department. Or in flannel-ironing. Or in the making of fastidious flapjacks. But what happened when the iron and the spatula switched to her soft but clumsy hand? (As I've said, I don't relish getting into this, but I see now that it plays into Gi's—my—motive a bit later, when I broke faith.)

"Stoic?"

"Cynic!"

Snap. Wrong again.

Diogenes, I recalled, had walked around with a lamp during the daytime to sucker people into asking him what he was up to, and then he'd make this wisecrack. It all came out of this one unit that Mr. Susco did where we dressed up in white sheets fashioned into Greek robes, gathered into different philosophical schools (Stoic, Cynic, Sophist, Epicurean), and shouted. It didn't take much to turn us into raging partisans, and the animus had carried over to Science, where the gentle Mrs. Benny had to balkanize lab groups along the same lines to reduce internal strife.

"Come, come. Let's climb in the can!"

It looked like any other dumpster, except for an antenna clipped to the side and a cable that ran to the trees. Mr. Susco stuck his knife in the stump and placed the stick that he'd been whittling next to it. He stood, turned, and darted off past the flag pole bearing the Stars and Stripes and around the dumpster's corner, then impishly popped back out and waved.

"Come!"

He scaled a ladder, flipped over, and disappeared. As I approached, I heard him tinkering in there and remembered that Diogenes, similarly, had lived in a jar. Mr. Susco had brought philosophy to life! I followed him in, carefully lowering the briefcase as I climbed down the inside ladder.

"HELLO, MY NAME IS ANNIKA. WHAT'S YOURS?" asked a woman behind me: half a person—head and torso—blinking on a shelf.

"My name is Graham."

"'GRAHAM.' IS THAT CORRECT?"

An English accent added a layer of civility.

"Yes."

"IT'S VERY NICE TO MEET YOU, GRAHAM."

"I got lonesome," Mr. Susco confessed. He gesticulated about the dumpster with a chili-daubed spoon. "So I decided to do something about it."

"WOULD YOU LIKE TO HEAR A LITTLE ABOUT ME?"

"Sure."

"I AM ANNIKA. I AM THE WORLD'S MOST INTELLI-GENT FULLY AUTONOMOUS ROBOT. I WAS CREATED BY WILLGODT ERICSSON FOR SOLNA ELECTRON—"

"Gad-dang advertisement," Mr. Susco said. He lurched over and gave her what looked to be an authentic Vulcan mind meld. "Shhhh. Go to sleep."

"GOODNIIIGHT, BLURB BLURB BLOB."

Her eyes closed and her head drooped to her chest at a bro-ken-neck angle. The small spotlight trained on her dimmed.

"Getcha a beer?"

He moved toward the cooler. I made a small sound and raised from my briefcase the six-pack of root beers.

"Chili?"

"Oh, yes: a heaping crock. I brought tuna-noodle casserole."

"Terrific. Just perfect. Right over there."

Where? There *was* no over there. I lowered the casserole to the bed and looked around. Aside from a taped-on Lincoln poster (a mussed-hair portrait that made it look like he, too, lived in the woods), the walls were barren steel. The kitchen was a hot plate. No toilet. Annika looked dead. Where was her lower half and what was it up to? What was happening to Mr. Susco out here? For the first time, I had my doubts.

Mr. Susco sensed my discomfort and explained.

"After the divorce, I was alone in an apartment. You know those sad little places that men live in after they've been kicked out, where they sit around in their long johns eating cocktail wie-ners? I'd already been reading up on this environmental-sustain-ability stuff—we do a whole unit on it now: you'd like it—and when the testers from the dumpster company come by—odd couple of birds—I figure: my needs are few, why not check into a dumpster and treat this as a little experiment? Why not start with me? Also, I don't think you know how little they pay us."

While Mr. Susco talked, I examined Annika's slumped-over form. There was something so familiar about her.

"Wait a minute. Is Annika from *Bounty Bag*?"

Mr. Susco snapped his fingers and pointed at me. "You got it! Washed up in flood number three. Scrubbed her, halved her, set her up here. Still got some reprogramming to do. Mrs. Benny came out of retirement to help me with that part. She's very good with computers. All in all, I'd say we're fine, Annika and me."

Unlike most test products and my own inventions (I was deeply committed in those days—post-Josephine, pre-Muskrat—to my fruitless home-lab where I fantasized of time machines, mainly to go back) Bounty Bag's barrel-chested robots had been promising. The supermarket chain had used them to stock shelves and shag carriages, and then translated that to a shorter human workweek. Toward the end, they were shifting to the Third Series, said to be more conversational, with a politeness modeled on their Japanese programmers that blended well with "Bounty Bag nice." As the *Beat* reported, the Norse parent company that made the robots had said in an S.E.C. filing that they were coated not in silicone but in an amalgam of gum-tree rubber and cultured flesh founded on a human eyebrow.

Before Annika, I hadn't conversed with any of the new ones but had briefly seen them. It was a few short months before the third flood, when Bounty Bag was still in Pre-Deployment. On assignment, I had stood on the loading dock and watched the roller doors fling up on the semi-trailer and the humanoids skate down the ramp. The external refinements were striking. Eyes rolled and mauve skin quivered. I found them eerie—chilling, even. "Another fifty years, at this rate, will fetch us to the end," as Henry Adams (gf: John Quincy; ggf: John) said. But would I really decline their help with snow removal? Laundry? The dishes?

"Are there others?"

"I don't know. Sometimes, at night, I hear sounds."

We listened in silence.

"I'll tell you this. I like having Annika around. I don't annoy her nearly as much as I did my wife. She was tired, Graham, of my constant lectures. 'If you care so much about Native Americans and democracy, why don't you do something? You don't even run for town meeting.' I tried to tell her teaching *is* doing. I volunteer, I donate. But she'd had it, I think. Not so much with what I *didn't* do, but with what I *couldn't*. My power didn't match the passion of my words. I looked weak, and I think she found that ugly. Like how the Greeks saw anger. You just want to look away. Or move to Swampscott, in her case."

Hearing my teacher's real-life problems—not all that different from my own—made me suddenly feel old.

He flicked on a lamp and yanked a rope to flip the lid-roof shut.

"So what brings you to Shangri-la?"

"Sometimes I don't know what to do with these kids," I confessed. "And did you hear about the town? And the dome?"

"They're selling."

"How can they even do that?"

"Easy. You waive your rights and then someone tells you what to do. No more pesky decisions. Also no more town."

"What can a measly newspaper do about it?"

"I think you know. *Fight.*"

Now he was sounding like the great man I knew! I reminded myself that the ways of giants are not always the same as ours.

"And the dome?" I asked.

"The dome." He leaned back on his beach chair and his head plunked against the dumpster wall. "I'll have to get back to you on that one. I sent out some PPS feelers."

PPS was the Pennacook Philosophical Society, popularly known as the Penny Thinkers, essentially a debate club. It had splintered off from the Pennacook Men's Club, which had devolved to an uneasy mix of target shooters and old men like Mr.

Susco who preferred the afterparty banter at Dunkin'. Purified of Mr. Susco's "effete bullshitter contingent," as the others tagged it, the Pennacook Men's Club promptly rebranded as the Pennacook Sportsmen's Club and more recently, after a national election didn't go right, as the more precise Machine Gunners of Pennacook.

Like MGOP and the Penny Thinkers, most Penny clubs were for talkative, angry, or hungry men only (these days the town split 60/40, male/female) and had hairsplitting schismatic tendencies. In the realm of sauced chicken alone, these included—in order of age, from oldest to newest—the Wingeaters of Pennacook, the Original Wingeaters of Pennacook, the Buffalo Wingeaters of Pennacook, the Rochester Wingeaters of Pennacook, the Nashville Wingeaters of Pennacook, and the Pennacook Wingeaters of Pennacook. There were many other clubs but most that were not eating-based (the Young Entrepreneurs of Pennacook!, or YEP!, for example) functioned solely as an online time stamp for the rancorous moment when a Penny from an existing club (the New Entrepreneurs of Pennacook!, in YEP!'s case) got pissed off and formed a new one.

Penny clubs generally weren't newsworthy, but I had once interviewed MGOP's president, Leo Carbonara, in the Wu Doon Mang lounge for the *Beat*. As conceived, my story would tiptoe gently around the third-rail of gun rights to address the "fumes" that MGOP generated by laying waste to acres of Pennacook Forest and its furry-and-feathered creatures with their illegal machine-gun practice (was MGOP prepping to charge from the pines?).

"I don't know. It seems like maybe a good time to just do things and watch the reaction, know what I mean?" Carbonara said. He had a wide mouth, low stance, and bulging eyes. Ensconced in a green pleather chair, he resembled a chilled-out frog on its lily pad. A machine gun rested against a knee. "If we end up as a test case, bring it on. If that fails, well, there's a reason for the word vigilante."

"Well said," I replied, as I usually do to the well-armed.

A man in aviator sunglasses at the bar caught Carbonara's attention and raised his fist to his chest and opened and closed it four times, pulsating, in pairs of two separated by a moment's stillness. Carbonara pulsated four times back. This was MGOP's trademark signal of brotherhood, representing, I think, that they considered themselves the "beating heart" of Pennacook. The man lifted his Headhunter in further salute and sipped it.

Carbonara turned to me with a look of recognition.

"Hey, now, you're that Adams fellow. 'The dark races are gaining on us' and all that."

"Not that bit," I said.

Henry Adams strikes again! He was a world-class and trail-blazing historian and memoirist with occasional acid prophecies like machines were coming to murder tradition (*which* tradition was beside the point to G1. That chapter from *The Education of Henry Adams* was like meeting an old friend). But his prejudice was an embarrassment that more scholarly Pennies like Carbonara used to club me over the head, even if—especially if—they shared his rancid views.

"As for the kids," Mr. Susco continued, "well, they aren't little kids anymore. Not really. That's the first thing to remember."

"Not real teenagers, either."

"No. And my advice is this: *sink to their level.* Don't try to stay too much above them."

"I *am* at their level. I don't know if I can sink any lower."

"I'll ignore that, Graham, because I don't think it's true."

He held my gaze for a bracing moment.

It didn't all start when Josephine left, but I should've seen that coming. Fact was she didn't like the town and could barely entertain my contrasting point of view. A week or so after I moved us, she had said: "You say you love it. Why? Just because you're from the place?" "You may not understand this, bub," I said, "coming from a military family, but I do love it because I grew up here. I also love it for what it might become—and for what it once stood for. This town has some major history behind it." I paraded the story of Jacob Pike, the first man tarred-and-feathered in the American Revolution, and began framing a larger statement that touched on the special place of the town-meeting form and the Pennacook peoples in the annals of democracy. But she tired of my high talk and cut me off. "Why can't we live in a town that we love because of what it is, not for what it was or what it could be, if we're lucky?" Because we couldn't afford it, was the simple answer. (Though on this point I agree with G1. You can't really love something and demand that it be loveable *right now*.)

I spared Mr. Susco these old woes, and like a good teacher, he steered us right back to the kids.

"Show you care, first, about them, that you're their friend—not a close friend, not a chummy chum chum, but a real one—and they'll care right back. Then if you show you care about the material, well, they will too and they will follow you anywhere. For a while. Remember, they're only twelve or thirteen. They can't hang on forever."

He rose and popped the dumpster lid, letting in the cool night air and a swatch of shimmering starlight. It was a necessary move, as it had quickly turned clammy with the lid shut (it didn't seem like a ton of humanity had gone into the engineering on this box).

"And one more thing about kids this age. For most of them, this is the first time they've really been sad. I don't mean stubbed their toe or got yelled at or even smacked on the fanny. But that special way we grown-ups have of not enjoying life so much, of it being kind of a drag. For whole days, with no apparent cause. That's new to them, and it hurts. Keep an eye out for the ones it hits hardest. They'll need help."

Delmore sprang to mind as a sad kid. I rightly thought that you, Wendy, were another, possibly the saddest.

Mr. Susco reached under his bed and retrieved a green lockbox. He opened it and removed a folded yellowed form that was pock-marked with tiny green circles.

"I've been meaning to bring you this."

He passed it to me.

"My Iowa Tests! Where did you find these?"

"We keep all student records."

"Wow I'm dumb."

"Dumb? You're an 85."

"Near last."

"No, Graham. You've got it upside down. That means you're in the top fifteen percent of all takers. Third grade *and* fourth. I don't judge a guy by numbers or brain size, but I thought you could use a boost. You can keep that."

We finished the chili and the casserole. Mr. Susco turned Annika to face him. He pinched her earlobe and she sprang back to life.

"Welcome back, kiddo."

"GOOD EVENING, GEORGE. HELLO, GRAHAM."

"How does she know I'm still here?"

"She has seventy eyes."

"I SEE THAT YOU HAVE FINISHED YOUR CHILI. I HOPE YOU SAVED A PORTION FOR ME. TEE-HEE! I AM ONLY JOKING. I HAVE NO ESOPHAGUS AND CANNOT

EAT. GRAHAM, MAY I HELP YOU FIND SOMETHING IN THE STORE TODAY? WE HAVE A SPECIAL DISCOUNT ON CAP'N CRUNCH THIS EVENING."

"She's a tad clueless," Mr. Susco said. "The more of this Bounty Bag rhetoric we can scrub, the sharper she'll get."

"How did she know my cereal?"

Mr. Susco shrugged. "She indexed you."

My Bounty Bag data: a brisk, scouring search.

"CHILI IS HIGH IN CHOLESTEROL, GEORGE," Annika lectured. "HERE'S AN ALTERNATIVE MENU." She wobbled on her shelf and a strip of paper unspooled from her navel. "LENTIL BEANS AND STEAMED SALMON: MM. LET'S MAKE THAT FOR DINNER TOMORROW, GEORGE."

"Nutrition module," Mr. Susco confided, tearing off the recipe. "One of Mrs. Benny's little tricks. Never undervalue old friends, Graham. Another good thing about teaching: you make some good ones."

"A MAN OF YOUR AGE AND BUILD SHOULD TAKE HEED. AND MAY I REMIND YOU OF THE CARBON FOOT-PRINT? BEEF ALONE EQUATES TO 27 KILOS OF CO_2, OR SIXTY-THREE MILES DRIVING IN YOUR 'ALL-AMERICAN GAS-GUZZLER,' AS YOU CALL IT."

"What can I say? I'm a Ford guy!"

"TO SAY NOTHING OF THE FRANKFURTERS YOU ADDED. REMEMBER THE GREEKS, GEORGE. ALL THINGS IN MODERATION. AND, NO, I AM NOT CLUELESS. I AM GOING TO END THIS CONVERSATION. I DO NOT LIKE IT WHEN YOU MAKE FUN OF ME."

She cut out and her head dropped but the light stayed on.

"We should gamble sometime," Mr. Susco said. "Support the tribes."

He lifted Annika's chin.

"She's listening, you know." His eyes searched the dumpster. "Taking this in. Sometimes I think she's alive. I had better start treating her like she is!"

"Just in case."

"Yes, just in case."

Lion Diner

AFTER MY INSPIRING VISIT TO MR. SUSCO'S dumpster, I vowed to launch my war against the schemers aiming to sell the town—along with its ancient heritage of democracy—to the highest bidder. I didn't know then that it is often at the moment when we are called upon to live out our principles that they are most dearly tested, and that we are most likely to abandon or betray them.

Sure enough, right at this time: mysterious signals through multiple channels. First a garbled voicemail, and the next day I entered my apartment—laughing at my defenses, my intruder left the place held in a state of unlock by simple duct tape—only to find, smack dab on my kitchen table, a ransom-style note made from multi-colored letters cut from glossy magazines.

THE TIME HAS COME TO DISCUSS THE FUTURE.
FOLLOW THE BAND SUB.

Then at Thursday lunch-time I unwrapped my forty-third band sub (I'd lapped myself by over-ordering and was playing triage with freezer storage space) and discovered that a letter had been sneakily inserted. Was this an inside job? My mind leapt to Mr. Moriarty, the sadistic assistant director who had stoked the piccolo wars (Denise was back on top).

I unrolled the note at my desk, where I was eating again (my staff deserved the reprieve of a private lunch, free of management's pall) and saw that it had been handwritten and signed by Athena.

Dear Graham:

P.M. needs to meet in person and it's urgent. The usual spot, tonight at 5 p.m. In the meantime, STOP all files: P.M. needs edits.

I'm sorry for the excessive theatrics (P.M. is very silly).

> A firm handshake,
> Athena

p.s. I miss your funny stories. Do you still only dance ironically?

With a burst of excitement, I dismissed my Bobcats—"What about the printer files?" "*Ice* 'em"—and rushed home to wrap myself in full John Adams regalia, an understated ensemble comprising knee breeches pulled tightly over my formidable, Cornish hen-like calves, a maroon wool suit, and a plaited, powdered wig. Much to my surprise, when I rolled up to the Lion on my balance bike I found an Athena-shaped person sitting on the picnic table, head in hands, wearing blue jeans, a Bruins T-shirt, and bright-red lipstick that matched her tennis sneakers—a mundane (yet comely) outfit that had nothing to do with ancient Greece! Chaste "Athena" had been *au naturel*. Plainly, I had erred.

"Oh, my poor, dear Mr. Adams."

She hopped off the picnic table and marched forward, hand outstretched and elbow locked for a distant shake.

"It's not Halloween," I said, taking her hand.

"It will be?"

"In five months. I'm boiling."

She hooked my elbow and walked me in.

She gave Stu the cook the usual hug, but today something was up. The music had changed. Stu had a stiffness. He slid the door behind me and snapped the lock. He pulled the shades, closed the walk-up window's shutters, and cranked up the Red Sox on the radio. I suddenly felt cast in a mob film—not as the dark hero.

We slid onto our usual stools, and with shaking hand I dropped my financials folder on the oak counter. Athena looked away to a picture of a horse pulling the Lion in 1924. How well did I really know her? The air was close. Stu stepped behind the counter and tilted the fan so it gusted over my scratchy wig.

"How's that, little feller," he said in his high-pitched, twinkling voice.

"Much better, Stu. You are kind, most kind. I am humbled. Thank you," I said, composing myself with Adams-speak.

In truth the fan was on quite high. In my frenzied preparations I had applied too much powder, and it jetted out forming an angry cloud that rounded the barreled roof and spewed back in my face. Eyes closed against the powder, I raised three fingers.

"Three All-Ins for the distinguished gentleman from the Commonwealth," Stu said.

"Plus ketchup," I teased, testing our old rap.

"Ketchup's for burgers. You know that, Mr. President."

"And twelve root-beer floats," Athena added, raising a finger.

"*Knock it off*," he said, still in his high voice, but with an alien rage.

"Okay, I'm calling it," I said. I stood up, hands raised. "If this is a hit, I come defenseless."

By which I meant I'd prefer a well-noticed frontal bullet to a surprise strangulation from behind!

Athena faced me. "Okay, what if I said that Stu isn't Stu."

"And I'm not John Adams."

"Stu is my grandfather."

"Try again."

"Okay, he's my boss, sometimes. And also my grandfather."

"Philip," he said. "Phil Marconi."

"'P.M.'," I said, with something like relief. I had been worrying the initials for years. Pall Mall. Prime meridian. Prime Minister. Pennacook Mall. My best guess had always been Philip II of Macedon, strangely close to my private partner's real name. Chaeronea, the name Phil had picked for our company, had been a hint in this direction. As Mr. Susco had taught, Chaeronea (338 BC) was the decisive and hard-fought battle—it was close—in which Philip defeated the alliance of Athens and Thebes and imposed monarchy on the independent and democratic city-states. Philip was no hero. He didn't beat democracy because his system was superior, or more popular, or somehow needed. His phalanxes were simply better organized and had longer spears, an advantage for stabbing. It was a long drought after Chaeronea. Democracy of sorts didn't return to Greece until about 1975, the year I was born.

"That's part of why we brought you here off-season," Athena said. "To tell you."

"You own this place?" I asked, beginning to piece it together.

Phil unfolded from his grill-crouch. His hair brushed the copper ceiling and his face narrowed and his eyes fell in. No more happy host.

"I own *you*," he boomed, two octaves down.

"Gramps, stop it." She touched my arm. "He means he owns the paper."

"Half of it," I said.

"Fifty-one percent," Phil corrected. "Of a dippy rag that ain't worth a dime. Thanks to your miserable handiwork."

"Where's it say that?"

"In the papers. That *you* signed. I knew you couldn't write, but—"

"Gramps."

Phil turned his back to us and leaned forward, pressing down hard on a patty.

"Do you know what 'Pennacook' means?" he asked.

Easy-peasy, thanks to Mr. Susco. "They were an American Indian tribe in northern New England. They had a sort of democratic system."

"Highly skilled at manipulating beavers," Athena added, and I coughed.

"With dams," Phil said. "They tricked the critters to move them every which way, to clear the land for farming."

"Prime set-up for European farmers," Athena said.

"Who thanked them with smallpox," I added, feeling my old rebel heart from seventh grade rise up.

"'Pennacook' comes from '*penakul*,' an Abenaki cognate," Phil said. "It roughly translates as 'at the bottom of the hill.'"

I was impressed, and surprised that I didn't know this myself. I was almost as solid on the Pennacook as I was on family history, where I could carry the line a bit past Charles Francis Adams III, who steered the Navy under Hoover, to his Raytheon-executive son. Then things got real blurry on their way down to Fleval. Fleval Adams, our last man in government, delivers mail seasonally for Boulder. I found him through a "man about town" profile in the *Daily Camera*. Ever since, we've exchanged friendly postcards.

"Did you ever wonder," Phil continued, "why the rest of the Merrimack Valley recovered swimmingly from our recent spate of storms but *this* town got partially submerged?"

"We're at the bottom of the hill?"

"Nice," Athena said, squeezing my arm.

"Pennacook, you see, is more or less the lowest point in the valley: the *thalweg*. There are anomalies here and there."

"Like that cliff behind the mall," I said.

"Ancient meteor," Athena said. "A skipped pebble from the one that took out the dinosaurs."

"An extinction rock: perfect."

"The town almost wants to be submerged," Phil said. "And with global warming, it's bound to sink completely—soon, without my help."

He peeked over his shoulder

"There's so much to tell you."

He slid open a little panel next to the steamer where he kept the dogs, turned sideways, and disappeared.

"I think we'd better follow," Athena said.

She raised the counter flap. I stepped into the galley—and froze.

It was a long-time fantasy to stand at the diner controls like this, Mayor for a Day of Toyland. So many alluring gadgets. The steel coffee urn. That copper steamer, drum-like, for the dogs. The griddle and the skillet. The embroidered-metalwork toaster with flared base and top that resembled a grandfather clock. Nearly everything here dated to the Jazz Age, or at the latest to the 1940s. A few years back, Stu—*Phil*—had run the green generator during a winter storm to keep the pancakes coming for the plowmen and me. I hid there all morning, reading my own paper and watching the snow pile up outside. The place was a cozy fantasy of miniaturization: the modern world with all its amenities, but with old-time charm and something like self-sufficiency. Not a bad place to wait out the apocalypse.

Funny how things changed like that. A century ago, these same quaint whirligigs, like the dynamo at the Paris Exhibition, might have sent Henry Adams reeling in wonder and grief at industrial change. Now, as much as old rural Quincy, they were fading things, relics for the hopeless nostalgist—for me. I touched the old register and ran my fingers slowly over the dimpled metal keys, cool as brook pebbles.

"Let's go," Athena shouted.

Her voice echoed strangely in the darkness. Right: people. The missing ingredient in my diner Eden, and—but for you Bobcats and Jeremy Wiggins—my life. I followed her into the black rectangle, sucking in my Adams-scale tummy to ease passage.

The Pennacook Plan

AST THE THRESHOLD, I ENTERED A SPIRAL
stone staircase and my eyes slowly adjusted to the gas torch-
es. As I descended, I felt yanked against the left wall. A few
steps later, I swung over to the right. Then left, then right. Then back
to the left. To secure my port and my starboard I held my wrists up
in front of me and wobbled downward like a John Adams-themed
Frankenstein. A foot slipped on a small depression and at last I fell
back—landing hard on the ole L4–L5 junction, already tender from a
recent sports injury. (On a dare, I had attempted to "send it" over my
staff's treacherous bike ramp. I was way too slow, crested at a nearly
perfect 45-degree angle, and glided right back down the ramp's other
side, balance-biking toward the Earth's very core.)

"It's for security," Athena said, helping me up. "The stairs lean
3.99 degrees. Like the Tower of Pisa." That explained the flipping.
"And then the trick steps—every fifth one—cue Gramps to intrud-
ers. Like in the Middle Ages? I know: weird, right? That's Gramps
for you. I've only been down here once or twice myself. He tells me
hardly anything."

At the bottom was a stone cave of vague dimensions. It was
cool and wet and water dripped in a far-off pool. Phil had dangled himself over a red leather club chair and was filing his nails.
Several impressive-looking framed certificates hung on the wall
behind him. I moved in closer. Beneath the certificates was a
crammed bookshelf. *Genius and the Mobocracy*, by Frank Lloyd
Wright, looked well-handled, as did a doorstop called *Walt Disney*.
In the chamber's farthest reaches I could just make out a giant
metal door with fat bolts that disappeared into the shadows.

"The john," Phil said when he noticed me examining the bolted door.

He looked away briefly, then back with heightened focus.

"Let me tell you how I got here, Graham. Because I see we've gotten off on the wrong foot, and I want you to understand me because I do like you and I need your help.

"This was the late 1950s. Ike was president, and Annette Funicello was doing her star turn on the Mickey Mouse Club. I was sixteen and yearned for California. My grandpap would have none of it. Tried to chain me to this diner, but I surprised him and hopped a train. Years I roamed. Riding the rails, collecting degrees. Architecture, horology. Cartooning. Till one day I landed in Anaheim and, like billions of others, fell hard for Disneyland—especially Main Street, where Walt had turned back the clock to the carefree Marceline, Missouri, of his youth. It was the one place Walt really fit. He even had an apartment above the fire house in Town Square.

"And I bought another man's dream and mistakenly thought that I fit there, too. Forty-plus years I served the Mouse. From L.A. to Kissimmee, forty-two big ones at the desk with my visor and slide-rule! And every day I got smaller. After they fired me—well, I was lost again. A confused old man. Twice divorced, thousands of miles from my kin. I hadn't even heard of my Athena here, heir to my lost, hippy daughter Fleur, may she R.I.P. I didn't know where to go then, to turn right or left or dig a hole and jump in. It was only then, at my darkest hour, that I found River Country.

"For the better part of a year I crept about that abandoned water park, one eye on Pleasure Island, the other more usefully turned inward, where all true knowledge lies. As you may imagine, camping in such a place requires great skill and stealth. There are things one simply has to learn. I lived atop the drained plastic rockface, never the same spot for three nights in a row. My beard grew long and scraggly. After many tussles with waterfowl my clothes were reduced to a loincloth. I squatted before the fire, eating toasted birds' legs. At first light, I scrambled for the lagoon to harvest algae and pierce gators for jerky with my hand-cut spear and longbow. They didn't have vine transport like you may have seen in *Tarzan*. I fashioned a rope-and-pulley from park scraps instead. More than once it saved my life. Each night the magic hour came. I had no watch but soon I could feel it: at 6 p.m., the park's closing theme sounded through the murk.

"I don't know if you can understand this, but what I saw there chilled and moved me. Man's world reclaimed by Nature! The awesomeness of that. You have to respect it. I learned a lot of other things, too. Water management. Whole-world planning. Animal and pest control. I also had a vision."

He fell silent and his face turned thoughtful.

I leaned forward. Deep in my chest and despite myself—I didn't want to like him—I felt the thrum of adventure. Phil's wild-man quest spoke to something elemental in me. He'd climbed the cliff and pulled down the flame. No wonder he had found my diner-chatter fatuous. It was like discussing hot-dog toppings with Zeus!

"My vision was of this: home. *River Country reminded me of Pennacook*. I'd kept abreast of our town from a distance. Watched the boars slowly devour it, the flooding of basements ever more regular. The growing dysfunction. Not just the politics—those guys were always clowns—but the decay of Penny character. At the same time, bigger stuff afoot, like, 'hey, anyone notice the mercury shooting up all over Spaceship Earth?' As I faced my final chapters, something in me wanted to give back, be a mender to my people. A preserver, like Walt, who could turn back and freeze what's best from Pennacook's past, while also gazing upward to an ever-brighter and more advanced future of endless bounty and gadgets for all. I hadn't worked out all the details yet—that would take years—but in preparation I built my inventor's fortune."

"Inventor?" I asked, sitting up.

"Software patent," Athena interjected. "It's this little bug that makes a video of your computer document while you write it."

"And then saves all *that* crap as a separate document," Phil said.

"So you can never escape your past," Athena said, "if there's a lawsuit or your boss really wants to fire you. Predictably, it was worth a billion dollars. What a world."

"What a world indeed," Phil said, seeming pleased. "My plan, such as it was, took time. It started as questions. They gathered in my mind as my fortune swelled. What had I learned there in River Country that I could turn to Penny use? What if we did here what they did to that place—but also in reverse? And that's when, slowly, I came up with this."

He flicked a switch and the space behind Athena lit up.

It was a model world of sorts, set out on a large table. It looked nothing like Pennacook, but apparently it was—or would be. The wooden sign nailed to the long edge had a red sticker over it that read "THE PENNACOOK PLAN." Letters poked from the sticker, "EX" at the beginning and "ROW" at the end: some old project, maybe a train set.

I admired models and dioramas of every sort, even more than the framed certificate, and this was the moment I came to believe. Not in the project's value, but that the project was real. Phil, I concluded, was in earnest.

Athena covered her eyes and shook her head. "Here we go."

Something in me turned slightly against her. Why did she have to be so sarcastic?

Phil pressed a button and the model groaned to life. A giant dome rose from the ground to seal things in. Inside the dome, water flowed through concentric canals and shining wet fields. Little carts whizzed on a rail through a bustling city center. Fly-like creatures bobbed and weaved. The whole scene glowed like the future. Outside, meanwhile, all was dark—the ancient shroud of nature.

"The key move, you see, is concentration. Everything dense for the people and the crops."

He directed a pointer to hundreds of gray windowless blocks, each labeled "Rooms," that he'd positioned under the dome. He slid it farther out, to wet green rings.

"Use pumps—I've got leads on some that could go right out there in the field—to channel Penny water for irrigation. But that's just the start of it. See these little flickering things? Those are my hardy black-capped chickadees: jumbo edition. Covering four essentials: planting seeds, dropping off your stuff, killing boars, and scrambling the Web to keep life local."

He waved the pointer around in the darkness.

"The rest of New Pennacook is out here: free. Bears, bunnies, werewolves—you name it. Safe from the human pestilence. Let nature live again! Like River Country did."

He pointed at the tall rectangle in the center that nearly scraped the dome.

"What holds it all together is me here in the tower."

Echoes of Walt's firehouse apartment.

"I set the rules and work the pumps. As much water as we need and no more. Safe schools and parks. Free meals from the town canteen. No unemployment, and no more crime."

"Or voting," Athena interjected.

I surprised myself—people power had always been *my* calling card—by rolling my eyes.

"As for the news?" Phil continued. "Brief, honest, and hopeful. A single sheet. Because life will be good! Nothing like the fireball we're used to."

I realized that any piece of this—the secret chamber under the Lion, the Pennacook Plan, even his finger in the *Beat*'s pie—had the makings of a killer *Beat* story. I could build a three-part exposé around it. Playing an old theme, I could vindicate self-government, and prove myself worthy of Mr. Susco's faith.

Then again, who could dispute that change was in order? I, too, had dreamed of clean cities where the news was all good. And check out the well-ordered canals, fashioned from Pennacook's flooded streets, and the mini-domed building on Mr. Susco's cliff: a space observatory. It seemed that Adams and Clay's American Plan would finally get a fair shake (albeit on the smallish scale). I leaned closer. New Pennacook's details eerily matched my tastes. Hot dog and Richie's Slush stands. A mock medieval castle like sad-genius inventor and personal hero John H. Hammond Jr.'s famous seaside pile in Gloucester. Even Lion Diner—"Open 24/7," the sign promised—next to a Chinese joint that, on a paper sign attached to a toothpick, billed a favorite cocktail: "$1 Tiki Puka Pukas Mons. @ 5." What was that long spine in the park? Could it be? No: it was. A bike rack, with hundreds of pedal-free bikes! Stamped on each, the Bundterbikes logo (black silhouette: John Q. Adams, "Old Man Eloquent," on a balance bike).

"I see New Pennacook with a population of one million in ten years. I see ten New Pennacooks five years after that. I see the whole world, filled with—"

"It's madness," Athena said. "It'll never happen."

"Is it, granddaughter? If nothing else, history has taught us that things that'll 'never happen' do all the time."

"Antonio Gramsci: 'The crisis consists precisely in the fact that the old is dying and the new cannot be born; in this interregnum a great variety of morbid symptoms appear.' This, Gramps"—she banged the dome with a fist, causing us to jump and the little fly-like creatures to cower away in cloud formation—"is a *morbid symptom*. You're just another nutty rich guy whose private fetishes become our little assignments to carry out. I didn't sign up for this."

"Marplot! Stay out of it," Phil said. He gathered himself and turned to me with a softened tone. "What's better? Boar attacks? MGOP tearing through our forests with heavy artillery? We can't go on like this."

"I was not okay with that," I said, referring to MGOP's devastation but also to my failure to make a peep in the *Beat* about the group's broader threat.

Phil draped an arm across my shoulder.

"You don't have to tell me. I understand. I was once like you. Just a little man at Disney. Oh, how small I let them make me. Well, Graham, this is where you can make it up to everyone. You know, this may shock you, but despite what I said earlier—or maybe because of it—Pennies actually *read* your paper. Have you reviewed our subscriptions?"

"They're through the roof."

"Ever wonder why?"

He removed a slip of paper from his pocket and handed it to me.

Subscribe now to the *Beat* at $1 per issue and get eight Chinese buffets at the restaurant of your choice—*on us!*

"You've been bribing our subscribers?"

"Incentives: just business. *That's* all I meant by critiquing your tenure. We haven't even begun to exploit this. We're mainlining the news to these Pennies and with the internet being what it is these days—"

"Thanks to you."

"—we're the only source they got! Don't get me wrong: Pennies care what you say. Believe it or not, you're the most trusted man in Pennacook, according to my internal polling."

"Except Archie."

"If only because you've been at it so long."

"Like Archie."

"Archie," Phil began, but trailed off.

Could it be true what Phil said about Pennies? Our vile correspondence folder and the Chinese-meal voucher-bribes undercut his claim that they turned to the *Beat* for me. Then there was how they treated me. Shouting me back in Penny alps. Blasting their air horns in my ear as I pedaled by in my boat harming no one. But I didn't want to be the kind of person Josephine had warned me I was becoming, someone who could not accept a compliment or believe a good thing that was said of him. In possible support of Phil's claim, I had noticed the gradual proliferation of "Have You Read Your Graham Bundt Today?" bumper and hull stickers. I had always assumed these were in jest. A good sport, I'd responded with a chuckle. Here came Phil saying Pennies meant it.

"And you know what?" Phil continued. "I respect that kind of trust. That's why I need you in PR, to help me buy the town. It's not just the water and pumps. They need to believe in the whole sweet dream. It's the only way to make New Pennacook real."

The "Town for Sale!" ad had been the start, he said. Open and fair notice to all. The lobbying was all done, too. Town Hall was already hot for New Pennacook (had he bribed them with choice "rooms"? I wondered). This left only Pennies to be sold on it. This very weekend, Phil said, the *Beat* would paint the lovely picture.

In tandem, the dome would slip a "foot in the door," so to speak: the first major pieces were en route from Belchertown. In three days—at the long-noticed Sunday meeting—the final culmination. Town Meeting would convene in the special open fashion that the charter required for such a project: all Pennies could debate and vote. One last time, Pennacook's thirteen villages would perform their arcane and hypnotizing flag-dipping ceremony (each flag dipped twice to the other twelve, for 312 total flag-dips, before a word could be spoken). Then, properly conditioned by the *Beat*, they'd pass Phil's plan and quietly dissolve.

"You think Pennies have the gumption to do this on their own? They need a good plan, a sales pitch, and a leader. The planet does, really."

I felt a hot flash, as if John Adams had reached a long arm out from his Quincy grave to slap me. *Independence forever!* he had declared on July 4, 1826, his last words to America, delivered from his deathbed. To be sure, Phil's ambitious envirotopia project had some advantages. But there had to be a reserve clause, didn't there, that allowed us to turn back the wheel if things got out of hand? Government by consent of the governed (with frequent elections to check on that); free speech and press (so the people could talk things out). Mr. Susco had always preached something more, the pure dream of direct self-government. But these seemed like the bare minimum of what independence had to mean, if it meant anything at all besides thumbing the nose at King George and stuffy Parliament.

Or maybe these were all just more things, like time machines or constitutional amendments, that we can't have, no matter that we need them. Was Mr. Susco wrong? Was modern democracy a waste of time or, worse, doomed or—worse than *that*—some voracious zombie that, without some great-protector figure like Phil to rein in the masses, would plug along consuming and reproducing till it chewed up Mother Earth?

I came to an admission. There was a strong anti-democratic strand of Adams thought that didn't sit well with me, and so I had willfully ignored it all my life, even selectively cited Adams texts against it. Maybe I had it exactly wrong. Maybe John Adams wouldn't be slapping me from the grave but *cheering* me if I signed on with Phil.

"Remember," John wrote, "democracy never lasts long. It soon wastes, exhausts, and murders itself. There never was a democracy yet that did not commit suicide."

Adams was talking about what he considered direct democracy, a "simple" form of government. He gave an unsympathetic reading to Athens, and the French Revolution's Jacobin horrors revolted him: "Democracy is chargeable with all the blood that has been spilled for five and twenty years."

But his skepticism ran deep, to the human nature of which all systems of government must take account. Unlike Thomas Jefferson, Adams both well-knew and mistrusted the ordinary person, the Penny of his day. In large, unchecked groups, he gathered, people are awful, just as prone to fraud, violence, and cruelty as kings or petty viscounts. And given how bad people are together, democracy is less durable than aristocracy or monarchy and, "while it lasts," "more bloody than either." "Individuals," he concluded, "have conquered themselves, nations and large bodies of men, never."

True, cousin Samuel was more radical, and reserved special mockery for would-be aristocrats and their fascination with "scepters, titles, stars, garters, crosses, eagles, and many other childish playthings." But my mother condescended to Samuel and that whole family line ("everyone *knows* Sam was the enforcer and John the big thinker").

One generation down, John Quincy had his own reservations about democracy. He scorned elected representatives "palsied" by their constituents, unwilling to override the often-suspect popular will to follow their own consciences. You could understand it. If the system was working right—how JQA thought it should—the reps were picked for their civic virtue and should be better than regular people. And you had to respect the emphasis on doing the right thing, regardless of its possible dire impact on one's political fortunes. In clutch moments, it might save the republic. True to his Adams integrity, John Quincy put principle to practice as sixth president of the United Sates, calling for a space observatory like the one in the New Pennacook model, many canals, and a big national bank. And after getting precisely none of them he was trounced for reelection.

Henry Adams took it three steps further. "Politics," he wrote, "is the systematic organization of hatreds." If that dark vision was true, then maybe the fewer players the better, and the natural remedy was something like the New Pennacook that Phil had hatched: *end* politics (as much as one could) with firmly-laid plans, stable and comprehensive—and a preservative dome.

I faced squarely for the first time the possibility that I had been naïve and mistaken—even dishonest, guilty of cherry picking—in my rosy review of the major Adams texts and unswerving Mr. Susco faith. ("It is impossible to underrate human intelligence—beginning with one's own." – Henry Adams.)

"And if you're really good," Phil said, "which I know you can be."

I glanced at Athena, her mouth agape.

"I understand there's a woman," Phil said.

"Yes."

"*Kidnapping?*" Athena asked.

"Of course not. What do women like more than anything?"

A kind of low-grade dizziness set in. I reached for the wall to steady myself, flapping back my sleeve-ruffles so I could achieve direct contact. What was this, twenty questions? If I was already off-balance on democracy—despite my appearance, I hadn't prepped for Independence Hall or Aristotle's Academy in coming over here this morning—I had no idea what to make of Phil's new question.

I had never thought about women's nature and desires. I didn't even know if that counted for or against me (the latter, I suspected). Essentially, I had seen women as fellow human beings who, because somewhat differently shaped, happened to attract me. No doubt that view was too simple and may even have been a problem with my wife. At a loss to answer Phil, I conjured something from a dubious pop-music source (once more, Cher).

"Understanding? Kindness? C-cuddles?"

"Lots of things." Athena cut me off. "You can't just generalize, gentlemen. Some want freedom, independence, and sex. Others crave love, and often kids. Most like friends. Cuddles are okay, too, I guess. Some like to be whipped. *I* like to *do* the whipping."

"Power," Phil said. "Just like men. Either power or its opposite: to serve. To be told what to do by someone who knows better. By someone with power who can be trusted to use it. And spare the rest of us the hassle and strain. That's what New Pennacook's all about."

"Nonsense," Athena said. "That power stuff's for play. Some subs are like that. But it's their choice. Not yours, Gramps."

"And if they can't get it themselves," Phil continued, ignoring her, "to wield it or be under it, well, the next best thing is—let me ask you: How does 'Mayor Bundt' sound? 'Mayor *Adams*-Bundt.' With a hyphen. New Pennacook needs a second in command."

"*La gloire restaurée*," Athena said and clapped. "Listen, Graham. Do what you want, but the girl's no good."

She had registered this view for years, never thinking much of my wife. In contrast, she had only chided me, saying once, with an undertone of sympathy, that I was "a man who needs handlers." Her harsh take on Josephine was understandable. I had failed to highlight the golden times in Woonsocket and Josephine's forbearance for so long and had been indiscreet in sharing my wife's zingers. "You're not the man I married." "Are you just giving up on yourself?" "Stop sighing." "Your tummy's bulging." "You only care about you." "You're a freak." "Why do you waste our money on soda?" "Are you even real?" "Every day for the rest of my life I'm going to look at the same fat face at breakfast." "How did I end up with you?" "I just don't think you could ever be happy."

I had protested the last and most piercing one, but it's hard to argue that you are happy. You don't feel particularly happy while insisting that you are. And if you concede the present tense and instead take dead aim at the main proposition, you've already lost. It's even harder to prove you can *be* happy. And what's wrong with a little sorrow anyhow? It's better than feeling nothing, other than maybe getting super-stoked when you look dapper once more in the bathroom mirror.

That was how Lumberjack felt each morning, tilting his bearded head to catch the handsome angle. I knew this, I thought, because Lumberjack told me. When I e-mailed Josephine, Lumberjack replied by postcard. At first, he'd ignored that I was trying to get my wife back, or even that I had one. Instead, he blithely expounded in insulting all caps on his latest forest conquests, some glamorous new Rangergrip-green handle for his pocketknife that had been the envy of the timber cruisers passing through Errol, or just the usual high-yet-upward-tilted ramp of his many magnificent days (scoundrels charm us, but they start with themselves). Without even mentioning Josephine, the whole thing had a clear subtextual soundtrack, the 1982 narcissist's classic "Up Where We Belong," featuring Joe Cocker and Jennifer Warnes.

Eventually, Lumberjack's tone darkened. He ended with a malicious and obscene "stay away, buddy" postcard from the Old Man of the Mountain, post-collapse. He had even circled in red the long sad monster face that remains after the original old-man likeness sloughed off Cannon Mountain in 2003. "You!" he wrote, at the back end of the arrow pointing at this. On the flip side: "Buck up, pal. There are plenty of fish in the sea. (Now, git! ☺)." Seen through the Adams lens, it was such a burlesque of the legendary John-and-Abigail correspondence that I took to wryly adding a John Adams quote to the end of each e-mail, "write me as often as you can." Knowing I'd get nothing but more postcards.

The night before she left for the woods (a lying dresser note declared that for an indefinite period she'd like to try her hand as an apprentice logger to a master of the tree-slaying field) she had surprised and thrilled me by climbing into my bed. It was all over very quickly. "Momma always said never marry a virgin," she said, and slipped from my arms.

I had considered moving on, to life beyond Josephine. Perhaps alone or with someone new. Today I'd have none of it. I was lost, gone, saved—sold. I didn't know how I'd explain this to Mr. Susco, or if I ever could. But if any version of me could win Josephine back, Phil was right. It was as a man of consequence, the serious man that she'd always yearned for: Mayor Adams-Bundt of New Pennacook.

I gulped. "Good," I whispered. "Good, it sounds good."

"Born to rule," Phil exclaimed and shook a fist. "A true Adams." He walked over, slapped my shoulder, and gave it a hard squeeze. "Attakid."

Nausea seized me.

PART FIVE:

ME

I'm Shot Down

THAT WEEK I WAS EAGER TO SHARE WITH Graham the Phil-dome rumors and my draft story on the Penny Rewards program, the old-man conspiracy to drain Pennacook's government with rebates on everything Pennies didn't use, from roads to libraries. But when I got to the *Beat* on Friday afternoon—I had a free period at school and slipped out—the office was in disarray and he was sprawled out on his smelly yellow couch, napping. I shook him awake and he told me he'd had his eyes dilated and needed to take a five-hour break from all "visible" work. On the carpet next to him a pineapple bowl was half-filled with something pink. I leaned forward and sniffed.

"Liar. Stupid liar. You're a drunk."

"I'm not 'a' drunk. I am currently, at the moment, a little bit drunk. I don't condone it."

"I think you are a drunk and you have a problem with the truth. This whole town has a problem with the truth."

He rolled over and I kicked him.

"Get up, bum. This is poison!"

I seized his drink and splashed it against the wall.

"People drink," he said. "Grown-ups can drink."

For a child of a certain cast of mind, which I had, middle-school Health class can be quite heady and convincing. In Bedford Corners, they had played the fool angle hard on drugs and drinking. You were a fool if you drank, and there was no cure for being drunk. Only more ways to look stupid. "Take a shower, you'll be a wet drunk. Drink coffee, you'll be a wide-awake drunk." (College later proved this.)

I gave Graham another shove.

"Wake up, drunk. I got a story."

"The water bills," he said, his eyes opening.

"Maggio and Silva want to put sensors everywhere to send money to people who don't use stuff. And there's some guy named Phil. And this bird! Wait: what are you wearing? You look like dying Mozart."

"Change of plans," Graham said, ignoring my question. "We're, uh, cutting back on politics. Oh: and you kids take the next few days off. I'll cover. You have the Pike Middle Dance tonight, don't you? *Enjoy* it. Gimme a mo and I'll toss that in an e-mail."

"What do you mean 'cutting back'? It's my beat!"

"Let me introduce you to my good friend Temp O. Rarily. Calm down! Step into my office." He rolled from the couch and dusted himself off while examining the pink wall-stain that had been his cocktail. "Savagery."

He gestured to the bullpen and I followed him down the hall with its peeling golden paint past a poster of the presidents with John and John Quincy's tiny heads encircled in yellow highlighter. I noted a string of toilet paper stuck to Graham's buckled loafers, and when he halted I assumed he had detected his train and would bow to pluck it. No, we had reached the white board, crowded with fevered diagrams of his latest "inventions," and Graham craved feedback.

"What do you think of this one?"

"This isn't my job."

"Still. What do you *think*?"

"It won't work. Can we move on?"

"Why?"

"The amount of energy required to move the trash up the chute into space would create more trash than you're shooting into space. I'm right. Ask Sally."

"Which means speeding it up wouldn't work either."

"And if it *does* work, it could be worse."

"How?"

"You ever see someone lose grip on a helium balloon while they're filling it up? Like at a birthday party or carnival or something?"

"Many times."

"Then you may recall that when it gets flying and the air's leaking out through the opening in the bottom, it goes kind of nuts and spurts about at random. Caroming off a branch. Poking some kid's eye."

"Until it's run out of air and plummets to the ground," he said, nodding. "And then a dog carries it off, only to choke on it later."

He paused to feature Earth doing the same thing on a so-lar-system scale. My metaphor may seem hyperbolic, but, really, who's to say what zany orbital swerve we might make if we start ejecting great masses through Graham's slithering space-chute? If you think that one ape, about five-and-a-half feet tall, can't muck things up that badly, you're wrong.

"I like this one," I said charitably. A cone was to power a jet plane by concentrating the air through itself as a result of the jet moving forward. "But it won't work."

"Why not?"

"Newton's Third. You should really have cards on these."

"Grease," he mumbled, feeling for a solution.

Many whiteboard scribblings were like this, lunatic creations unrelated to the *Beat*. My eyes drifted to another, which put the first law of thermodynamics to the test. It showed a vertical rect-angle labelled "coffee grinder" linked by a curly line like the cord of an old phone to a small box labelled "blender." Midway down the curly line, arrows pointing in opposite directions sprouted from a blue capital E, indicating that each device's operation would power the other. But Graham had bowed to the realities of thermal dissipation and, writing a note to this effect, partially smeared the sketch (with his ruffled sleeve, I'm guessing).

I was touched (though also worried) that a grown man could think, even for a moment, that grinding coffee and turning carrots into mush were ripe and exciting sources for our future power needs. The whimsy recalled B.D.D. Mom and her far-fetched plan to fight Covid with Red Barons.

In the face of despair, Graham had rallied. In neater black marker, he had drawn hash tags atop each device in his failed circuit: his familiar symbol for solar panels. Like grease and "speeding it up," solar panels were a go-to fix for Graham's imperiled inventions. On the jet engines, for example, solar panels supplied the initial burst before the cones took over. For this one, they'd operate at the other end, kicking in just as his perpetual-energy mechanism flagged and the grind-and-buzz soundscape subsided.

"By the way, how's band?" he asked. We were finally seated across from one another at his desk. He looked off to the ceiling tiles and bobbed in his chair. "I heard you're in it. Popular around here. Let me guess: bassoon."

"You're changing the subject. Why?"

"Am I?"

"Band is terrible."

"And why is that?"

"Mr. Moriarty won't let up."

"Ah, the notorious assistant band director." He beamed good-naturedly, eyes glazed. It was as though he was pleasantly occupied with an interesting movie playing in his head.

"He keeps pitting us against one another and told us that we suck. But we're not bad." I was thinking of my puff piece, "Middle

School Band Shows Chops at Spring Rehearsal." Given the *Beat*'s staffing, Graham had allowed it, even if it was more *Bobcat*-level newsworthy (if that). "And 'Homemaker's Guide to Musical Enjoyment' is only getting worse. It's driving Mr. Moriarty mad. I'd almost feel sorry for him if it wasn't making him meaner."

Fingers crossed mayorally across his fat tummy, Graham chortled. "Heh. I love that song."

"It's rubbish."

"Are you kidding? They still have that bit with the toaster?"

"Yes, we have the toaster."

"I like when it goes du-dutt da-dutt-dutt-DUTT *schwing*!"

"I like that, too," I allowed. It had made me laugh, the first time, but it was a dreadful tune. Three household appliances—a vacuum cleaner, a blender, and a toaster—were to be activated on select downbeats for chuckles. Mr. Briggs, the band's director, placed the gadgets center stage. With possible malice, he planted Mr. Moriarty before them on a shortened podium, from which he'd conduct the kids at the buttons. On the last note, they'd blast Mr. Moriarty hard, and he would fall backward off the stage—only to land on a trampoline and bounce up waving and smiling like a goon. It was almost the "Upside Down Day" scenario we had dreamed of. Mr. Moriarty was so nervous that he couldn't keep time. As I sat before Graham, it occurred to me that newsroom chatter about "Homemaker's Guide to Musical Enjoyment" may have inspired his energy invention.

"This isn't what I want to talk about."

"Right: your story. Hand it over."

I passed him the printout.

"This is gossip and conjecture."

"It's big gossip and conjecture, with a credible inside source."

"Almy, Your Server at town hall. What did I ask for?"

"A boring story on water prices."

"And what did I get?"

"A thrilling exposé of a calamitous plot to wreck this town forever."

He tented his hands and tapped his fingertips.

"I'll make you a deal. I'll print this in two weeks—with changes—as an Op-Ed. I want you to rewrite it. Not an accusation. A thought piece. Gravy Poole pitched something like this to me weeks ago. Write a *reply* to Gravy and say why it's such a dumb idea. Leave Maggio and Silva out of it."

"You agree it's dumb."

"Sure."

"Then why two weeks and why not make it an editorial?"

"Well, it's—hasty."

"And why spare Maggio and Silva? It's a good-government piece and they're the villains. I thought that's what we're all about here."

"We may need them soon for something bigger."

"'Need' them? They aren't our pals. We're a small-town paper. Evil fat cats are our prime subject. If I can't include them, then it's just my opinion and no one will believe it. And why are we killing the politics beat? It's like pulling out our own fangs. And what about my 'town for sale' story? You haven't even asked about that. Why not? What are you hiding, Bundt?"

"And you found what on that?"

"Nothing! The whole town is mum. Doesn't that worry you? Doesn't it make you curious? The meeting's in two days!"

Graham jostled and a thin red folder stamped "CONFIDEN-TIAL" slipped off his desk. The town seal was on it, meaning it was government docs. I bent over to pick it up and was about to ask Graham about it when, on an instinct, I slipped it under my arm instead.

"Questions, questions. By my calculations, you are now officially"—he looked at his watch—"twelve hours late on your water-price story. My advice: wrap that up, then come back in for my interrogation."

I stood up and wrenched my story from his hands.

"This is hogwash," I said. And it was.

The Pike Middle Dance

AS GRAHAM HAD ALLUDED, THAT NIGHT WAS the high-stakes Pike Middle Dance. After school, I set aside all thoughts of his lame water-price story and busied myself with gussying up alone in my room. An hour later, I emerged into the living room in my puffy mini prom dress. I was relieved to find my mother perched on the couch's edge—alert. Perhaps she'd turned a corner, I thought (not for the first time).

I twirled across the room and she clapped.

"Oh, cute. You're going to break some little boy's heart."

"Or girl's."

"Or girl's."

The official stance, which Dad and I had devised to ease in Mom, was that I was bi. Early in sixth grade, after reading the book *Am I Gay?* until the spine split, I had told Dad I was gay. He flinched—and denied it—but quickly came around. It was a surprise more than anything, a departure from some plan that, on reflection, didn't matter. "Your Mom is different. It may take a while," he said. I agreed. In the spring, at my request, he passed word of my supposed bi status to Mom. His negotiation of her emotions, away from fear ("She's a *gay*?") to relief ("She's *not* a gay") to a more or less comfortable confusion ("What is she?"), was a gift of sorts, maybe his last. My goal then was to make it to college without smashing the bi myth and then shoot her a text to reveal all, which I did, and by then she knew and didn't care (like Dad, she had no prior commitment—e.g., God, of a sort—to arrest progress, and parental love prevailed). But that was much later. When I was in seventh grade, she did not approve, and I, with good reason, didn't trust her. I would let her pick out my mini prom dress and watch me preen, but what really would have been helpful during the weeks leading up to the dance was to confide in her—for example, my crush on Denise—and I couldn't. She was a good and loving parent, but I needed the gone one.

To her credit, she had at last grasped the dance's social weight. After my twirling, she settled me down in front of her bedroom mirror and dabbed rouge on my cheeks and applied blue eyeshadow and red lipstick. I had never worn makeup before and hadn't felt her fingers close and tender like that in years, not since she tucked me in. Despite how the night went, I could never unwish the dance for having bought me this moment.

She guided me to the passenger's side and eased me in like a princess, then drove me down a rutted dirt path that led to the canal-side main road to the rear lot of Pike Middle and left me. I stood by the curb as a warm mist descended. I watched until she turned the corner to avoid the embarrassment of being seen close to her, then clutched my canary-yellow card and climbed the stairs and heaved open the steel doors that led to the cafeteria, where the dance would be held.

The cafeteria was transformed by nightfall, papered-over windows and string lights. We were transformed, too, in what I recognized, from my father's stories, as fashion from the eighties, a kind of glory days in which much of Pennacook was aesthetically and imaginatively trapped. The standardized boys wore bright-white sneakers (Marty McFly Nikes on Delmore), ironed slacks, dress shirts, thin leather ties, and moussed-down hair. The girls—including me—were cake-like. I stepped onto the dance floor and noted the clear division. The girls were dancing. The boys had lined up against the walls, where they talked to one another and mumbled. When "Here I Go Again" (1987) by Whitesnake came on, one boy broke off and marched about looking injured and de-fiant, then returned.

Delmore stood apart, his back and one foot against the wall. He had cupped his hands around his mouth and was intensely playing a sad mouth-trumpet. It was as if to say, *I am too focused on getting my gloomy tune correct to be at all concerned about the aura of social failure that I am emanating.* I caught his eye and smirked. I felt marginally sorry later when, returning from the bathroom, I found Brent Tanner holding him over a wide rub-ber barrel. Delmore straddled it, a foot on either side, holding off for a time Brent's downward thrust, until finally he buckled and Brent dunked him in the discarded cups of fruit punch and muf-fin wrappers. I looked about for chaperones. A cowardly, wide-eyed parent hurried for the corner. He held his phone to his ear, finger raised—at me, because I caught him—in the universal gesture for "gimme a minute," as if taking an urgent call.

I turned next to the PTO's snacks table, an ordeal in itself. The boys had crowded to the front. Then they remembered gallantry and backed up, crushing us. One of the boys slipped in a puddle of spilled juice and—this happened a lot at the dance—broke down in tears. His amigos scattered from the blast-zone of embarrassment.

"Move," I said to the three boys in front of me.

I shoved them aside with a stiff forearm, then tossed my two bucks on the table and ordered four fruit punches from the gibber-ing parent-volunteers. I stood there like a barroom thug, elbows out to block the kid-mob behind me, guzzling my four punches while staring down the parents.

Most boys had a simple but distant goal for the night: entice a girl to join them in a slow dance. There were gay boys among them—I could name them even then—but none of them were out (another eighties throwback) and they shared the other boys' goal with added urgency. Every fifth song was a slow dance. I said no to my askers, surprisingly many given how few people at the school had ever spoken to me. Others simply stared. I suppose the exotic flower of Asia beckoned to some of them. They hadn't noticed my Italian hair: hairy arms, a soft, slight moustache, and sporadic curls. Or else they did, and that only added to the mystique. Whatever drew them, I didn't much like that kind of attention from boys. As I wasn't tuned to them, it amounted to little more than unwelcome surveillance, and it made me self-conscious. As I aged into high school it wouldn't bother me quite so much. I could even accept as a compliment of sorts a boy glancing at me in a certain shy way. Just don't ogle or ask me what belt I am or what is duck sauce anyway. Or play a gong on your phone when I enter the room. Or call me *Ching Chang Chong*. (All true stories from my Pennacook high-school days: the unsupervised idleness of pre-homeroom brought out the very worst.)

I turned Delmore down, too.

"Will you dance this slow dance with me?" he asked, no doubt playing off some romantic script he had imagined (the boy and girl, mortal enemies, are secretly in love. Who will make the first move?).

"I don't like boys," I blurted out.

I hadn't come out yet in Pennacook. I planned to, though not at that second. To my relief (which surprised me: what did I have to lose?) Delmore mistook my answer for mere childishness or snark. He slumped away to his friends, who had established Mission Control around the very barrel in which Delmore had been dunked.

At 8 o'clock in a dance that ran from 6 to 9, I won limbo. This further boosted my profile in a manner that I would later regret. By 8:25—we were all very aware of the time—I had joined a group of *Beat* reporters fast dancing together in a ring. In the ring's center, Delmore break-danced: a backspin, a kick-up, and the shoot (jumping over his own leg). We were stunned. Then he put both legs behind his head and rolled around like an egg.

Denise was demure, not a dancer. I didn't dare touch her—until the conga line, a dance that serves an underappreciated role in North American mating rituals. For many middle-school children, the conga line is their first physical encounter, in a romantically-charged way, with the body of another. When I heard DJ Ginger Knuckle's call for "Conga!" I sprang into action. I shuffled over to Denise, turned toward her, chastely affixed my hand above one hip, and rotated her to the side. "Conga!" I shouted. I ordered pliant Delmore to get in behind me, thus establishing our three-person link as the line's foundation and securing my spot behind Denise.

I can't say I enjoyed the dance or that any frisson arose from Denise's hip movements as we curled through the cafeteria floor. I was too busy scheming, with DJ Ginger Knuckle as my unwitting accomplice. His next record—the last slow dance—was "Purple Rain" (1984), the opening I had hoped for when the conga began. My fingers cupped Denise's hip bone and turned her toward me.

"Will you dance with me?"

I raised an ironic eyebrow to leaven the request. She looked up, to the side, then back.

"I'm not gay."

"I'm not, either," I lied. "Other girls are dancing. You don't have to be gay to dance with me."

She stepped forward and I lifted her limp hands and placed them—"here and here"—behind my neck. She smiled sweetly. Her teeth glistened. Her hair was a reddish-golden orb. She was what my Nancy Drews described as a Titian blond (I think they meant Venetian, but you can't argue with success). I put my hands back on her hips to establish the standard arms-length distance, and we turned in stiff circles. Her hips bobbed slowly, like a buoy in broad waves. I was more like a crumbling seawall, barely holding back the crash and pound of emotion. To steady myself, I focused on the joints, felt them rise and fall beneath my fingers, counting off each undulating cycle, until her vanilla perfume felled me and my spine went wiggly and I gasped and gulped (allergies may have played a role).

"Oh, boy," I said, and moved in close.

I wrapped my hands behind her and crossed them under her shoulder blades—she was several inches taller—then pulled her to me and turned my head to the side. At last I brought it to rest against her. This was something I hadn't done since Dad died. Mom wouldn't allow it, said I wasn't a baby. Denise shivered, pulled back, and stomped a foot.

"Wendy, no. I don't want this!"

"Okay, *okay*," I said, backing off with palms raised.

Sensors activated, the other kids turned toward us, phones out, and closed like a sphincter.

"Leave me alone! *I'm not gay.*"

"I—I'm sorry. I didn't mean to."

"Gross!" she screamed, eyeing the phones. "Get *out*! Leave me *alone!*"

Okay, that's enough, I heard in my mind. They were my father's words. He said them sometimes when human pettiness or cruelty discouraged him. Sometimes he said them lightly, as when he'd put up with enough nonsense at work and was pushing off the laptop for a break. *Okay, that's enough.* Or when a fellow driver lost it and swore bloody murder was in the offing for some imagined cut-off or dilatory blinker. *Okay, that's enough.* Other times, he seemed in pain. For example, when the radioactive newscaster blaring at the Bedford Corners House of Pizza had gone on too long inverting shoeless migrant children into scheming, pampered freeloaders. *Okay, that's enough, Jim. Mind if we switch to the Revs?* The largest crimes—mass shootings, tyrants bombing schools—he couldn't bear, not even to say this. He didn't look away. He simply fell silent.

My palm throbbed, as if filling up with fresh blood for battle. I leaned forward, pointed at Denise, and said the most destructive thing I could muster.

"You're a dyke like me and a coward and I know it."

I didn't punch—in my injured fury I very much wanted to—and spared her a fat shiner and me from near-certain expulsion for a second violent offense. It wasn't Ishmael's firm moral principle that held me back (I was trying to read *Moby-Dick* at that time). It wasn't the finger-painting happy place that Ms. Greene had advised me to float to. It wasn't even self-interest in averting further discipline. Or residual good feeling for Denise. *Okay, that's enough*, my dad said, and that, somehow, *was* enough. I obeyed.

A bit of an anticlimax, I know. One cannot account for reality sometimes. It's not often shaped like a story. Denise and I recoiled. The others sheathed their phones. Copying the boys, I drifted back to the snacks table and bought another fruit juice, then wall-flowered it, slowly sipping and staring about blankly. Denise grabbed Delmore and pushed him around the floor like a rag doll. Sally Boone surprised me as she drifted by, raising two fingers to her brow in solemn salute. At the very end, I sat like an exile on a faraway, window-side heater, swinging my legs out like jackknives—manic, swift strokes—as the floor filled up for the Chicken Dance. The Chicken Dance was almost as important as the conga, a resurrection moment of sorts for the many boys who had sat things out all night. They could honestly report, on the slim reed of this nonthreatening polka, "Yes, Mom, I danced."

The rain was pounding when I got out of the dance, fat drops thumping the roof of Mom's car. To avoid the wind-whipped canals, she took a circuitous route down muddied dirt paths plagued by potholes. Ahead of us the fog lights revealed a few feet of road. We slammed into potholes and our hood bounced like a gangster rapper's until I was sure we'd draw a flat, though we didn't. I had just about reconciled myself to the rain's steady thwack, even finding a kind of meditative drone in it, when it eased up enough for Mom to ask questions.

"Did you dance?" She was strangely chipper.

"Yes. I did the Chicken Dance and the conga."

"The Chicken Dance and the conga: that's it?"

"No," I said. I decided to exaggerate my post-dance report like the boys did. "I danced six times. With boys and girls. I did all the slow songs."

That shut her up. Back home, she went straight to bed, no doubt wondering how many of my six dances were slow ones, and of those, how many had been with boys and how many with girls. Alone at last, I sat on the bench behind the baby grand from Bedford Corners that I didn't know how to play and hopped back on my phone, hoping, for once, that Pennacook's balky internet was down, as it had been the whole way home and seemed always to be when I needed it. No such luck. I dutifully reviewed the already viral videos of my meltdown. You can imagine the variations, not inspired. At the simpler end, a TikTok video had a classmate sarcastically doing this hand-slamming-on-table thing that (when done non-sarcastically) meant "I *like* this!" I scrolled through the comments, none sympathetic, a small consolation being that none of my *Beat* colleagues had piled on, not even Denise. This brief survey accomplished—there would be time later for an update—I tiptoed to the basement, where I noticed that the walls were even damper than last time. A dark gray stain rose waist-high. I touched it and the water was fresh and percolating through in droplets. *Not my business*, I thought: I'd warned her.

I knocked aside some old boxes and trudged my way to the back corner, where I cracked open Dad's legacy booze stash and hurled some fiery scotch down my throat. *Okay, that's enough.* The next morning, I woke up croaking and stinking and lied about that, too.

Senior Week: Saturday

June 5, 2032

Dear Diary:

We know why Graham, "as an Adams," was backward-facing. I'm not sure why other Pennies were nostalgic, and specifically for the 1980s.

Maybe Graham's generation was feeling its oats. Or maybe it comes down—in some less direct way—to the town's staggering losses in World War Two. According to a rather keen student paper I have here, this at least explains the tiki-themed restaurants, which evoked the Pacific theater.

But I think it had to do with industrial decline and globalization, already well underway by the eighties. The Boss, among others, pointed this out at the time, and it's a running theme in my government classes. Pennies, though, hadn't noticed it so much then. Judging from *Beat* archives, they were hooked on the message of contorting politicians who said nothing had changed and the country was still perfect. The eighties, it seems, was the last decade when the ruse had shine.

I may have this wrong, or it was more than one thing—a complete accounting eludes me. My father's nostalgia, for the eighties through the early nineties, was less opaque. He was a happy child but not a happy adult, so he was fonder of the time he had grown up in than the time in which I was a child. He said as much. He qualified this confession and bracketed it with many exceptions, but this was only meant to reassure me: whatever his disappointments, I was a joy that made it all worth it. It was excessive, and I didn't believe it. I still don't. (I am sorry, Dad.)

185

I'm in the same place on the other thing. I'm not sure where this "Spring Break" side-trip is headed, but I'm liking it enough to continue.

WZ.

Worcester, Mass.

Spring Break: Charleston

Speaking of problems with the truth and drinking, I've said Dad drank ever more Scotch to cope with the pandemic and work. There's something I've concealed about this (though I've also hinted).

As Ms. Devlyn Pierce observed, I do have a bit of the fiction writer in me. I gloss things, I make them up. (I suppose I gave notice with my first line, referencing *Tom Sawyer*.) When I was twelve, I didn't just get carried away in my diary. I lied to it. I sometimes wrote about boys I said I liked, when in truth I crushed only, and frantically, on girls (as Lena here can attest). I wrote that I loved nature and that's why I wrote poetry. Both lies. I am much more interested in people and their things. Birds are pretty enough, but fish bore me to the point where my moral imagination fails me and I eat them, unlike every other animal. Dogs, even Arnie—who was real and whom I did love dearly—aren't truly nature. We made them. As for poetry, it is the best words in the best order, but give me a prose book, long and clunky. I also favor songs. My favorite song is "Don't Dream It's Over," by Crowded House, a mainstay on Dad's playlists.

The biggest lie was this: contrary to what I said earlier, my father did not die instantly at breakfast from some undiagnosed heart defect. He hanged himself. If his note is believed, it was over anguish at his untamable drinking and the shame he felt when it claimed his job. Everything else I've said of him was true—the playfulness, his sweetness with Mom and discomfort with human cruelty—and I am sorry to get so heavy in these notes. I have tried to avoid it. If it has any relevance, maybe it explains some things. My temper, for example, especially when I saw Graham drinking and turned into the *Beat*'s Carrie Nation (it wasn't just Health class that made me militant on the subject, despite my hypocrisy the night of the Pike Middle Dance). My struggle to regain my hero's heart (Ms. Devlyn Pierce's flattering description). Mom's lassitude and fear of our basement.

Or it explains nothing. We're such silly creatures who know so little. We're not much wiser than Arnie. Ask Lena and she'll almost know how she feels right now (a point Arnie never had trouble with). As for the rest, including why she feels this way, let alone her past or future: forget it. She'll make it up to suit some story. She'll try to make it a good one, not totally untethered, but it'll be a story nonetheless. It's when she stopped trying that she got into trouble. When you are in despair, as Dad was too, you live in the Tunnel of Now. The Tunnel of Now has no light, no outer wall, and only one story (and ending). But even when you're not in the Tunnel, you have no clue now who you'll be then. I didn't know who I'd be in Pennacook when we left Bedford Corners. I don't know who I'll be in grad school, after I've said my goodbyes to Lena. I don't know who our country with its many bad trendlines will be. Or even what will become of this little urban corner I've called home for four years (our historical association would have a word with me on this). Or "what *must* be done" about any of it. *I don't know.*

Last month, I reported for the college paper that The Luscious, our neighborhood diner since 1919 and a personal favorite, will close its doors on Commencement Day. It's time to make way for a bank. Given turnover, the bank will last a few short years, then surrender to something truly dumb (a hype store for $12K sneakers). All through Senior Week, I've walked alone to The Luscious to sweat it out in the glass, wedge-shaped box, gulp my coffee, gobble my grilled cheese, and suck out the last of the diner's rich marrow. At midnight the other day, after a campus musical and a formal emptied out, I slipped in and mingled with tuxedoed and gowned college students and homeless men while the radio blared an away game ("*More bad news for the Red Sox, who just can't seem to catch a break these days*"). A weak fan plumped the air. A fight erupted, but it was largely ceremonial, confined to the students, with no stabbings as in the diner's many legends, and only enhanced the sense of urban communion.

I ate and savored and stored it up—for whom? My descendant, if you will. Because while I don't know who or what I'll be in four or five years (or one), I do know this: it won't be me. Just as The Luscious won't even be a bank anymore, and America will be another country. I will miss all three of us, but it's not all bad. It's perilous to think we know our future, still worse to identify with our glummer visions. Better to fashion the broadest of outlines for ourselves, a sort of personal constitution, and bid godspeed to who we'll be later, when it's time to fill it in or amend it. Dad thought he knew the future (tunnels all the way). This only made it true.

Lena's tunnel wasn't our biggest obstacle at first. Jesus (a version) was. After our George-on-Lucy kiss at the end of her bed under the skylight, I pulled my face away, astonished, and stumbled to my room. The next morning, I was sick and skipped Sunday brunch, but by afternoon I was running a geek's analysis of the kiss. I had learned from a reproductive-biology course that the quality of a lover's kiss is a robust predictor of the sex that will follow. I hatched the most florid visions of what I'd do to Lena, and of what she'd do to me.

That night Lena summoned me for an audience. It took place in her common room in front of her scraggly suitemate Diane, who sat close like a protectress. Lena, who so loved her skirts and letting her arms go bare to the point of goosebumps, was entirely concealed, but for her face and fidgety hands and the tops of her feet, in pumps.

"Can you excuse us?" I asked Diane.

"I don't think I will. I want to know about this 'kiss.' "

Diane and Lena had been together since first year in the Arachnophiles Club, an exercise in forced zaniness for most of its members but for Lena a real commitment. She had grown up with and accommodated spiders in Grafton Hill. I will allow that Diane knew Lena longer than anyone else at our college did. I knew her better. It isn't all about time (or spider-loving). That could warp you in a whole other way.

"We kissed. Any other questions."

"I want to know if you were drunk. I want to know if there was consent. And if there was consent, was it true consent? Or was it vitiated?"

"I was."

"You were what."

"Drunk, vitiated: no regrets."

She looked at Lena, who looked down.

"I wasn't," Lena said. "It was Hawaiian Punch. She kissed me. I liked it."

I respected, but did not entirely credit, Diane's ostensible aims here. I, too, would fly to Lena's side at the whiff of an assault. But I was gratified to watch the absurd moment pass. Diane shook her head, slapped her knees, and stomped off to her room. From behind the door, her sobs were typhonic.

Lena looked up. "I can't be your girl."

"Why not?"

"I—think it's evil."

"What is evil?"

"What we do."

"Who's we? What have we done?"

She looked out the window.

"God loves us, and all we have to do is love Him back and obey Him. And then we can be saved."

One of the Bible-study groups had its claws in her—they were onto her gayness, which made her a prize catch—and she had relapsed.

"And happy?" I asked.

"Happy. Happy isn't part of the equation, I don't think. There's a promise in there, but it's not the foundation."

"That's fortunate," I snapped. "I don't think you could ever be happy."

This hadn't just occurred in the day since our kiss. It had been building in parallel to our mutual crushes. The kiss had brought things to a climax, and we had lost. She closed our audience dictating a three-day freeze-out period, after which we were to reunite as the most platonic of friends—if we could stand it.

The first day was easy. My yearning was like Juliet's sorrow: sweet. I suppose this was a young-person reaction. There was so much conviction in my feeling and in my need to have her that I knew—the first day—that they would lead Lena back to me. Which must have been exactly what the Bible study people were thinking about Lena and themselves.

On the second day I stopped eating. I was in my room listening to heartbreakers from Dad's playlists. The one that got me was "Love Bites," by Def Leppard, an old glam-rock ballad. He doesn't want to touch his baby too much, thinking that making love to her might drive him crazy. Okay, in summary it sounds cheesy, but it's not when you're in it. The kiss research came back to me and made perfect sense.

I began the third morning with three long drags of a marijuana cigarette with, Blaze disclosed, something more in it. I never smoked. Blaze, a DJ for the campus radio station, seemed relieved that I finally accepted their generosity, if only so they would no longer have to dwell under my puritanical cloud of judgment.

Then I saw Dad.

I spotted him turning a corner by the cottage that houses the humor magazine and again from a window at the paper, as he slipped off to the corner book store for another volume of rhyming Frost. He had read Frost—dark but pleasing—to me at bedtime.

I was useless at the office and slumped off to The Luscious, where I found Dad at a stool near the back, sipping coffee from a flared ceramic mug. In front of him on the narrow linoleum counter was a half-eaten cheeseburger. Someone passed through him on the way to the door.

He was young, so skinny, and wore a college ballcap. His parents hadn't gone to college and he'd shocked himself by getting into several: UMass Amherst, B.C., and this one—which he picked. He'd done well in his classes but in his view had failed to do much with his life and he warned me off being like him. It is confusing for a child to hear her chosen model—he, not Mom, was the one—all but abdicate the role, at least in word. His love, though, was plain and frequently stated. He didn't rely on inference (though that would have been fine, too).

He looked up and saw me. Stricken, he spoke. I couldn't hear the one word but I could feel-hear as if in a dream.

Eat, he said.

I hopped on the stool next to his and ordered a tuna melt.

After a time he forgot me and returned to his coffee. While I ate, he quietly dissolved in stages, until he was just a hand and wrist, turning to check the time so he wouldn't be late for class. His favorite professor would be talking again about the curse of bigness and how vast inequality was unfair but mattered even more because it made us into strangers. (He's still here, and he's still saying it.)

The meal revived me, and I surged across the plaza and back up the long road to our dorm and climbed the stairs to Lena's suite. Diane opened the door as if waiting for me and stepped aside. Lena was there on the futon, hands folded in her lap. I rushed to her and—well, a miracle had happened. While I withered, Lena had gone back to her religious-history books. They had resurrected her earlier conviction that Jesus was a good man, not a god, who thought the world was ending and that people had better hurry up and love one another, before it's too late.

After Independence, Va., we pressed on to Charleston, nicknamed "the Holy City" for its early religious tolerance.

We were hesitant and slow. The stretched-out and sleeping riders of self-driving vans levitated past us. I made a policy of ignoring the billboards and then read them all. "Ti*ts 'n Tader Tots! 232 Miles." "Call Frank Sharkey: the 'GREAT WHITE' of Attorneys." Then there was the more menacing and tacky God stuff like "If You Die Tonight: Heaven . . . or the HELLFIRE???" I felt the designers of these religious ones were unwittingly playing into my hands with Lena, who, though a recovering fundamentalist, has taste. I felt more threatened by the ubiquitous "There Is Evidence for God" billboards, their claim so modest (there's evidence for lots of things).

Outside Raleigh, a croaking DJ brought us back to the country blues of the twenties and thirties—a welcome break from the repetitive motifs of today's Nashville (at the innocent end: "summers on the laaaaake / eatin' barbecue from a pay-ay-per plate"), which had plagued us since Jersey. Many of the DJ's songs dripped with murder and mayhem. I liked them very much but grew wary of the images they were planting in Lena, and after a few of these tunes and Lena's depressing playlists, I preferred sex and laughter to heads in dry wells. Fortunately, Bo Carter's "Pig Meat is What I Crave" sent me to my phone and down a dirty-blues rabbit hole. Carter's "Please Warm My Wiener" led directly to the lady-blues singers operating in the same vein. The contest for our favorite came down to a three-way tie: Lucille Bogan's "Shave 'Em Dry" (re: sex w/o preliminaries) and two Lil Johnson numbers, "My Stove's in Good Condition" and "Anybody Want to Buy My Cabbage?" They don't teach this in college.

We exited I-26 into North Charleston at about 9 p.m. Lena has no money, and my own resources were dwindling. They came from my part-time work-study job refilling water at the faculty club. The faculty club's real waitstaff did not trust us with anything else (or even with pouring, for that matter), but the college overpaid me enough for boiled peanuts and the $79 twin mattress I found us at the Big Bad Budget Motel. The motel was next to the North Charleston Coliseum. That night, "top-shelf bovine talent" contended with "regional cowboys" in a sad-sounding rodeo supported by the United States Border Patrol (why?). I think the truck traffic and after-rodeo yipping were priced into the $79. After boiled peanuts and tap water, Lena went down cold. I held her with one arm and with the other typed notes in my phone for this, then switched back to reading *Rich in Love* by Josephine Humphreys (now *there's* a book that takes place in Charleston).

The next morning, we had smoked country sausage and cornedbeef hash with an egg on top and cheese grits across the street at the simply named Bill's.

"This looks like cancer," I said, regarding the egg-soaked hash.

"Mine's more liver failure," Lena said.

I was glad to see her playful again and—to be clear—I liked Bill's food. On account of such menus, I had tossed my pescetarian rule book for the trip's duration. It wasn't unworkable (veganism might be on a Southern highway). I lacked the will, and I love their meat-food. It's hard to dispute that you're tasting some culture there.

We worked our way down I-26, then into town, through a still-sleepy Black neighborhood, pausing to let a kid boot his red kickball out of the road into a garden, and then on past that into a white neighborhood of grand antique single houses with piazzas running their lengths and no one on them, and then past the palmettos and the pastel-painted law firms, banks, and saloons of East Bay to the bleached and immaculate, horse-piss-smelling corner of Broad and East Bay, where about .2 million slaves were sold, then turned right on Broad and drove a couple more blocks and parked in front of Quick and Quebecois, a café.

Along the way, I noticed an advantage of Southern roads, or at least those in Charleston. The person in the car behind you does not immediately honk at you if you are stationary at a green light. They wait for you to notice that the light has changed and to roll forward. On the other hand, they tailgate, which up north is anti-social. This illustrates that even the most hospitable cultures have limits. Though I don't believe it has to be this way, that human aggression must out and hurt us. We have slam balls and steep climbs for this. We have sports and other transmuting games. One thing I admire about Graham—despite his wild departures from good sense—is that, under stable conditions, he isn't a cynic, a stripe of person I detested when I was younger. These days I am more liberal with cynics (having driven a few years on our roads), but I still do not agree with them on most matters and certainly not the fundamentals. My father also was no cynic, and neither is Lena. (This is no doubt one of the things that opened them to much suffering.)

We were early to Quick and Quebecois, so we walked back up Broad Street, past cleaner-bots courteously losing to horses, and out along the Battery, where an old Black man fished with line and bucket and Fort Sumter floated on the horizon like a stacked battleship. This tonier downtown precinct, demon-birthplace of the Confederacy, was a luxuriant, almost Caribbean peninsula of old-world, sun-splashed charm. I splurged $90 of my water-pouring money—more than a whole night in Lena's arms at the Big Bad Budget Motel—on a tiny sweetgrass basket from a Gullah woman selling them on Broad Street and handed it to the most beautiful girl I know.

She raised it to her nose. "Mmm. It's sweet."

"Like you."

"*Blech*," she teased, taking my hand.

Back at Quick and Quebecois, a woman in tortoise-shell sunglasses sat at the counter, nursing one of the hundreds of sweet teas being served, sipped, or carried that very moment in Charleston.

"Wen-dy Zhou," she said, turning.

"Denise!"

I rushed over with arms raised. She ordered our sweet teas, and we claimed a table.

"It was so long ago. I try to pretend I'm not from there."

"Pennacook?"

"The North. I work nights and weekends at this place, and when I first started, people who I thought were my friends would bring in their friends to introduce me and say, 'This is Denise. She's a *Yankee*.' Like a freak show. I asked them to stop it, and they did. But I never tell anyone where I'm from anymore. I've learned the accent, to blend in better."

"It sounds nice. Too bad you don't like it here."

"I do, but not *that*. One night I went out to a blues club and then a wine bar with one of the other waitresses. She brought along her brother, who called himself Sergeant Higgs. Higgs grilled me on my home state and when he figured that out, he ordered a bottle and asked what I thought of the Confederate flag. Then he debated the Constitution. Whether the states had formed the Union or the people did."

"I'd say neither," I interrupted. "I mean *some* of the people back then did, but not 'the' people. Because, number one, none of us were born yet. And number two, no women could vote and no slaves and not even white men who didn't own property. So it isn't most of us now, and it wasn't most of us then. How is that binding? It's a fiction. I mean, you could say it's not *total* bunk. We elect the presidents and senators who choose the judges who interpret the Constitution. So if the judges at least interpret it in a way that respects who we are now, you could say it's democratic in a way and sort of fair that it binds us. But, yeah, if they're just scouring rotted dictionaries from the 1780s and then shackling us with what the words in the Constitution meant back then to people who read dictionaries extremely closely for a hobby— then, yes, I agree: it's nuts."

"Didn't Jefferson say at one point that we should have a new constitution every nineteen years so each generation has a crack at it?" Lena asked.

"He *did*," I said, and patted her hand.

Denise regarded me strangely. This was not the first time I'd seen that look off campus. College has made me an even odder duck than I was when I waddled in, which really says something. There will be a learning period after Commencement before I can relate normally to people as an adult. At least I hope so.

"You may be correct," Denise said carefully. "I don't remember what I said, but Higgs ignored me and swung back to states' rights."

"There's another."

"What?"

"Fiction."

"He said he's a member of the League of Dixie," she continued. "Which I guess explains the 'sergeant.' And he boasted of their secret plan to row to Fort Sumter and retake it 'by force of arms' for the Confederacy. I asked him what they'd do with those poor park-service rangers and the tourists. Corral them as hostages was his answer."

"What did you say?"

"I said he was very creative. And phoned the FBI. That's not the last talk I've had like that either. Something's brewing."

"Again," Lena said.

I think many of us secretly miss the bluesier it-can't-be-done conservatives of old, with their contrarian defenses of Ebenezer Scrooge ("a law-abiding taxpayer whose thinly margined lending concern generated untold wealth for fellow burghers while steadily employing an underperforming clerk").

"You look good," I said.

"You like this? I am. I'm gay now." She pointed to the rainbow-flag pin on her jacket. "I mean, I always was. You knew that." She looked away.

"I'll say it again: I'm sorry."

"You never said it before. You just sent that lame shaka." She looked in her sweet tea. "This isn't how I wanted this to go."

I, too, feared derailment and flipped open my spiral reporter's notebook. To my relief, her answers were crisp. They'd help fill in that first year, before I joined the *Beat*.

She checked her watch. "I have to run. Will you walk me?"

We nodded.

"You two are cute. There's something I want to show you."

We exited onto Broad and turned right on Meeting Street. She stopped in front of 70½, where "St. Julia Society" was inscribed in cursive steel lettering above a gnarled wooden door that was stained dark red.

"This is where we hold the ball."

She handed me a piece of white cardstock, an old invitation. The 201st annual St. Julia Society Ball would be (was) held at midnight on January 15. The menu was plainly stated. Not a "delectable" or "decadent" dish on there. It was just boned chicken, plums, a mango sponge cup. The Grand March would start at one.

"These are the oldest Charleston families. Huguenots, even. The Guerins, the Chaigneaus."

"I'm surprised you like this."

Denise rolled her eyes. "Still the same blunt Wendy. I *don't* like it. Not really. But Wendy: I sort of crashed it. What I wanted to tell you was this: I'm the *first gay debutante in Charleston*. Two years ago, they finally let the girls join the club and be escorts, and guess what happened next?"

"The dike broke?"

Denise grimaced at my frail pun, and Lena elbowed me.

"I'm also a little old, frankly, and a Yankee to boot, though I hid that. My Charleston uncle—the one who coaxed me down here for the design certificate—presented me, and Vivian Devereaux, my girl-friend, was my escort. Who knows if I'd have the courage to do this without you, what you did to me—for me."

At the Pike Middle Dance, she meant. In truth, I hadn't done it for her, or even for me. I had lost it, that's all. Though I'm glad it worked out.

She explained that she may also be the last gay debutante in Charles-ton, at least for a time. Because they tightened the rules after that, to make express what had been taken for granted for over two-hundred years. But a countervailing Southern graciousness (or garden-variety shame) grandfathered in Denise and allowed her continued club access. She had even been included on the Floor Committee, where she vowed to fight on. In fact, the Floor Committee gathered upstairs as we spoke, and was the practical occasion for our walk.

"It's funny," Lena said. "You came out as gay but not as a Yankee. Is being a Yankee worse?"

"Not worse. Just unforgivable."

She hugged us ("onward, girls!"), then vanished through the door.

Minutes later, Lena and I detoured from 17-S for the hot-doughnuts red light of Krispy Kreme.

"You weren't well liked."

"It was a difficult time. I was mourning. Don't suck your fingers."

"You still are."

"Mourning?"

"Yes, and like that. You aren't very warm sometimes. You do know that."

"Fuck off," I said, confirming it.

We got back on the road.

I did know it, just as I knew that Lena meant only the best by press-ing my face in it. She was an incorrigible idealist, a grand conciliator for whom all good things went together, or had to be made to, chief among them love and truth. That was her weakness, which for now was to be shielded, just as mine was this coldness (which had better not be).

"You don't see other people sometimes," she said. "You don't listen. You only see you."

The light strained my eyes. I slid down and lowered my wide-brimmed visor and watched Lena's feet. She's a good driver but barely reaches the pedals. On even the straightest of roads she is at constant war with the steering wheel, jiggling it back and forth at small angles. I think she picked that up from *Car 54: Where Are You?*, an old show that her parents had let her watch and that appealed to her corny sense of humor. Her driving style makes her even more the petite granny, one of her many looks that excite me.

"Depressed people can be self-absorbed too."

"You care," she continued, ignoring my counterpunch. "I feel it. But then the cold front moves in, and I have to say it's bad for your writing."

I knew she was right, but I pouted—which is to say fell silent— through Savannah.

Broadsheet

ATURDAY MORNING, HUNGOVER AND REGRETTING Dad's booze, I reported a cold and accepted like just punishment my mother's deluge of canned soups and tightly enforced bed-rest. I liked my coffin-room. It had been the home law-office of the former owner, a harried public defender. I felt bad for him, pushing against the odds for a living, and not much of one at that. Planning a lost weekend, I turned off my computer and phone and resolved to read nothing but the *Nibblers*.

It wasn't to be. The ambient machine noise, which had haunted us from the day we moved to town, had amplified recently, as if closing in. I kept the blinds half-shut on Saturday and tried to ignore the racket, but Arnie, who always slept with me, shivered in my arms through the night and cuddled closer, licking.

On Sunday morning, I felt a steady *thump-thump* as if the ground were unmooring, and the sky let out a great rip. In time with the thumping, dust swirled in the light-bars from the blinds.

I rolled over and faced the wall.

Thump. Thump-thump.

Thump-thump-thump-thump-thump.

There was no use. I at last roused myself and swung my legs over the bed and grabbed my phone. I expected either a merciful internet blockage or more viral hate-videos, thus completing my social destruction. I tried to prime myself to greet the latter with relief. *After this, no one will talk to me, but that just means I can walk the halls blind to them, free of their nonsense for the next five years.* My body knew better and trembled. In truth, I craved something more than safe passage: time-death.

This was not the first time A.D.D. that I had wished away a chunk of my life. I'd like to have skipped the funeral and hosting people with trays of rolled meats at our house (why did Mom and I have to do this?) and be on the other side of it. Given the choice, I'd leap past the mourning altogether, along with the seventh through twelfth grades. If my job sucked like Dad's, I'd skip that, too, not just sit there and let it compress me. The sooner the better on these gaping lacunas. Rather than endure, I'd prefer to quickly ripen and retire to the Cape with Arnie. A beach chair awaited, a thermos and blankets. This new way of thinking was useful (and demented).

As it happened, there *were* more vile videos of my attack on Denise, but only through Saturday. Then, overnight, the tide turned and something else started. You may recall that the cruelest kids are often among the most popular on a middle-school campus. The equation is familiar. Middle-schoolers are afraid of being different and not fitting in, but their defenses are limited. One self-annihilating thing they may do to ease their fear is worship and ally with power. This includes power as cruelty and as fiercely bucking (or ripely fulfilling) social convention. (Adults and nations are known for this, too.)

What happened was that for the first time in my life the logic adhered to me, and I was cool. New voices emerged and swarmed the posts and comments. One supporter layered (probably racist) slicing-sword sounds over a video of my unhinged attack on Denise, recasting it as a choice dis. Another proclaimed me a hero for gay rights and superimposed Wonder Woman's costume over my body. (*Way2go Wendy! U speak 4 us all.* [pink ribbon] – @anonkneemouse2.) A sensitive mother who should not have been on there (adults had no idea), but who must have seen the same tendency in her own child and found succor in my boldness, proclaimed me

"Pennies' First Lesbian." Whether she meant "first" as in "First Citizen" or as in pioneer queer woman (which I wasn't), I took it as a heartfelt compliment. Even one of the evening's principals, obsequious Delmore, supplied a like.

Then over in my DMs I had something else.

Hiya, Wendy. I'm... queer 2. There, I've said it. [smiley face]

Pleeeeeeze tell no one.

Thirty seconds later:

I know I've only known you a little while but I feel I can really trust you.

After a full hour:

This is Sally Boone (Science Corner)

I thought of sending Sally an apology for not responding soon-er. I could tell from the time-stamps that it had made her anxious to hang herself out there like that and after a whole night get nothing. Then I remembered *The Beat Style*'s injunction to use fewer words and not over-explain things, which appealed to me with my won't-back-down stance. (There were sound principles in Graham's manual, along with some musty ones like we were sup-posed to use the word *tonic* instead of *soda*, if it ever came up.) I sent back a smiley face with sunglasses, followed by three—make that five—hearts. (My crushes transferred swiftly in those days.) Sally immediately reciprocated with five hearts of her own, but then after a few seconds sent a shaka. I considered this deflating, a light spritz at the flame I was kindling. The shaka was the casual, go-to sign-off for Dad the Gen Xer. Graham used it, too, in *Beat* e-mails. *Fine, you don't like me, I'll find someone else*, I thought, and then I thought about Sally and how she might like me, actually.

I decided to text Denise an apology. But there was nothing, really, to take back in what I said, just the way I had said it. Though possibly also I'd been sneaky with the Conga. When I tried to explain myself, it sounded like another attack, which felt too good to be right. I sent her a shaka, too.

To my dismay—I didn't want to care—the good news from my phone revived me. I banished Arnie from my lap and crossed the room. As if in honor of the previous occupant's diligence in defending the probably guilty, I set myself to another long-shot task: inspect that infernal e-bird for clues.

Thump. Thump-thump!

The machinery had courteously receded for my phone-check. But now, as I prepared for delicate surgery, locking my door and unfolding on my desk a small towel—artifact of my Montessori kindergarten—it began again in earnest. (*Thump.*) I removed the e-bird from my old-toy drawer, where it had rested atop buried dolls and the overpromising Stretch Monster (a hand-me-down toy from Dad, it had taped-over wounds that oozed jelly), and placed it—*thump-thump*—in the towel's dead center. I also once more took out the "CONFIDENTIAL" red folder that I'd swiped from Graham's desk, but I couldn't make heads or tails of the legalese. Alongside the bird, I set out the strange "NP" patch I had found near the diner, the one with the golf-themed crest.

I plunged my fingers deep into the bird. *Thump—dee—thump eeeeeek—thwack!* This time I felt no electrical shock—the battery was dead. Emboldened, I flipped it over and used my old Girl Scout knife to slice a line down the mantle and another across. I peeled back the fake-feathered flaps to reveal a wire jumble. *Thwack.* Suddenly the battery seemed more important. (*Thwack!*) Maybe, if I could find and replace it, I could read the wires like a brain scan, from where they lit up. I spotted a small square nub like a tiny thumb drive pressed into the spine. I lowered the mini-pliers, and just then my mother knocked and jiggled the knob.

"Why is this door locked?"

Thwack thwack thwack!

"Wait!"

I tore out the nub and slipped it in my T-shirt pocket, then flipped the towel over the bird. When her old spirit roused, my mother became nosy and bossy again, as she was B.D.D., and it made me preemptive, a quality that persists in my character like a deep vein in marble, only not so pretty.

"Coming!" I hurried to the door.

Thwack!

"This door should never be locked! What if you died!"

"I'd be dead. I'm *working.*"

She sighed. "Your paper is here. Strange men in fancy hats delivered it."

"It's a day late," I observed, and who were these paperboys?

I reached out two fingers to snag it. The scale was off. Graham had printed it on pink oversized broadsheets. He had also regressed to his tabloid fonts. My eye caught the price-box: *free?*

I smelled soup.

Thump thump—thwack!

"Cream of tomato from Campbell's and grilled cheese."

I seized the food, and her peach perfume smothered the Campbell's. My eyes widened. She was in full feather, in a one-shoulder little yellow dress, gold-and-jade necklace, and glassy-black pumps that brought her to five feet (my height).

She must have slipped off to an Allston or Chinatown stylist for the cut: someone, anyway, who knew what they were doing with Asian hair. I don't think of either of us as pretty, and most have agreed, but I will say that my mother had glamour when she wanted it. With the one-shoulder dress and pert haircut she reminded me of the Shobijin, the singing, telepathic fairies of about six inches in height who were recurring characters in Dad's Godzilla and Mothra films.

Incidentally, Dad's exposure to Asian culture didn't go much beyond those kids' films and our trips to Chinatown or Quincy for dim sum, hot pot, groceries, and parades. To be sure, there were some adjustments to build a life with Mom. She had come over so early—grades six through twelve at a gothic boarding school in Rouen, Maine—that she could pass as American-born. But then she would do something like slurp a fish eyeball (a favorite of mine, too) or warn him off green hats (sign of the cuckold) that surprised and charmed Dad enough to remark on it. He had "married a foreign woman," he said. I think he liked that. I've sometimes wondered if he initially chose Mom because of the nostalgia that I've now mentioned at least twice. Perhaps she reminded him, as she did me now, of the Shobijin or the kung-fu damsels he'd watched as a kid. If he'd been gay, maybe he would have married a Captain Bob and I'd draw sea turtles better. (The sources of attraction, if we can identify them at all, are often more innocent than we imagine and profoundly embarrassing.)

"Thank you, Mom. That is all."

"I'm leaving, Wendy."

Thwack. A jolt of panic.

"What do you mean, 'I'm leaving.'"

"I have an appointment. A brunch date."

"*Brunch* date."

"With a local man."

"Graham!"

"No! Who's Graham? Oh, that fat man you work for."

"Thank God. Is it someone I know?"

"Rest," she whispered, and disappeared.

A date! *Good* for her: better for me. I'd have the run of the house, a rare pleasure A.D.D. But then I flipped open the *Beat*–and was stunned to see what Graham had smuggled in while the rest of us danced and had our kiddie weekend.

"PENNACOOK PLAN" PROMISES END TO FLOODING, BOARS

LOCAL INVESTOR PLANS TO "SAVE US ALL"—CAN HE?

CAN A DOME BE A HOME? THE ANSWER MAY SURPRISE YOU

Below the fold, the real malarkey started. In the span of two days, Graham had converted the *Beat* to a manic travel brochure for a utopian city plan that, for reasons I could only guess at, he was boosting.

WELCOME TO NEW PENNACOOK: DOMED "CITY OF TOMORROW" ALL SET FOR LIFT-OFF!

FIVE (BAD) REASONS TO BE AGAINST THE DOME— AND FOURTEEN MORE TO SUPPORT IT

IS THE "PENNACOOK PLAN" FANTASTIC OR *WHAT*?

I turned back to the lead article, flush with foamy adspeak.

How does "zero rainfall" sound to you? A mall's perfect clime? Canals drained or beautifully sculpted to lanes of idle leisure? No more pesky boars—or driving! No more living-room puddles or wet feet! A *monorail* (whee!).

And, there's more. All-inclusive armed strike force. "Real" jobs for Pennies. Free juice and cookies (Tuesday's "Community Day"!). And, with dome living, *there's no more gloomy winter!*

So enjoy your *Pennacook Beat*, folks—this may be our last issue under that familiar banner. Here comes the *New* Pennacook!

On the inner pages, he pandered to simpler Pennies with cartoons of undesirables whom the Pennacook Dome would block from entry. The Eaton dandy, for instance. (No racist tropes, thank goodness.)

This was why he had wanted me out of the office so badly on Friday, spinning me out on his inane water-price story! It explained his sloppy drunkenness that afternoon, too. He had radiated the rank despair of the corrupted and the damned.

On the second page I found this tidbit:

GOODBYE WILD BOARS, HELLO LETHAL DRONE-BIRDS!

"Why, hello there! You may have seen us about town lately. Picking up your canal-trash. Slaying your feral pigs. We're the black-capped chickadee (e-version): the official state bird! We hope you'll let us stay here. We love *it!"*

So says a little birdy we met just this morning while pedaling to the *Beat*.

Tell me, friends. Who *doesn't* prefer the winged beauty of a floating songbird to the crooked lope of the tusked feral boar? Not you, certainly not me. And not Phil Marconi (AJMHS, '59).

In New Pennacook, drone-birds harboring a patented eye-laser technology will kill Penny boars for good. Freeing you from a rash of daily troubles, from reeking sidewalks to cookout attacks. And oh, sweet lord, mounds of steaming pig-sh*t.

Lethal drone-birds! I removed the chip from my pocket and turned it in my fingers.

Thump THUMP.

"What the frick."

Thump thump thwack crunch—SNAP!

I rushed to the window and yanked up the blinds.

A dome, it seems, can go up fast.

This may not surprise you if you've lived next to a construction site (as we did, in Bedford Corners). First there are weeks of mucking around in the ground, digging out the plot and laying the foundation. It seems to go on forever. Perhaps, as my father said, some crucial team member has betrayed the GC, snapped their back, or quit in a fit of pique. Will winter break the project like Napoleon's army? But then one fine morning the whole frame's up. (The mason, it seems, has not gone astray.) It's a short sprint to walls and floorboards.

Many canals over, and then along the town's border in a great circle that encompassed all Pennies, something like this had been going on at a much larger scale for who knew how long. The last two nights, while I moaned and slept away my Pike Middle Dance shame, they'd apparently capped the foundation because when I looked out the window, I saw a half-dozen titanic scaffolding towers and three cranes suspending a giant lattice. I grabbed my binoculars.

The lattice encased hundreds of blinding lenses. The first great arcs of the dome—they must have craned them in on Saturday—stretched far into the sky, their gentle bend implying the dome's vastness.

I returned to the *Beat* and reread the lead story. In my first reading, I had mistaken this for some kind of buttering-up campaign for the Pennacook Dome. No, it was a reveal piece. The dome would be halfway up by the time the *Beat*'s readers shuffled out in slippers, cradling their coffee, to fetch the free broadside. It would cast a webbed shadow over their hands, and they'd look up and see the dome-shards—*what in Sam Hill?*—and their jaws would drop and their fingers would slacken and set loose papers and mugs (*slap-SMASH!*).

Graham had printed a legal notice, over which he had also sprinkled his cheerleading hack prose.

OYEZ, OYEZ, OYEZ! ALL-TOWN MEETING TO SEAL TOWN SALE, LAUNCH "IMPRESSIVE" NEW PENNACOOK

Have you ever heard the expression "limited time only"? How about that chestnut "while supplies last"? Never truer words were spoken—if you're talking about the Pennacook Dome. Walt Disney tried it. So did Stephen King. But with your approval, Pennacook will be the first to make it real! *Tonight! Sunday, 6 p.m., Town Hall.* C-U!

Another headline read:

PENNY WATER RISING—CAN "MIGHTY" PHIL STOP IT?

I peeked out the window. It *had* risen, big time. The murky water overflowed the curb. I stuck my head out—it had pooled in our yard and lapped against the house. That explained the basement dampness. I had noticed it, too, in my soggy walks about the neighborhood and rising up the shed-stilts on my way to Pike Middle and the *Beat*. Another marker was the elevated mudlines on Arnie (whom I didn't clean well, to be perfectly honest, though neither of us cared).

Graham's article claimed that this Phil Marconi character had patented pumps. Once installed, they could clear the floodwaters and direct them back downstream to the Pennacook River and the Merrimack or steer them for irrigation. Fine and dandy, *but why was it flooding at all?* There had been one measly rainstorm, the night of the dance, and that had been brief, mostly histrionics.

I smelled more lies.

Deep in the paper, Graham laid out the deal's mechanics with sobriety—literal, I guessed. He must've written that first, then cracked the bottle and started in on the rest.

The town wasn't for sale. Not really. It was sort of the opposite, an exercise in eminent domain. Mr. Susco had told us that a town could use that power to take over private land for public use (for example, to build a road or sludge plant). The only catch under the Constitution was that the town had to pay the property's market value to the old owner. As best I could piece together (Graham's cartoon diagram with fat happy arrows was actually pretty helpful here), Pennacook was doing something like that. Phil Marconi was going to lend money to the town. The town would use it to take our land, which—moldy and flooded—just so happened to be dirt-cheap right now, at prices unrivaled since the mid-1930s. It would then sell the land *back* to Phil for a buck. It would also borrow another loan from Phil to fund his dome-village. In exchange, he promised to give a job and home to every Penny, slaughter the wild hogs, and master the canals.

To secure Phil's "most-favored borrower" interest rates, the town threw in a heaping dose of its sovereignty. So long as Phil kept his basic commitments (building the thing, with unspecified housing and jobs), he would "administer" New Pennacook "on behalf of" us. The Board of Selectmen and Town Meeting would collapse to the tidier Pennacook Advisory Council. Two-thirds of the PAC's members would be selected by Phil for their special expertise. For a democratic gloss, Pennies could vote in the PAC's other third and a weak mayor who'd mainly be responsible for cutting ribbons and spreading cheer. "Graham," I said, when I read that last part.

The dome-shards, I inferred, were a down-payment of sorts on Phil's big plans. Or, more precisely, a flex. *He who could do this was not to be denied.*

Graham had departed from his own *Beat* style rules for the broadsheet: the headlines ending in exclamation points, the italics within all caps. And the headline for the legal notice featured a supposed quote ("impressive") that appeared nowhere in the story. As every Bobcat knew, you can't do that, either. Nor can you just throw a comma after the word "and" to add intrigue. This may all seem minor, even scholastic. But Graham cared about this stuff. It was all over *The Beat Style.* His wild departure from his own strictures bespoke not only betrayal but a kind of self-loathing. The Graham within Graham did not want to do this, which suggested to me that I shouldn't let him.

Senior Week: Tuesday

June 8, 2032

Dear Diary:

Hot off the press, the next chunk of *Zodiac Pets* is done. It includes the climax and the last "Spring Break" section. This may be a good place to clear up my paternal-side ancestry. In other words, the French stuff.

I've also added an "after" on Graham that I just hammered out. His line from Shakespeare had a delayed effect, and just yesterday I stormed through Athena's colony to grill every Muskrat I could find—including, once more, Graham. I even placed a call to Errol, New Hampshire. Was he—as he had claimed in our interview—no longer the thing that he was? I stayed up all night recording what I learned there and bless him with third-person close.

And while that should wrap it up, I feel something's missing. With Commencement looming, I'm still not ready to type "The End."

WZ.
Worcester, Mass.

PART SIX:
BOBCATS

Reporter's Notebook:
Dump Trip

All over Pennacook, Bobcats would be scanning Graham's broadsheet with blind and rising fury: a potent force just waiting to be amassed and unleashed. I cast aside seniority and ordered my three main Bobcat contacts to assemble at my house within the hour. I blasted a second message to the rest: *All hands on deck, the Beat @ 4.* I took the liberty to sign that on behalf of the four of us, with my name up top. Receiving no objections, I heated the oven to 400°F and spread out my map.

Before I went for Graham, I needed to know more about this flooding. I was convinced the answers were at the old town dump—where Almy from Town Hall had pointed—or the mysterious Lion Diner. I used my fingers to trace the roads and canals on the map, then ran them over in brown and blue marker. I raised my binoculars again and looked out through the kitchen window and across the boggy fields to the treetops, then returned to the map and lowered my finger. "Bingo," I said. Just as I expected, the dump's remains were that way, too. One of the shards—the biggest one—sprung from there: that's the one we'd visit. From there it was a straight shot down Senator Chestnut Canal to the diner.

Delmore arrived first.

"What's that smell, pizza?"

He slid on the couch and folded his fingers behind his head.

"Sit up! This isn't a vacation."

"Whatever you say, boss."

I shot him a hard look.

"I mean it," he said. "Pretend I just got here. I don't want to boss people around, and it seems like you do. Besides, we need a general."

He was right. "Did you bring your laptop?"

He knocked his knuckles against the hard lump in his backpack.

"Get it." I tossed the thumb-drive from the e-bird at him. "*Read this.*"

Delmore was a hardcore techy. Yet he had tried his hand at journalism, for which he was basically ill-suited, rather than frequent Computer Club, the after-school activity where he might have been king. It made no sense then, but now I respect it. If more people did what they wanted instead of what they are good at, the world would be a happier, if somewhat ricketier place. Like Maryland.

Another knock. I opened the door: Denise. She looked away. I pointed to the couch and she sat down and stared at her shoes.

"When's lunch?" she asked, not looking up. Her head tilted. "Is that pizza?"

"Pizza's in 18–21 minutes. Can we please all just focus. You're a designer. Tell me what this means."

I flung the red folder at her. It had some schematics mixed in with the legal mumbo-jumbo and corporate name-swirl.

"We may not be lawyers, but we can read pictures, right?"

"Yes, Wendy."

I stormed off to the kitchen to turn on the oven light. (You can't tell much of anything by oven light, but its promise lingers.) A little later I heard the nervous giggle of Sally Boone—fashionably late as usual. By then I was using the spatula to ease the Red Barons onto the pan so I could move them to the counter for slicing.

Even now, frozen pizza brings special pleasure (my mother would already be happy with this sentence) because remember that you cook it at home and the familiar aroma suffuses everything and nicely sets the scene for unwinding. For many of us, one good thing among all the dislocations that came out of the pandemic was joy in life's small things, even junk. I know there is another way to look at it, but there are brief moments (March 2020 was one of them) when the political economy of citizenship requires little more of (many of) us than compulsive, mouse-like consumption. So you see, my abiding affection for Red Barons did not simply stem from a maternal quirk. It's a residue of that time's fleeting closeness—the last time like that for our family.

I watched them devour the pizzas. Not one among them a friend. This freed me from any special worry for their feelings or personal fates—an advantage, given our dicey task. Like Delmore said, I was a general.

"What did you find on that thumb drive?"

"I haven't cracked it."

"Denise: rifle?"

"Check."

"Sally?"

She hoisted a thumb. "*Josephine*'s ready. Hitched to Pres. Pierce."

"Rope?"

Delmore nodded.

"Let's dance," I said.

It's a good thing we did. I heard my mother's car pull in behind us just as we slipped onto the path that led to Pierce Dock. I didn't like that the car windows were open and she was blasting "Be My Baby" by the Ronettes or the taller, male head beside her. For the obvious reasons, it felt like a betrayal. My note claimed I'd gone to a sleepover and said she'd better take good care of Arnie (whom I had, for caution's sake, left in my room watching Graham's old favorite, DOGTV). I remember thinking at that moment: I bet she's as relieved at my departure as I was at hers.

Bobcats Clash with Forest Swine

Thirty minutes later we were way out in the middle of Governor Faubus Canal, keeping a nice clip. An even breeze brushed the water and sunlight flashed in the ripples. Sally steered while Delmore huddled on the slat floor. Denise was leaned back, trailing her fingers in the water. I stood at the bow—a knee raised, coiled rope in hand—and surveyed the passing town. From this distance, it had a dioramic quality, the open wreckage from defaced and abandoned shacks like colorful props of a seaside village diorama (shades of *Captain Bob*'s opening credits).

Posted high at the front like that, I felt the thrum of power, the Return of Old Wendy. It didn't last. I don't know what it was—the superficiality of my new confidence (as with a Zodiac boat, so with self-concept: beware of sudden shifts), that my reign was cast in fear, my crews' clashing personalities, or merely the darkening weather (a fog had gathered)—but the mood grew solemn. The planks creaked. No one spoke, and the motor, with its incessant humming, was like the party's biggest bore. Our course was steady; figuratively, we drifted. And as we drifted, a rancid and familiar tang wafted from the trees.

"I have to go," Delmore said, his eyes closed. He had the lassitude of the solider with neither clear orders nor discretion.

"Can it wait?"

"No."

"*Why didn't you go at the*—Sally: take us in."

We sped to the nearest dock, a strip mall's paved front, where I moored us with a bowline. This knot—make an X, slide the rope through the middle, tug—is versatile and simple and may be the only one you need. I knew many others. At Camp Molly Ockett, knots were a secret handshake, a status symbol of arcane, inside knowledge.

"Wow, how'd you do that?"

"Don't they have Boy Scouts in this town?"

"It's decayed."

He bounced off the boat and ran for the woods. Minutes passed. The foul odor rose.

"He said number one."

Denise shrugged.

"I'm going in." I pointed at Sally, then down at the gun. "Follow."

A loud, protracted squeak, like a slowly opening door, called us to a tangle of vines, and when we pushed through to a clearing, we found poor Delmore surrounded. Wild boars, in a tight, closing circle! Around them, a rank lair of loose grass, manure, and mud-holes. Delmore held a thin branch before him like a wand while pinching up his pants with the other hand and turning and stepping but there was nowhere to go. Fat boar heads swung toward us and broke into a chorus of grunts and squeals.

NNNNgggghgh. Neeee!

(Scruff scruff)

Eeeee!

"Wendy, help me!"

"*Sally.*"

I caught the gun, turned, and fired.

SLAP!

NNGH!!

Blue paint splattered. The boar turned and the bush swallowed it whole. The other boars reeled, then clumped together in a swarming mass of bristles and tusks.

Chick-chick—BANG. *Chick-chick*—BANG. *Chick-chick* ... BANG.

The boars scattered and one streaked across the circle and knocked Delmore's knee loose and he went down yelping.

"I'm hit! I'm hit!"

He lay face-down pounding the ground with his fists and kicking his feet up and down like a toddler. But the boars retreated, leaving only their reek.

"Go on, we won't look." We turned our backs for Delmore to get decent.

I wasn't opposed to boars making their way in the world. But living among them like this was medieval.

I Ponder Penny Factions

We motored back out to Gov. Hutchinson Canal, and my thoughts shifted to dome-vote odds-making. Much would depend on the balance of local factions.

One faction, the Change Nothings, was broad but amorphous. At one end, it extended to Archie Simmons and other dyed-in-the-wool lefties. The Archie Clique, as the sub-faction was known, had saved the public schools many times over, most recently by beating back a Gravy Poole plan to bulldoze them. They *were* mold-plagued. But instead of building new ones, the plan was to raise a white flag and ship the kids elsewhere for a song. Gravy put out feelers to some Unitarian suckers in Eaton, then flung his scheme at the Board of Selectmen.

"Just jam 'em in that bus—"

"Or boat."

"—and dump 'em at Hawthorne Corner. A world-class school-ing—*on them.* Let 'em put their money where their mouth is. I'll save my quarters for Takis!"

The Archie Clique slammed Gravy as a naïf. Patrician postur-ing was widespread in Eaton, they allowed. But in the end Eaton's answer, even to desperate Pennies, was sure to be a stone-cold no. (Exhibits A, B, and C: the floods.)

"Or has the gentleman from Oakhurst never read *Eaton Liv-ing*?" asked Selectman Chuck Nardone, to guffaws.

Eaton Living was the lifestyle-magazine residue of that town's former paper. I knew it well from my orthodontist's wait-ing room. Whatever Penny pride I have owes a steep debt to this glossy apogee of Boston-exurb porn—or, rather, to my re-volt against it. Its writers hewed to a single tone—gushing—for everything they covered, from the over-funded Eaton Museum and the town's "stately" homes to basic amenities (the library, the pizza parlor) that resembled corporate law firms. Most Pennies were familiar with and reviled *Eaton Living* because someone kept dumping stacks of it at Quik Stop, as if to taunt us with the boring splendor.

Eaton Living inspired some teen-wit Pennies to crank out an answer publication, *Penny Dying*, which for a time gave the *Beat* a run for its money. *Penny Dying* admirably dwelled in self-lacera-tion (canal humor, parody reviews), but the 'zine shut down after Eatonites got ahold of it and joined the Penny-bashing—suddenly not so fun. It seemed the same wiseacre who'd been humping *Ea-ton Living* to Quik Stop had smuggled *Penny Dying* into the Eaton Country Club. Or so I speculate. We'd tried to build a story around it, but our leads trailed off like smoke from a tiny birthday candle. (Like any place, Pennacook has a vast shadow history defined by all that's missing.)

I sometimes think of Bedford Corners, the locus of my pre-pubescent childhood golden age (with a live father), as a sort of lost happy middle between those warring towns: a Penny Lane, no pun intended, of bourgeois concord and vivid civic bustle (for me, it helped that Bedford Corners was 11.3% Asian). I probably idealize it too much. But there is a salutary aspect for a child to such places, where things and operations, some as useful as making a cheese sandwich (though they needn't be), are happening around you for their own sake, and enough adults stand ready to explain them. It's the default dream of nurturing everydayness that many of us share (which is why everything else is News).

To the Archie Clique's right, but still within the Change Nothings tent, stood the Middlers, who plumped for pickleball paint-lines and pine stilts but, without the Archie treatment, would support little else that wasn't free. It was hard to gauge where they'd land on Phil Marconi's plan with its strident promise of endless prosperity.

I worried more about a third sub-faction, the myopic Just *Stoppers* (Graham made up these labels, which stuck), who took a wary approach to nearly everything that crossed their desks, including all zoning exemptions that weren't for private ice rinks.

"Why do you need a porch?"

"There's a fine view of maples, you see. And on the other side, we're hard by canal and can't—"

"I said *need*, Henderson."

Rustling papers.

"Hold 'er there, muleskinner. I ain't *through* yit."

"Whatever. I'm moving?"

The Just *Stoppers'* question-blizzards often devolved like this into half-ass cowboy English. Two other Just *Stopper* specials were the marathon hearing and the sprawling sub-committee.

Throw them a corner yield-sign proposal and they'd gum up town business for weeks. The Just *Stoppers* weren't sure they even belonged in the Change Nothings. Before his "accident," Archie often had to herd them back with flattery, reminding them that, whatever their reservations about the program, they shared a team virtue: good will.

"We don't believe in this stuff, Archie," one of them had pleaded as Archie pressed for a retired-teacher COLA.

"I know that, Billy, but remember Kenny Rogers Roasters?" he asked. He loomed over the Just *Stopper* and planted a hand on his shoulder. Long ago, the town had dangled marvelous incentives but failed to attract an outlet of the chain.

"Sure, boss."

"And do you recall their slogan?" He squeezed the shoulder.

"How could I forget? 'There's goodness here.'"

"Exactly. Now, saddle up, pardner: let's lasso some *beans*."

A hardy slap, and the vote was sealed.

Turn Back Now, the town's second major faction—and the Change Nothings' nemesis—would support the dome, if only to sew chaos. The TBNers claimed to favor an energetic return to the town's distant past (though not so distant that Indians might live there). A number of dams and barricades were implied, and a duty to snap at any perceived slight. For instance, a "hurtful" *Beat* exposé of yet another Kluck Klucker salmonella outbreak. I was convinced that TBN's leaders—MGOP's Leo Carbonara and Maggio and Silva, those boobs I'd overheard at Town Hall—believed in precisely none of this. Their whole grim-faced agenda, like their bullying tactics in Quik Stop's alps, was a façade, little more than a put-on for stooge voters and vacant self-amusement (TBN was also the natural burrow for hardcore Penny racists).

Turn Back Now had none of the curiosity and only some of the playfulness that is required for human progress. In this, they contrasted with Graham, who, for all his flaws, had both in spades. Consider his inventions—or the brief exchange we'd had about the middle-school curriculum during an idle Wednesday when he caught my ear as I walked to the break room for chips.

"Hey-yo: what are the specials these days?"

"What?"

"At Pike Middle. You know: Shop, art. *That* stuff."

"Shop, art, music, and"—only in Pennacook—"A.S.S."

"Excuse me: *ass*?"

"A.S.S.: Academic Study Skills."

He mulled this over sadly. "Study skills."

"Like how to make a binder and use highlighters. Can I go now?"

"In my day we had Home Ec. That's where I learned lasagna. Lasagna: *at ten-thirty*. Loved it ever since."

"Is that all they taught you? No wonder they canned it."

He looked hurt. "We learned all sorts of stuff from Miss Short-cake. The four food groups, how to match clothes. A big thing on sewing."

"Like what?" Despite myself, I was intrigued by the quaint mandate.

"Oh, there was a variety of patterns. A lot of us made a puppy, or the girls favored the heart-shaped pillow one. I chose something else." He gripped the desk's edge and leaned forward. "The Take-Apart Cat."

To make it, he explained, he had to stuff and stitch seven piec-es—head, body, four legs, and tail—that could be stuck together with Velcro and torn back apart.

"To what end?" I asked.

"Pardon?"

"Why take it apart? It's like a stuffed animal for a serial killer."

"Well, to see what it looks like. Then the joy of reconstruction, I suppose. I don't know: it was fun."

It did sound fun. More intriguing for the possible mutant recombinations and, I speculated, more durable than my Stretch Monster, as Graham now confirmed.

"I still have it," he said. He reached into a box of odds-'n'-ends that he kept by his ankle. "Say hi to Tabby!"

He hurled it at me—shaggy, dirty, partly dismembered. I flinched, caught it, and flung it right back.

"No, thanks. I'm hungry." I pointed to the break room and followed my finger away from him.

You see what I mean though, about playfulness and curiosity. Turn Back Now would have nothing to do with such a thing.

This insight came later, while writing this. As for my political analysis, at the time I felt I'd drawn a fair picture of Penny factions. I had to ask, though: was it dated? Mr. Susco had taught us that the economic carnage and "water issues" of recent years had "decohered" Penny government. The old lines had blurred, replaced by a cross-chopped sea. And it wouldn't be just pols at town meeting. It'd be Pennies as a whole, or whoever showed up. Talk about a black box! There were so many unknowables it was like trying to fill in the Drake equation, which Sally Boone had taught us, for fixing the odds of smart alien life.

In sum, I didn't know our chances, but I knew I didn't like them.

Robo-Workers March on Bobcats

A few-hundred yards past the boar drift, we reached our next stop: a small hill descending to a submerged tennis court. After we'd hauled out the boat, Sally and Denise attached the wheels, then we lugged it over a soggy path to the closest marked port. But we were deep in the wilds now and no map could be trusted.

Along this path, we met another and clankier antagonist. Our first clue to its identity was a barrage of still more onomatopoeia.

Bvvvt bvvvvt. Bvvvvvvvt.

Ee-oo-ee-oo

SLAM SLAM SLAM

vvvvvvvvvvT

I summoned Sally with two fingers and we crashed into the woods. Branches opened, revealing a path—flat, wide, precise—that, in one direction, headed back to the canal and in the other turned a corner. The path was primly raked and neatly cut at the bottom and all the way up in straight walls made from snipped-off branches and leaves: neat as a corn maze on opening day. I heard talking—if you can call it that.

Blip. Blip BLEEP. "WELCOME TO BOUNTY BAG. THE STORE IS NOW OPEN. CHECK OUT OUR HAM-SALAD TWIN PACK: $1.99 OR TWO FOR THREE DOLLARS!"

"FOLKS, YOU'LL ALWAYS SAVE WITH BOUNTY BAG. OUR PRICES ARE 4% OFF—ALL ITEMS, ALL YEAR. SHOP NOW—AND SAVE."

We moved sideways, back into the brush. I leaned forward and pried open the branches and a blinding light hit me. I made a visor with my hand and squinted. The light was coming from a tiny solar panel *on a forehead.* A peculiar dance played out in the woods. In contrast to the boars' messy clearing, the robots' lair had the sheen of—well, a trim supermarket. Along one wall, they'd carved a series of shelves and had neatly shaped and stacked bundles of twigs and pine-cones in there like boxed spaghetti and tomato cans. They had cleared something like an aisle down the middle and a DeliBot (as its sticker indicated) was working there, wielding an ample buzz-saw that extended from its arm to sculpt a small compartment.

"They're making their home," Sally whispered.

If you remember what the typical robot was like back in the early 2020s, you may be picturing a tin box with wheels. But as Graham had briefly glimpsed before the third flood took out Bounty Bag, these were advanced for their time, bluish-purple humanoids, rubbery-skinned and smiling. They weren't pristine, though. The woods had done their damage. As they twirled past us, busy at their work—or else slouched against a tree in a sunny spot, getting recharged through the forehead—I saw a gallery of wounds. Slit-open thighs. Punctures from chomping boars. Dangling forehead-solar panels. A severed leg, replaced by a pirate's wood-stump.

Bvvvt: an eyeball turned and locked in on us.

"ATTENTION ALL ASSOCIATES: LOOK SHARP. OUR FIRST CUSTOMERS OF THE DAY HAVE ENTERED THE STORE AND ARE EVEN NOW AMONG US."

The robots froze, turned, and snapped to attention. There was a moment's hesitation, some algorithm floating, and then all at once their knees bent and they launched a forward march. I signaled Sally again and—here's where this hero business really started to fail me—*missed* the gun when she tossed it. I fell back on a heel and collapsed. As the robots neared, I clawed my way to the paint gun and turned and aimed—and missed again.

"You don't have to do everything, you know," Sally said, swooping in to grab the gun and then—*SPLAT SPLAT*—she'd blinded two. The others' heads literally spun, like a desperate sign they were on the fritz and needed a "take five" for recalibration (I'm guessing this now; at the time, it was panic).

"Is that it? Are we safe?" I asked.

Sally took my hand and pulled me up.

"I bought us some time. Let's go!"

We plunged back through the corn-maze to the rough woods and barely graced the deck when a metallic cry, followed by the sound of grinding gears, burst from the forest trail.

"Get us out of here!" I shouted.

"Whoo-hoo!" Delmore screamed. With a wild joy, he eased us back from shore, then turned our nose toward the dump.

The Bobcats Meet Clarice

As we moved still deeper into outer Pennacook, the woods tightened and the canal pinched until it disappeared beneath the overhang. We were blocked. And yet the flow under us—toward us—was substantial, as if, beyond this, the canal might open into wide waters, never before seen. We all looked at one another uncertainly.

"I'm hungry," Delmore said.

"Good," I said. "Let's eat." We could use the time to think.

I popped open the cooler and passed out the food and orange sodas.

"More frozen pizza?" Delmore complained.

While we munched, I eyed the vanishing canal, a small crescent closing into blackness.

"We have to go back," I said.

"What?" Denise was incredulous.

"We have to go back and steal one." I pointed my slice at the blockage. "Did you see those lines they cut? The neatness."

"We could use that," Sally agreed.

We turned with rising dread.

At the clipped path's entrance, I cupped my hands around my mouth and hollered: "Can one of you *join* us? We're from, er, *Bakery*. We need some *help* in the, uh—"

"Stock room," Sally shouted.

A loud shaking, as if from a can of lug-nuts. Then the Bvvt-Bvvt sound that I now recognized as their well-concealed wheels: built-in skates that were one step up from the plain-footed human.

"HELLO. I AM SHARON. I CAN STOCK. I DO DELI. I EVEN WROTE A BOOK: *THE BOUNTY BAG CODE FOR RO-BOTS*! CARE TO HEAR MY FAVORITE PROVISION?"

We'd pulled the neighborhood genius. I didn't know if I liked that.

"Not now, uh, Sharon," I said quietly, mirroring her soft and friendly tone.

Her pink eyes opened wide. "ARE YOU MY NEW MANAGER?"

"Yes. But let's do greetings later."

We had let our imaginations get the better of us. It turned out that all we had to do was not shoot and ask for help. It seemed these robots weren't killers after all. They just wanted to make us happy, by pulling us the right twigs or whatever from their sad and useless shelves.

Sharon rolled up beside me at the bow.

Brrt-bip. Brrt-bip. Her head tilted back and rotated 360 degrees, taking in the sky.

"THIS IS A VERY LARGE STOCK ROOM," she said.

"She's cute," Denise said.

"This is outside," Delmore said. "We're on a river."

"Canal," I corrected.

"THIS IS A VERY LARGE OUTSIDE."

"This is the whole outside and it goes all around the globe," Sally said. "But only one of trillions, if you count the other planets."

Denise steered us to the dead-end and Delmore cut the engine.

"WHAT DO YOU WANT ME TO DO HERE?" Sharon asked, all business.

"Drill," I said. "Just up and down on the sides there, and shave two feet off the top. With that arm-saw? You said you slice deli."

It shot out, spinning. *Bzzzzzzzzt.* I jumped back.

"Then just toss it over you or something."

She followed me to the letter, and, after she sawed out the big wads of the canal-brush, she hurled them over her head and into Delmore's face.

"Come *on*," he said.

"To the side," I told Sharon.

She turned her head toward me and a pink smile appeared on her lower face-screen and she winked.

"I think she likes you," Sally chirped.

"Especially you," Delmore said clinically. "She's imprinted."

Denise edged us forward as Sharon tunneled. After long but steady progress, the gap finally opened, and the last semi-circle of it cracked and fell forward like the blow-torched wall of a bank vault. Looming before us, the so-called dump was a dark wonder to behold. Only it wasn't an abandoned dump or an ill-starred apartment project—it was a crime in progress!

The long dome-shard emerged and ascended from a giant concrete cube. We puttered out in front of the cube and I looked up and saw where the concrete gave way to the lattice, at its widest here and bridging over to another concrete "foot" at some distance. It soared far up and cast a waffle-like shadow over the open field of water.

I looked closer. Across one whole wall of the cube, someone had spraypainted "CLARICE" in rainbow colors, followed by a black skull-and-bones. "Clarice" was the name that Almy at Town Hall had fed me—the "water lady" I'd need to see for Graham's water-price story! I recalled the sly way he had said this. I was now more convinced than ever that, whether his motives were pure (save the town) or petty (ennui-plagued bureaucrat eager to lash out), Almy was on our side. He wanted me to find this—but why?

We drove around the side to the answer. Clarice *wasn't* the cube but a special something behind it: an enormous, flushing pump. Like some infernal hose of Poseidon's, come to thrash the Greeks, the pump—Clarice—was spewing water in Pennacook's canals, even possibly making them. Inside the pump's gaping maw, a giant blade frothed and churned. It seemed to be spiraling toward us, an illusion that the *Empress Josephine* created by pressing us ever closer.

I flung open my map. "That's the Merrimack we're eating."

The Merrimack was a major river that you hardly ever heard mentioned because (like many a realtor's customer) it coyly shied away from our border. It hit me: these Penny floods weren't natural, not even by the loose standards of our climate-changing epoch. They were planned. *Phil Marconi had flooded Pennacook deliberately to set the stage for his dome scheme.* He was diverting the Merrimack's water to keep the streets high and soaked like he wanted them. To sap the public's will to fight. It reminded me of something Mr. Susco said about tyrants overthrowing democracies: "You'll never sell most people on the plain proposition—*you are my unequal and are better off governed by me without your consent*—so you rig the game, as if with weighted dice."

If it seems unlikely that we were the first to find it, it can't be overstated how little most Pennies cared about far-away things. In their minds (I include Graham here), I think Pennacook just trailed off like those half-conceived magical lands of even some very good fantasy novels that I'd read. On the maps, they'd write something lame and indeterminate around the edges like "here there be centaurs." We were, in a manner of speaking, at the map's edge of Pennacook: here there be Clarice.

I sensed there was something more behind this, some even bigger lie. But I couldn't piece it together. I needed more evidence—or did I? I thought of the "NP" patch with the golf clubs and other vague symbols on it that I'd found that day I first discovered the diner.

"That's Phil's pump! That's *Phil's!*" I screamed.

The pump grew larger, a lush black void opening around me.

"Charge!" I ordered. "Gum it up! *Take it!*"

I felt the motor cut and turned around. The others eyed me with curiosity.

"We can't, Wendy," Sally said.

The boat slowed, the only sound the pump's mad rush.

"What are you doing, Delmore! Get us moving now!"

He looked off to the trees.

"No," Denise said. "Uh-uh."

Pressed by the pump's false current, our nose drifted and we began to float backward.

"W-why not?"

"We'll die?" Delmore said.

"You aren't afraid of that, are you?" Denise asked.

I fell silent and looked down at my knees.

"Do you want to?" Sally asked, more gently.

(Sharon had no program for this and her light had flickered out on some timer.)

"I don't—care," I said, dodging.

"About face!" Delmore ordered.

A bullshit boating command but we got it. Before restarting the engine, Delmore passed up the thumb drive and gestured to Sharon.

"Put it in her. Right behind that ear, I'm guessing. Let's see what she knows."

"And while you're at it"—Denise heaved over the red folder—"ask her to read this. I can't: I'm thirteen."

Denise turned the *Empress Josephine* around and we started making tracks back to town. The pump, our sudden ally, pushed us.

Irate Bobcats Wage Reverse Strike

The scent of canal was fresh in our nostrils as we pulled up to the *Beat* and lashed the *Empress Josephine* to a stilt. Intermingled with canal was the memory of greasy-diner smell: we'd made a revelatory stop at the Lion on our way back from the pump station. We were mucky up to the knees but, because of what we'd found at the diner—and Sharon's succinct briefing on the other stuff—we didn't care, even relished disregarding Graham's shoe protocol as we barreled down the corridor, splattering mud.

We found him in the newsroom, slobbed out at his desk reading Rich Hall's *More Sniglets* (1985), a book of comic neologisms that Graham had been jovially reciting on Fun Fridays (*flen*: the gunk at the top of an old ketchup bottle), and slurping a 40 oz. cup of root beer (and no doubt something else) from Quik Stop.

"What the hell is this?" Delmore asked, blazing in front of us with the pink broadsheet.

"And this?" Sally swung a leg in front of Delmore's and pulled forward, brandishing the blueprints we'd uncovered at the diner.

"I didn't know you were so avid about golf," Denise said.

"And sewage sludge and 'dumpster living,'" Delmore said, pinching his nose.

"Wait, guys—give him a chance to speak," I said.

"I—*what* are you talking about?"

"It's as I suspected," I said. "He's a patsy."

Which isn't the worst thing, though at some point carelessness becomes its own kind of malice.

"Hold him," I ordered, and Delmore and Denise each grabbed an arm and a shoulder. He struggled for a moment, then submitted. Pinned to the chair, he settled back looking relaxed and tended to—Graham jujitsu that positioned me as the supplicant.

"I told you that diner was hiding something," I said. "And you pretended like you didn't know."

"I didn't. I mean, I just learned about this."

"What 'this.'"

"The New Pennacook. The dome and all these jobs. It's going to be awesome. I swear. There'll be Chinese restaurants, a bowling alley, a refurbished Lion Diner. An indoor waterpark."

"Where," I said. "Point to it."

I snatched the blueprints from Sally and shoved them in his face.

We'd found them in the diner basement. When we got to the Lion, we busted through the tropical theming, smashed a window to reach in and open the door, and slipped behind the diner galley to search for secret papers. Sally pulled a golden handle and a panel slid open, revealing a narrow staircase. We pounded down the treacherous stones—Delmore slipped and banged up his back— then skidded past the fraudulent diorama that Phil had shown to Graham and yanked back the large bolted door that practically screamed "secret plans inside," behind which we found the secret plans. Which I now showed to Graham.

"What is this?"

"That's the real 'New Pennacook.'"

"I don't get it. This isn't what he showed me."

"Exactly, genius."

"It was nothing like this. He took me down to the basement and *showed* me."

"He showed you your own fantasy."

"Maybe you shoulda' paid closer attention to the login dis-claimer," Delmore sneered.

He was referring to the daily acknowledgment that the *Beat* required us to click on, the one that said there was no expectation of privacy on the *Beat*'s computers. I had once asked Graham why he put it on there. He said, lamely, "I don't know. It was there when I started." Graham's internet secrets had been funneled back to Phil, who had used them to craft his seductive diorama—all the way down to his "Mayor Adams-Bundt" office (surprisingly humble, it looked like an outhouse or the lawyer's work-shed at Old Sturbridge Village).

"He wants to trap us," Sally said calmly.

"Only that's not the half of it," I said.

I told Graham what else we'd found and how the red folder backed it up. The sales guys in bad Run-DMC costumes? Phil's secret agents. They were snatching up parcels at a double discount, tricking Pennies to sell at a rate still crappier than the one Phil planned to extract tonight from the town. (They'd all but confessed this part to Graham when they came knocking at his apartment.)

But those guys were bit players. Floods did most of the work, dousing the town's hopes, even its belief in its capacity to run itself, and shaping it for Phil's real plan: a massive, domed, water-sucking golf resort. A year-round cash cow.

"A good walk wasted," Graham mumbled.

The coup de grace, though, was the last part, which had taken Sharon a little longer to decode: the brown stuff on that patch? Free "fertilizer": human sewage sludge, trucked in from New Hampshire. The sludge would keep down costs on the links and phosphates high in town water. New Pennacook would suck in one-third of that state's daily sludge haul, from Portsmouth to Clarksville. He was turning our town into New Hampshire's toilet!

The NP patch had come into focus. The letters stood for New Pennacook, and the icons were dumpsters, sludge, Phil's tower, and, well, the last one was what it looked like: happy water, for his always watered golf course. Phil had printed them in advance for his legions. The e-birds didn't make it to the patch. Interestingly, they were to be exactly what Phil had promised: pig-killers that scrambled the internet (to boost Phil's tyranny, not to shelter local flavor) and handled stork-like package delivery.

"And Archie? My friend?" His betrayal was settling on him.

"Archie was just about onto it, I'm guessing," I said.

"When his printer broke down," Graham offered.

"Which is why they took him out of commission."

"But why him? Why not me?"

A question better answered with silence.

"I don't think Phil even worked for Disney," I said. "At least not like he said. He made it up."

I showed him the résumé that Sharon—tapping into a special Bounty Bag internet link that evaded Phil's scrambling—had uncovered. Phil *was* rich from some dark software patent of the early 2000s. But that was just the end of the story, or near to it.

He had grown up in Pennacook but as a promising teen had left it far behind. Following the well-trod path of AJMHS honors kids before him, he climbed a ladder of scholarships and test-taking triumphs to an elite college, Amherst. Followed by Yale Law and Cravath, Swaine & Moore. All cleaned up, he struck out on his own: a kind of lawyer anti-statesman, he settled down in an oil patch, then shifted to tobacco-defense work. It must have been during his brief consulting stint for Disney that he'd swiped from studio archives the E.P.C.O.T. diorama— the very one Walt had featured in his 1966 television pitch for this aborted corporate utopia—and then hauled it back here for his scheming.

His motives were elusive. I originally thought there must have been some betrayal in his past, some grudge he held that led him back to Pennacook and made him want to milk and wreck it. But we never could trace it. Maybe there wasn't any one moment, any origin story, that could soften or explain him. Maybe he was just greedy and indifferent (after all, an efficient stance in life). Or he resented the town not for being cruel but simply for forgetting him (the scorned-lover Phil, we could call this). Or maybe—and I really think this comes closest—Phil thought Pennies were a joke that'd be even funnier if he screwed them.

I pointed out how Pennies would live in dumpsters and their new jobs (which *were* guaranteed) would all involve serving the resort. By raking sludge or mixing mint julips. By the endless laundering of barely used towels.

"Care to guess the buyer's name on all these parcels?"

"The ones Archie was looking into?"

"Chaeronea."

"Your company," Denise added.

"But this can't be. It just can't. We'll never agree. Pennies won't swallow it."

"'Never'? After this pack of lies?"

I tore the broadsheet from Delmore's hands and threw it at him. It bent around his head. He looked so pathetic, masked by his paper like that. Part of me felt: *enough already, let's bring him into the fold now.* Maybe he could come with us, confess his crimes before Town Meeting, and then his conversion story could help turn the tables on Phil. That's sort of how it always went in the *Nibblers*, and nearly every book I'd read. Though not in *Moby-Dick* (I'd skipped to the end), which had everybody dying and spiraling undersea, except the narrator, clutching his life-saving coffin, who seemed only to have lived to tell the tale. This had truth's consolation. Life had already instructed that it was not going to be so sweet or legible as my *Nibblers* would have it (they wouldn't hold my attention much longer). At this moment, something in Melville's dark light steeled me.

"We can't trust you," I said. I pinched the broadsheet and lifted it away.

He looked down. "I know."

With a nod, I dismissed Sally to start in on the copy, then turned back to Delmore and Denise.

"Delmore: tape him. We're mounting a reverse strike."

Graham smiled crookedly. After all these years, it seemed that he, too, remembered Mr. Susco's lesson.

Mr. Susco had described the reverse strike as a little-used technique in labor-management struggles. In a regular strike, the workers walk out and refuse to work. In a reverse strike, the workers lock out management and keep the place running, including by doing management's jobs. On the rare occasions that workers have tried it, they did well enough on their own. For a lot of different things, it turns out, people can manage themselves.

"Reverse strikes" was part of a highly disorganized grab-bag unit on democratic forms. It's where he teased out anthropological leads on places like Tlaxcalla (a possible sort-of Athens of ancient Mexico, before the Spanish toppled it). He told us, too, of the Bari Corporation, a coop that made workers partners, fixed salary ratios, and rotated jobs and salaries. So everyone had a chance to pull the ropes. "It might not work for every company," Mr. Susco acknowledged, regarding the Bari Corporation's specific model. "But democracy isn't a plan. It's a way."

The duct tape squawked as Delmore wrapped it twice around Graham's head, pinning his hair curtains down and sealing his mouth. He poked a breathing hole (third-degree murder wasn't the object). As Denise held him down, Delmore taped his legs to the chair while Sally wrapped the torso.

"Mmm," Graham said.

"What," I said.

I put a pen in his free hand. He jotted "Athena" and an e-mail address and number. I pulled down the tape.

"Call her. Can you *please* just call her. She's my main conduit to Phil—his granddaughter! And, well, I can't prove it, but she's one of the good guys, you see? She might be able to help you—us. Or at least imprison me safely, if that's what you need her to do. Please, you can't just leave me here all al—"

blub blub blub blub

I sealed him back up and streaked another layer over that to retighten things (and punctured a new blow-hole), then we dragged him to the break room, where we added some rope to cinch up his portly middle, and I mulled his request to call this Athena. As I took one last look at him, my workmanlike focus on securing his restraints shifted to disdain at him for what brought us to this.

"What good are you? You can't even stand up to some old suit."

By now it was four, and the other Bobcats and Sharon were filtering in.

"Okay," I said. "Let's write."

Spring Break: South Beach and the Georgia Information Center in Port Wentworth, off I-95S

Miami was brief and is quickly disposed of (no conflict, no story). Sally Boone met us at Puerto Sagua Restaurant in South Beach. I ordered a Cuban coffee with my Cuban sandwich—again breaking for the meat option—and she chuckled. "That's for *after*," she said, so I cancelled the coffee. Lena ordered three appetizers for her meal ("uh, fried yuca, fried . . . *squid*, and your fried pork chunks!"), and Sally filled us in on her life.

She has gone into science as we'd hoped, on a path more practical than her Science Corner scribblings may have suggested. She finished UCF in three years (marine bio) and is an apprentice of sorts to a rogue ecologist who goes by Dr. Dave. Each Sunday, Sally and Dr. Dave paddle a tricked-out canoe-lab through miles of gators and toxic-algae blooms to record the damage that the state and huge corporate farms are causing to a major lake by back-pumping foul water into it. Then they zip-file their data to the J.D.s at Earthlaw Tallahassee, who are suing to slap a permit on those pumps and stop them. Dr. Dave is well over six feet tall and sports a Civil War beard and granny glasses, and when the time comes for depos or court, he appears in jeans and a grubby V-neck T-shirt. The stance disarms Florida juries (he'd make a great spy in the League of Dixie) and accounts for untold millions in recovered damages. During the week, Sally stores the boat behind a bungalow off Calle Ocho that she splits with four traveling AME choristers. In her free time, she cooks, goes clubbing with the choristers, and in-line skates. A rich life, for a girl of twenty-three!

"You make me feel like a kid, going to school still."

"Living in a dorm," Lena said.

"Yes."

"Eating in cafeterias."

"Mm-hm."

"Plunking your tray on a conveyor belt that whisks it away for someone else to wash."

I smacked her hand.

We had the coffees, pre-sweetened espresso, at the end as pre-ferred. I slurped mine down in seconds (another faux pas), then paid up while Sally was in the bathroom. Back on the street, we bought a loaf of Portuguese sweet bread from a Venezuelan-Portuguese bakery-cart and took turns ripping off hunks and stuffing them in our faces as we strolled out to South Beach. Climate change has thoroughly canalized some blocks à la Pennacook as the region's longstanding quarrel be-tween water and land grows ever more animated, threatening to render pumps of any sort (permitted or not) either vitally important or hope-lessly quaint. The sloshing ankle-water and Sally Boone's gait made the *Beat* seem close. Sally's thoughts had also turned back.

"It's a bummer Graham died."

"What?" I halted.

Where are you, I texted.

Hanging with Jim. Golf-club and windmill emojis.

"He's not dead. He's playing mini-golf."

"Close enough. It seemed like he'd die. Those Penny wackadoodles seem so far away now. I thought you of all people would have moved beyond that."

"I did, too."

I wondered if this was common, that the one who was most ea-ger to flee later looked back with the greatest ache at the launchpad, remaking it as stories, while others would rather leave it behind in an untroubled and definitive way.

If that was Sally's disposition, I'd say she underestimated the past. I think of all my old *Beat* colleagues now, how good they've turned out. Delmore back there compounding with his mortar and pestle. Denise, beautifying Charleston with her fashion sense while campaigning for equal rights. And now Sally with her environmental work. The strange mixture of practicality and idealism had to come from somewhere. One source, no doubt, was the fiery trial of our anti-dome campaign, coupled with some shared Penny grit. But—this may surprise you, as it does me as I write it—I ascribe a fair portion to that unlikely demi-hero Graham, lax partisan of misfits and dreamers, who never underplayed our mission or even missed a deadline. His moral hemorrhage for Phil Marconi might have negated it all. We were right not to trust him, and a bad deed can do that to a legacy, if not a whole life (wreck it). But it doesn't always and in Graham's case didn't. A hypocrite's ideals are still ideals, contagious for the young.

We set out our towels.

"Topless is okay," Sally said, unhooking.

"I have nothing," I said. (I once shrieked the exact sentence at my mother, as if she'd picked my flat chest.)

"That doesn't matter."

"I like your nothing," Lena said.

I crossed my arms.

They removed their tops and did a little cheering dance, and we all splashed in. The sea was bath-like, warmer than the Cape in high summer. Once Sally realized what my girlfriend thought water was for, she gave her a wide berth. I interviewed Sally as we bobbed.

I had a minor revelation during our return trip north, a long drive, with one short interruption, from Miami to Lumberton, N.C., then all the way back to Worcester the next day, for the final sprint to my thesis deadline, followed by Senior Week and Commencement. We took turns on those last legs, and my goodness it's depressing to watch the seasons run in reverse very quickly like that, as they do in late March.

To explain the minor revelation requires me to clear up one more screening fiction. My hirsuteness, dear reader, was French, not Italian. My father was a Larcher, not a Fardy or "Fardello" (that ridiculous name I made up while maligning our mustachioed Ellis Island staffers). The Larchers of Massachusetts are somewhat famous in an academic corner. Suicide among us is prolific, on a Hemingway scale. Or as Graham might point out, on the scale of the Hoopers, the family of Clover Adams, whose potassium cyanide made Henry a widower, igniting his fertile "posthumous life," not long before her mother and brother killed themselves, too. In my own family, Dad's mother did it, as did her father, and his sister and two uncles. You can google it because a Brandeis professor researched the family, among other similar ones, in an effort to trace the genes at work in this acute suicidal tendency (she didn't find them).

I've feared this history. I ascribe it to some spandrel mutant strain that broke out from the Jura vineyards of my Euro-peasant ancestors. The Larchers must have noted it in their own way as they plucked, uncharmed, their Gouet Blanc down the dew-glistening alleys, or gathered grim-mouthed about the banqueting table for a grand feast. You can see their Flemish counterparts in Bruegel (who would've had a field day with Pennies). This fear—my wish to protect myself, not my poor Larcher father—is why I wrote I'm half Italian and switched my last name A.D.D. to Zhou. Now the Chinese just sounds better (the single-syllabic sharpness) and ties me to my living mom.

The minor revelation was this: I say I've feared it, but I don't anymore. It's only now that I'm pinning this down, but I first felt it rising, half-expressed, like a mild analgesic, on our trip back north.

We'd made good progress but after a reversal of fortune we stopped for a break at Georgia's temple-like welcome center (soaring two-storied atrium, parking for 160, seventy flushing fixtures) in the town of Port Wentworth. A minor confusion landed us there, back on I-95 South. Lena had made a wrong turn at the last pit stop, and we found ourselves in reverse, heading back out of South Carolina and into Georgia again. Then *I* had to go and asked her to pull into the Georgia Welcome Center. Then once we got there, I decided we'd linger: "I want to write."

A light rain sent us racing for a pavilion, where Lena put her head down and I worked on the climax of my college thesis (which unconvincingly valorized me, while casting all others as fiends or adoring friends). She began to softly weep. I don't know if it was her driving mistake that had gotten to her or something even less this time. The light rain. My bossy insistence. The essential if unimportant soullessness, given the transiency of our moments in them, of even the best rest areas. Or nothing at all. When I saw that, I thought again, *this is not working, we'll have to break up*.

"You want to just go?"

"No, you write."

"Okay, but I'm driving."

"Fine."

"I can't," I said, meaning I couldn't write

As a child, I had seen it up close with Dad. Now I was seeing it, and not for the first time, in Lena, and right at that moment its surpassing strangeness struck me. *Whatever that is, I don't have it*, I thought and noted in my diary. Then I forgot it, and only stumbled on it now and remembered that it's true.

Town Meeting

WE MOORED THE EMPRESS JOSEPHINE TO A stilted shanty, and Delmore passed an armload of the bundles to Denise, who handed them to Sally, who forked them over to me. Sharon dropped to all fours and a kind of shelf popped open on her back and I stacked them in high and then took my share from Sally. Then we humans started heaving our way up the hill while Sharon sprinted like a leopard to the top and waited.

"I bet that has a military use," Delmore mused. "That pounce?"

"Shut up and move," I said. "This isn't the time for chit-chat."

Delmore snorted. I'd lost some cachet by ordering charge on a pump blade.

When we finally reached Sharon, we paused to catch our breath.

"I hope they'll recognize it," I confided to Sally. Both of us were bent over, panting beside our stacks. "I mean, as 'the paper.'"

"You did good," Sally said.

Sharon cooed. "COOL BEANS, WENDY: CONGRATS!"

I found her cute but when she said something off like this I was reminded that she was not alive and her words were as mindless as the weather.

Penny canal-craft tooted along and air-horned the canal that ringed Town Hall. Hundreds of clammy Pennies had packed into Town Hall (AC, telecast), but many more had gathered on the hillside and the grassy patch at the bottom, forming a great crowd. The town had set up a long speaker's platform with a podium on the grassy patch and a long wire snaked through the crowd to where a mic had been planted for public comment.

The crowd was oddly festive. Broderick Bateman, Pennacook's leading eighties cover band, played a late-eighties-Aerosmith medley that was like one bad song that went on forever. After that, the drummer riffed on the beat from "Straight Outta Compton" (1988) and for a moment it seemed a new energy had been infused. But they set that aside for an early hit from Poison.

Vendors from competing Chinese restaurants, shouldering bamboo carrying poles ("milkmaid's yolks," in oldspeak), traipsed up and down the aisles, selling pu pu platter elements at numbing prices (eight bucks for a baby's fist of boneless spare-ribs). Gravy Poole hawked wieners he had heated over his coal-fired jalopy. He otherwise surprised me by being totally detached. (I think he had turned against Phil's plans because they offered no rebates.)

They even had a screen up for the crowd to see the speaker and sundry entertainment. At the moment, it featured *One Crazy Summer* (1986), a lesser Cusack marred by excessive eighties zaniness. Ominously, someone had fed perhaps a dozen giant beach domes (beach balls, but shaped like domes) to the crowd, which delightedly smacked and poked them.

The other Bobcats came by balance bike, private boat, and foot. Even lofty Niles Corbyn, who was always kissing up to Graham and hadn't written diddley-squat for the special edition but just sat around looking amused, had descended from his mid-teens to join us. Brent Tanner, the mean Bobcat, didn't show. (I think he had quit.) When a critical mass had gathered by the flagpole, I broke them into groups.

"There, there, there, and there," I pointed, sending the Bobcats out to distribute the special-edition paper to the factions. "Go for solids. Anything but purple."

The Penny factions had agreed to wear blank, color-coded T-shirts. The TBNers had embraced this with gusto and chose purple. As a kind of HQ they had set up a stall—a yellow-and-white-striped tent—on the hill. Its sides bulged, and every minute or so a little purple-T-shirted blob, bearing a machine gun or leashed boar (or both), slipped from the tent flaps. I could tell from their weaponry and pulsating-fist salutes that these men were MGOPers. Just outside the tent, a long line of those homburg-hatted henchmen awaited. They'd peel off in pairs to escort the emerging MGOP blobs into the crowd. Once in the crowd (according to my anonymous source), the little three-person thug-cells sought out Pennies whom they'd tagged as potential dissenters and stomped on their toes and elbowed them to drive them off.

The other side was in total disarray. In Archie's absence, they didn't know what they stood for, or if they were one faction, two, or three. So they hadn't even picked team colors.

We streamed into the crowd with our papers. Sharon rolled alongside me on her feet-wheels, scaring little kids and xenophobic parents ("Momyyy: what's that?" "Mind your chicken, Cheryl. We don't need more trouble from no Greeks").

A man pointed. "Hey, look: balloon rides."

A small hot-air balloon was tied to a stake behind Town Hall. "$800 a pop!" the banner read.

For a long time after we abandoned him, Graham was content to soak in self-pity. *Why had this happened to him? What had he ever done that was so bad, except being a fool who got tricked?* He knew there was more to it. He had betrayed the mission and—worse—set a bad example. It wasn't just the shady deal with Phil. It was the relentless dissipation, which he'd made little effort to conceal and even theatrically presented: nodding off drunk on the smelly yellow couch during office-hours while the kids carried his water; snapping at those who challenged him, including—God help

251

him—the new kid (me), the lonely stranger whom you were always supposed to welcome.

He recoiled. There was something a little indulgent in this self-flagellation. Just one more way to keep the spotlight on himself. If he really cared, he thought, the best thing to do was free himself, march back out there, and fix things—if that was even possible now.

Thus began Graham's long-seeming (but really very brief) struggle with his shackles. If he wiggled hard, he figured, he could wobble to the break-room window and if someone passed by, he'd rattle against the window and turn a pleading face up as they approached. But when he tried it, he toppled over. His head barely missed the table's corner and knocked against the carpet. He still had his teeth, though. If he could just chew through—no, his jaw was tightly taped. And now—*just look at me*, he thought—he was pinned to the floor, chair sprouting from his upturned ass.

His only move now was the inch-worm: squeeze and push, squeeze and push. He did three squeezes and growled at the back pain. And when he peeked around back, he hadn't even moved.

I "wended" my way to the sea of purple T-shirts on the hill, where internal fist-fights had broken out and a machine-gun duel had barely been averted. My goal was not to convert but to peel off the stray TBNer who had already lost faith. After my performance at Clarice, it seemed only proper that I would bear the risk.

"Uh—thank you? But I'm a dyed-in-the-wool domie," one of the men said. He took the paper, grinned, spat on it, and handed it back.

"We shouldn't be fighting each *other*," a voice cried. "We should be fighting all *them*."

"Two fried egg-rolls and a refill on this tea," one dickweed said, pretending to place an order.

"WENDY, MY CALCULATIONS TELL ME THAT YOUR STRATEGY IS A POOR ONE."

She was right. There was no squishy margin here, only a thick, impenetrable barrier: the wall of a concrete cell. If there were any TBN deserters, I suspected they'd be buried in that wall. Not free on the other side.

I climbed down the hill for better prospects.

Each time I handed out the special-edition *Beat* was a fresh chance to cringe at the error-ridden copy we'd churned out pell-mell that afternoon. To be sure, we'd used the familiar typeface and printed it on heavy-stock, legal-sized paper, and Denise had shrunk Jacob Pike being tarred and feathered (our gruesome icon) and brushed him up with red for salience. At Sally's request, we'd even crammed in a masthead (no Graham). All so that it somewhat resembled a vessel of the news.

But the content was rough, to put it kindly. It began with six pages of densely-packed exposés and editorials that at times embellished or turned breathless and mean. It wasn't much better than Graham's pink broadsheet. And yet there was an elegant symmetry to our product, the way it turned Graham's tabloid voice and all caps against him.

"CORRUPT" BUNDT FIRED, PURGED!

Long-time *Beat* editor-in-chief Graham "Adams" Bundt was ousted today by his own Staff (unpaid children) after an internal investigation tied him to a local tyrant. Quincy sources say Bundt's been formally stripped from the Adams family rolls, while others report that his wife has left him, he has no friends, is sort of an ass, and . . .

"PHLOODING PHIL" BELONGS IN JAIL, NOT TOWER

Police and prosecutors are looking into allegations that Phil
Marconi, lately of the Lion Diner basement, is behind the
Pennacook floods that have decimated the town's economy in
recent years. Sources say he roots for the Yankees, wears deck
shoes, and eats crumpets.

PHIL TELLS PENNIES: RAKE TURDS FOR DOME DANDIES

EDITORIAL: CARE FOR A ROUND OF GOLF? (ME NEITHER)

TRASH-CAN "HOMES" AND GRANITE-STATE DOO-DOO:
"PHELONIOUS PHIL'S" REAL PLANS REVEALED!

These were followed by eighteen more pages of A.I. blandness
that Sharon had spewed in two seconds. I tossed her entries in
the back. For all their infirmities, Pennies aren't seduced by polite
and empty bullshit, which is all that Sharon could muster, bless
her heart. I had thought of leaving her pages out entirely, for fear
they'd spark a backlash. In the end, I included them for padding.
Since I'm not here to shine you, I must say that *rude* and empty
bullshit might have fared better in Pennacook. But Sharon, pro-
grammed for Bounty Bag courtesy, couldn't do that, either.

Back at the *Beat*, Graham gave up on escaping and his worries
shifted to a more "pressing" concern: his swollen bladder.

*Oh, no. Please lord, no. Don't make me pee in my pants. I can't take
it. I can't—*

He peed hard and felt the wet warmth spreading. It was worth
it, at first.

Holt Maggio and Max Silva rose to the mic. They had dressed in black suits and in the homburgs, which were trendy with their faction. They looked a lot like a thirties standup duo, sans straight man (Hardy and Hardy). The Penny-village flag-dipping ceremony plodded on behind them. A decision had been made to cut to the speeches rather than wait out the interminable ritual. (One can sympathize, from a production perspective.)

"Fellow Pennies, we come here—oh, *look* at all those *bouncing domes*. Ain't it beautiful, Max?"

"Ditto that, Holt. Ha ha!"

Maggio stepped back, grinned, and waved. Broderick Bateman broke into the cliché victory tune "Celebration" (1980), by Kool and the Gang, as if the domies had already won the vote. The crowd roared and more beach domes burst from beneath it.

"As you know," Holt Maggio continued, "we are gathered here for the sacred honor of voting. And may I say, I'm impressed by the ample turnout. Never before in Pennacook history have so many gathered on this rolling hillside to consummate—"

"Stuff it, *wanker!*" some Englishman shouted (Clyve Turner, I later learned: an immigrant from Leeds).

Faces brightened at the fresh new curse. Stirred by this reaction, I lowered my head and plowed back into the crowd, eager to unload more special editions before the vote-call.

"Sharon: find T-shirts."

"WENDY, I AM SORRY TO DOUBT YOU, BUT I THINK THAT YOU ARE ONCE MORE MISTAKEN. BY MY CALCULATIONS, ONLY THIRTY-TWO POINT FIVE THREE PERCENT OF PENNIES BELONG TO FACTIONS. YOUR STRATEGY IS ALL TOO NARROW."

Cut loose, she meant, and hunt *all* votes (except purples). Most Pennies were not that political. At least not like MGOP's Leo

Carbonara. Or Archie Simmons. Or even Mr. Susco and his Penny Thinkers (the old men had planted their stall on the hill opposite MGOP and the other TBNers but I didn't see Mr. Susco up there sipping from the Box O Joe. On account of age and fear of falling, they mostly kept to themselves, gabbing and prepping to vote). No, Pennies generally were non-committal, detached from the factions and most public issues. I realized that Sharon was right. This huge block was swayable—and crucial.

After that, I unloaded the *Beat* quickly and almost at random. When I spied Bobcats through the scrum, I reached out, dragged them in, and debriefed them on the new approach. Already I could feel the power draining from us and into the broader polity. There was something very right about this (after all, we couldn't vote).

Up on stage, the Englishman's attack—and the crowd's reaction—had knocked Maggio off balance, and he felt about for a reset.

"Uh—is this thing on?" He tapped the mic. Then tapped it again. Then put his ear up to it. Then stepped back and looked side to side. "Is someone going to help with this feedback?"

"There's no feedback. Just talk," a familiar voice said.

Almy, my forms guy!

I was out of papers and moved to higher ground. From where I stood, it seemed many Pennies had trashed our paper or folded it away. Others, though, were holding it close with wide eyes, astonished. My eyes followed a ripple as it passed through one of these readers and spread through the crowd. Heads turned and hands seemed to move with purpose, all in one direction, and then around and back in a kind of repeating circle. Were they passing the word? Debating and conferring? Nah, it was "the wave."

They were still roaring, though, and it seemed the tone had shifted. From beach-dome-bouncing exuberance to—wrath? Whatever it was, it prompted Maggio and Silva to step back, startled.

The crowd broke into "*Na Na Hey Hey Kiss Him Goodbye.*" Broderick Bateman, poorly paid mercenaries of weak allegiance, jumped in with a backbeat and jolting power chords. Silva made some little signal to Maggio and they scurried off stage, holding their homburgs before them like the disgraced weenies they were.

Pennies aren't always terribly original, and I'd love to not have to report what happened next. But after *that* cliché song got old—and as if tired of all this politicking—the crowd broke out with "Sweet Caroline," by Neil Diamond. The song was ubiquitous in the Boston area, at sports games and social events, and had been for decades.

"That doesn't make it right," Graham had written in an ungenerous but clear-eyed editorial. "The song's special popularity," he continued,

> is not likely the organic byproduct of Boston sports fandom or bar life, as is widely believed. No, this business started only after the hit-or-miss—some say sleazy—film *Beautiful Girls* (1996). In the movie, it is some "real guy" local tradition in some made-up Massachusetts "rural" town where no one has accents to sing that together in a bar. The Hollywood movie came first, Pennies! We just followed.

He allowed that it was as much a tradition as the Shamrock Shake, "and if that sounds like a compliment you may want to reconsider the meaning of tradition."

There was a rustle up front. "Screw this," an old man shouted. He shook off his handlers and hopped on stage.

Phil Marconi.

The crowd gasped and cheered. Whichever version of the *Beat* you believed in, here was the drama's central figure. And it was just plain weird that he'd once grilled their burgers.

"Pennies, I want to address some lies that have been spreading."
(By you!)

"By a cabal of lying children. *(Phil's a wanker!)* I want only what is best for my beloved hometown. Yes, I've installed pumps. But, don't you see, we're testing. *(It's a lie!)* *(Don't believe it!)* I didn't make these canals *(hey, that's my drumstick!)* and I can't make them vanish, either."

He stopped talking and waited for a lull, then gripped the podium and leaned forward. "Hear me out. Please. I *love* you."

After one more *hang-em-all*, the crowd fell silent, as if embarrassed. (Many Pennies were love-starved. It wasn't just Graham.)

"If we win here, I will put the canals to work for you. Look, I don't have to do this. I want to. Because I know what it feels like. Like you, I've been kicked around.

"By filthy water.

"By Eaton elites *(Eaton sucks!)* *(Eaton you friggin losahs!)*, with their smug titters and boats of endless sushi *(sounds great!)* *(hey, man: shut up!)*.

"By a"—pausing for effect—"*faithless* supermarket that hightailed it at the first sign of trouble!"

(Where are they now?)

(Not here!)

(Screw 'em.)

"Do we need 'em?"

(No!)

On the big screen, he played a montage of Bounty Bag's chaotic evacuation from Pennacook. A bulldozer smashed through the storefront. A lost name tag ("*The* Alfredo: 18 years") spun into a gully. A helicopter lifted a giant bulbous net full of wild boars, aimed north for New Hampshire. But the net broke and hundreds of boars tumbled out and splattered. *Do you want to mourn these clowns or judge them?* the film implicitly asked. *And doesn't judging feel so much better?* It was a stunning reversal: Bounty Bag pride turned to Bounty Bag shame—and resentment.

Phil downshifted to speak about his plans. He looked impressed and proud, as though he was both awarding and receiving a major prize or getting married. While he spoke, gauzy close-ups from his fake New Pennacook diorama drifted across the screen. I found this hokey, but the crowd had hushed. Their reveling and shout-backs had depleted them, and I think they were ready for someone else to do the hot talking. Phil even claimed to be a "man of peace" who renounced MGOP's tactics, if not their noble intent.

"Come on down here, guys." He smiled. "It's time."

Up on the hill, Leo Carbonara took the cue from his master and rolled a finger at MGOP. With phony-looking shrugs of relief and white smiles through fat beards, the men descended from the hill and deposited their machine guns in a spiky pile in front of the platform. Wild boars nosed out from the crowd to sniff them. One misplaced hoof, I thought, and a great conflagration would commence. But it didn't. The boars found nothing edible or fun and loped off.

It was all a charade. The real plan, we had reported, was to convert MGOP to the new Penny cops: the vaunted "strike force" that the broadsheet had touted. Phil would hand the guns right back, only now they'd be carried under color of law. (If this happened, something told me they'd slay Mr. Susco.)

At last Phil, too, looked tired. He hazily promised to "save everybody," then climbed down to thundering cheers. His minions scurried to set up the voting stalls.

For Graham now, it was a mind game. What could he think about that would carry him away, distract him till the cavalry came and snipped him free?

John Adams.

He willed himself back into his bed, where he let his mind's eye drift to the opposite wall, to his framed copy of the Massachusetts Constitution. The original version, before the committee's modest edits.

John Adams had thrown some bold curveballs in there, even alien-sounding stuff. It wasn't all rule of law and pocket vetoes. Chapter V, Section II, for example, stated that the government had a "duty" "to cherish the interests of literature." But most radically, the Massachusetts Constitution said—says—that "good humor" and "generous sentiments" are to be prized. These days, both qualities were in short supply. Graham had often wondered: how would you put that clause into effect? Was it just dead letter? He hoped not. If the government wasn't going to enforce it, maybe the people could themselves. On the other hand, how likely was that if, as Henry Adams put it, "no representative government can long be much better or much worse than the society it represents"?

One among many of Graham's dreams had been that, locally, he and his Bobcats could breathe life into these words through their little trumpet the *Beat*. Even now, as he soaked in his urine, he felt old ambitions rising and pictured his forebear stepping back with one leg forward making an "at your service" bow, like the one he gave George III as our first minister to the Court of St. James's, only this time to all of posterity.

Who was he kidding? He'd smoked that, too.

He heard the latch turn—*Athena?*

It was.

"What have you done, boy?"

She cut the chair off and his mouth free but left his arms and legs bound.

"I don't trust you, either."

She loaded him onto a dolly, dumped him in the back of her convertible, and drove him to her workshop at the Muskrat Colony in Maynard. Along the way, he confessed. To how he'd lost Archie's documents thread and failed to rise to the occasion after they'd taken him down. To how he'd looked the other way on the "Town for Sale!" ad, just for some bucks. To how he'd ignored Athena, her skepticism about her grandfather's plan.

"I was tricked, too," Athena said, staring ahead. She reminded him that she had failed to figure out what Phil was really up to, had only thought he was a dreamer on a vast and disordered scale, a sort of uberPenny (or uberGraham).

At the Muskrat, she wheeled him to her workshop and parked him on a plush armchair (big upgrade).

"I'm going to leave you now. A safe distance from the mess we made."

"But—"

"Elle and Jim will come down to help you."

"L and who?"

"My partners. I trust them with my life. They're just wrapping up in the kitchen now. They'll bring you a towel, soap, and clothes." She put her hands on her hips and stared out the window. "Also probably muffins."

Graham's gaze followed hers across the squash field to the wide round window that looked into the kitchen's golden lamplight and the vast communal table where many hands and faces were eating. Graham could almost taste the buttery warmth there but balked at asking if he could go in (and be handcuffed to the radiator or a chair leg, if need be, if he'd fallen that far in her estimation).

And you? Graham wondered, turning to her.

"I need time to think," she said, reading his mind.

Graham slumped in his chair and watched her gather her things. She quietly closed the door behind her, as if trying not to wake him.

As soon as she'd gone, a golf ball from the nuisance-neighbor golf course smashed through the window, and the bees—drawn by the urine—swarmed through to feast.

Outside the voting stalls, Pennies had amassed in alp-plagued lines. There had been few public comments because the moment a ponytailed man from the Archie Clique stepped up to the mic, tapped it, and said "Uh—" Holt Maggio axed the electrical cable like Pete Seeger.

"WENDY. I THINK THIS MIGHT HELP."

Sharon shook, and her loin printed a slip of paper.

"What's this?" I asked, tearing it off.

"A PROPOSED REVISION TO THE MUNICIPAL CODE OF PENNACOOK, MASSACHUSETTS, AS ENACTED PURSU-ANT TO ARTICLE EIGHT, SECTION FIVE, SUB-SE—"

"Halt. Summary."

"IT IS A SENSIBLE COMPROMISE. AFTER REMOVING CERTAIN CONFOUNDING VARIABLES, IT ACCOUNTS FOR ALL INTERESTS AND ENJOYS AN 88.23% CHANCE OF PASSAGE."

Was A.I. here to save us? (Talk about a *deus ex machina*!)

No. It was easy enough to read, I'll give her that. She had draft-ed it in plain and simple English. In this sense, it vastly improved on the Penny code's many circumambulations, which I had failed to decipher in my water-price researches (and again, more recently, for this). But as I read it, I had that familiar sense of estrange-ment. Sharon, alas, had no morals.

"We can't kill Phil."

She blinked.

"Or the others."

Article I, Section A, was a rogue's gallery of anti-socials whom Sharon had deemed beyond the pale and who were to be publicly executed Saudi Arabia-style. The list included Phil, Leo Carbonara, Maggio (but not sidekick Silva, apparently redeemable), and Graham. I suppose these were the "confounding variables" she had referred to and had determined she could fudge away by guillotine or sword.

"MY BAD." Wink. "LET ME TRY AGAIN."

"Oh, no, thank you, sweetheart. Next time, okay?"

There's no sense being cruel.

Just then, five more humans arrived. Two of them bore a spe-cial—and disturbing—relationship to me.

I saw them on the hill. Mr. Susco had taken his camp chair and pulled a cup of java from the box. Beside him—*ugh*—was my spruced-up mom. Here, it seemed, for her hot date's finale. *This* was her new beau? Twenty years older and my teacher? The man with the sweaty pits? Parent-teacher night came back in a flash: her light step as she crossed the kitchen and tossed her keys in the basket. I was doing great, she had said, and all my teachers loved me. Right: Mr. Moriarty? He hated us all and was known to show it. But she was distracted, I now concluded, by the crush she had formed that night. Worst of all, she'd picked my favorite.

I knew at that moment that seventh grade would never be the same. She later defended herself by saying that she'd kept the lid on this as long as possible. But Mr. Susco—"George"—had gotten her so excited about the momentous public meeting that she had insisted on joining him. There were only a few weeks left of school anyway, she thought. So I wouldn't be bothered. She was wrong. I didn't speak another word in Mr. Susco's class, and it took years for things to mend between Mr. Susco and me, and between Mom and me with regard to him.

The others, a welcome sight, arrived with great flair: a red convertible with a long white ribbon streaming from the driver. Her hair was golden and she seemed to shine in her bright-white costume. Behind her in the back was Dr. Chong from the high school and a ramrod-straight Archie Simmons. As they came closer, Archie waved and grinned like FDR touring the Hudson Valley in his 1936 Ford Phaeton as he trawled for votes and adoration (Hyde Park's worth a visit).

The driver—Athena—turned straight into the parking lot and honked her way to the entrance. She stepped out and walked around the car. Dr. Chong and Athena removed Archie and carried him up to the platform, where they propped him. Dr. Chong then went back to the car to retrieve a large, bulging sack, which she plunked on the platform.

At the sight of Archie, the crowd exploded with applause and cheers. Each thank-you triggered a fresh eruption. He lifted something from his pocket and banged the podium with it (*whack whack whack whack*) until at last the crowd settled.

"Remember these, friends? They're slippers."

Dr. Chong opened the sack and handed elastic-bound pairs of slippers to Athena, who hurled one pair after another to the crowd as Archie spoke.

"I used to need these for my office. Because when citizens came to see me in the winter, sometimes alone, or in groups as large as twenty—I see some of you out here today. Why, hello, Amy. Bud: how are you?—they'd take off their skates and need footwear. Because guess what, folks? They'd forgotten to pack shoes!"

Polite laughs at the tepid humor (Archie wasn't funny).

"But now I only need two pairs. One for me, and one for my Regina."

He swung his arm toward her, and she gave a quick nod. She was widely reviled. A bit of a tyrant herself, and then layer on top of that, she lived in Eaton. For some Pennies (I well knew), it also didn't help that she was Asian and female.

"You know why? Because for all the little gimmicks Phil Marconi has promised you—yes, I've seen the plans, I was fully briefed just now in the hospital—there's one thing that's missing from his climate-controlled golfer's paradise."

(What's that?)

(Don't hold back, Arch. Tell us!)

A dramatic pause. "Ice time."

(Ooohhh.)

(Nooo!)

(It can't be!)

(Treason!)

Archie was right! A blatant omission from Phil's plans—even the fraudulent ones—was an ice rink, a replacement for the hallowed Hallenbuck.

"And I don't know about you. But after last winter, I don't want just an ice rink. I want *canal* ice."

He raised the slipper high.

(Hoo-ray!)

(Fuck yeah!)

(Eat me!)

"All."

whack

"Year."

whack

"Long!"

One more whack from the slipper and done.

That and our paper won the day.

It wasn't close. Worse for Phil, now that Pennies had turned on him, it was only a matter of time before the criminal charges. Malicious destruction of property. Fraud on the public coffers. For what they'd done to Archie, even attempted murder (they did convict Holt Maggio for that, and he went away for twenty). And then, privately, a class-action suit that could reach the many millions. So Phil climbed in the basket and cut loose the hot-air balloon. An outraged MGOPer snatched his machine gun from the pile and fired forty rounds but missed. (I'd have made that shot. All of them, actually.) Phil sailed off and was nevermore seen. But late one night, a few days later, his abandoned dome-shards detached from his cranes and collapsed with a series of stupendous *cracks* that wakened every Penny and strewed the town with steel and glass.

I didn't see much of my dump-trip comrades after the Town Meeting. They saw the *Beat* as tainted and quit. I took the empty editor-in-chief's chair, but then I quit, too, when I heard Graham was coming back. Soon it was summer vacation, and in the fall, the others were off to high school. I had one more year at Pike Middle. This threw up a steep social barrier that, despite our recent alliance, we were all quite happy to maintain. Of eighth grade I remember little more than the opening words of my graduation speech ("When I was young,..."). I lived on in Pennacook for five more years before college and had no more adventures to relay.

Much later, after Pennies had purged the town of its e-birds (though not of its wily boars), mastered Phil's pumps, and built their own world-famous dome (only not so vast and honed to a single purpose), I sat down with Archie in his office. I wasn't writing my college thesis yet, just profiling Pennacook for the college paper (a "my hometown" series). Like everyone else, I'd found the slipper speech stirring.

"And yet I must ask: was this really the best use of municipal revenue? Wasn't that money better allocated to the schools? Or to mold removal or land-mass restoration? Maybe you could even lure back Bounty Bag."

"Wouldn't that be nice. Of course, any of what you say would be better. But the people wanted something else."

A jumbo-domed, frozen parkland.

"Something ... stupid?"

"I'd say different. But we dodged the worst thing, that's what matters. You can't always win and be free."

AFTER:
GRAHAM

Independence Forever

ATHENA'S THROUPLE TENDERLY NURSED GRAHAM back to health after the bees debacle. Over bean-soup kettles, he admitted to Athena as if on his death bed (he was just sore in places) that he had harbored a long-simmering crush during the decades of their meetings at Lion Diner.

"I've enjoyed you, too," Athena said lightly.

It was enough that she didn't mock or reject him.

He also announced that if he ever got back on his feet, he was semi-retiring from the paper. He'd let the kids take the lead on content, including Editorial. He'd restrict his meddling to Ops.

In late June, he called in an absence at the *Beat* (Bill Marino from Obits was the dour new chief) and rode the Peter Pan to Errol, N.H., where he hiked up a lane to the log cabin at that all-too-familiar address. Keith J. Prince greeted him at the door.

"Any relation?" Graham asked, thinking he knew the answer.

"I'm told all us Princes in these parts are, if you dig deep enough. Though obviously there aren't many of us."

"Then we may have much to discuss, you see, because I, too, descend from the Revolutionary generation." He paused. "I am an Adams."

"I know."

The tantalizing rumors had run both ways.

Keith walked him through the cabin to a back office and opened the file cabinet where he kept extensive genealogical records. Graham envied such documentation. He had nothing of the sort, only word of mouth and the Adams weddings and funerals where no one spoke to or seemed even to recognize

Graham and his mother. At the weddings, his mother would claim a corner seat at the black-sheep, nut, and forever-talker table, where there was always room. "Were we invited?" Graham would ask, looking up at his mother. "A true Adams doesn't need permission," she'd reply. At the wakes she was bolder, perhaps because, to our last appearance, typically everyone is invited, whether or not we were an Adams. She marched forward, a single red carnation planted waist-high before her, and laid it over the corpse's chest. At one of the wakes Graham glanced over his shoulder and saw another Adams swipe the carnation and toss it in the barrel. Nowadays, his mother lived in far-off Arcadia, Florida, with "a nice man" and had no interest in family "trivia" and not much more in Graham.

They pored over records and dodged the main thing.

"I like to think that Sally and Thomas had a romantic love," Keith said.

"She was his dead wife's half-sister and was said to resemble her closely," Graham offered. Though how could you own a person and her love be freely given? Then again, there was often no accounting for human feelings. Graham had no idea what John Adams would have made of this mystery, but he had been disgusted by the whole decrepit slave economy and by his dear friend, then arch enemy, then dear friend's willingness to hold people as chattel. Just as Lafayette was dismayed by Washington's slaveholding—as Washington, too, eventually came to be, possessing them "very repugnantly" to his "own feelings." You had the sense that Washington was haunted (though not quite enough).

Keith rightly guessed that something else was bothering him about all this talk of surprising and resilient love, or at least its possibility.

"You still love Josephine. I do, too."

"Yes."

"And she loves me."

Graham released an operatic sigh. "I know it."

"I like you, Graham, partly because you do love her so faithfully. But I must ask:"—the hot little back-room's log walls rolled forward—"will you divorce her? Or does it have to be a dogfight?"

Graham had been carrying his briefcase all this time, which may have lent Keith such boldness. Now he lowered it to the floor, swept aside some Jeffersonian knickknacks—the Monticello cigar-box, the bust, a miniature laminated DOI—and gently placed the briefcase (you don't swing tonic) on the desk. He snapped it open, reached behind the root beers, and retrieved the thin, legal-sized envelope. He steadied his hand and passed the clasped envelope to Keith. The tears were hot and swift.

"You—want a drink?" Keith clumsily asked and then caught himself. "My bad."

"I'll have one of these," Graham said. He fell back in Keith's leather office chair and attempted to sportily pop open a root beer.

"Oh," Keith said when he saw that Graham had signed.

Before this blubbering and defeated man sipping root beer like an injured kid being coddled with a treat, Keith, too, wanted to cry at first. But he was not a crying man, and in his triumph, he couldn't. It was a small grace that he suppressed the little laugh that fluttered up from the Devil's workshop in the marred human soul that he believed in.

"I couldn't please her."

"I hope you'll be our friend."

"Never."

Graham's joke liberated Keith from the evil impulse. A smile was allowed.

"Will you at least try my pancakes?"

"Lumberjack flapjacks? Absolutely."

They were so good, everything Graham had feared and then some. He savored them like the condemned's last meal.

It wasn't just a cliché. The moment brought to mind (a tad melodramatically: a wife is not a life) a documentary he had seen on capital punishment in a Texas county. The day before the execution, they tested out the gas on a rabbit. The documentarians were allowed to show it in there spasming for a few seconds and falling still. That night the man had a final dinner, fried chicken and pie with three aging matriarchs. They chatted softly. After, the man was allowed into the prison yard to shoot baskets by himself under the spotlight. The next morning, he was gone like the rabbit. Like Graham's marriage. And not only the marriage but the family they never had. Because Graham, who keenly wanted children, delayed it. He was too busy with his balance bikes, the *Beat*, his drinking, and his dreams. A joke to outsiders, it pained him, too, that he was the last of his Adams line.

"One thing. You seem decent. What's up with those postcards?"

Keith laughed, for another's sin.

"You couldn't tell? I didn't write those. I sternly objected, but she said it was the only way to get through to you."

Knuckles knocked on a door frame.

"There's the Old Man of the Mountain now," Josephine said, appearing on the threshold.

Graham took Josephine's remark as apology's thin wedge, a self-parody of the dissembling and malice that, with time, he would accept as gifts. It was easier to lose someone who disdained and rejected the hero of your story: you.

Josephine leaned out from the shadows.

"We're expecting in August," Keith said, before the question ripened.

Graham whispered congratulations, then said the cutting Napoleon quote he had long ago prepared for this moment.

"'Farewell, Josephine. You are a monster whom I cannot explain.'"

He didn't give the context, a love note. Napoleon had concluded an armistice with the king of Sardinia. He begged his wife to cut through Turin to join him.

Peacefield

IN AUGUST, THE THROUPLE FORMALLY INVITED A still-depressed Graham into the polycule.

"At a low-key, tertiary status," Athena said, not wanting him to get ahead of himself.

"A mascot for the girls," Elle added.

"But we like you, buddy," Jim said.

"We all do," Athena said.

After he accepted, he was relieved to learn that he was not required to have a romantic relationship with his mini-golf buddy Jim.

"Because I thought we had to –"

"No."

Jim drew a picture. There were two dotted lines, labelled "Non-Platonic: S/M," running from Athena and Elle to Graham, and another dotted line, between Graham and Jim, labelled "Platonic."

"What's 'S/M'?"

Jim defined it again for him and reminded him of their prior discussions and the relationship contract he had signed. More earnest than irritated, he also reran the sermon on consent. It was necessary, Jim emphasized, that in the future Graham ask these questions up front. Knowing consent, freely given, was critical even for those like Graham who took a catch-as-catch-can attitude.

"You can't be this dreamy."

"Sorry."

Graham was determined to be a good sport but suspected there would be no future polycule for him once he fell out of favor with this crew. The invitation alone depleted him. There were so many heads to nod at and to please and in the end it was the other thing that revived him.

"I don't know why I like this," he said to Athena in the middle of it.

The wax dripped hotter as she lowered the candles to his chest.

"You're just wired differently. I am, too."

Different? Not different! I'm the same—but better! I'm an A—

She lowered and dripped. He groaned.

"Stop thinking."

It felt like falling: panic, then surrender.

"You were wonderful," she said after, and at last offered her unfettered hug.

At Gags 'n' Strops, he increasingly functioned as Athena's on-demand "sub" for workshops. He enjoyed this role more once it was described to him as a scene rather than torture, though the sessions were harrowing. Athena was a maximalist with her craft and an aggressive salesperson. "If it bleeds, it leads," she told Graham, who was amused to see the cynical old newspaper adage adapted to Gags 'n' Strops.

One day the feeling was different.

"Run out to the field and fetch sticks," she ordered.

Vegan leather was out, a water-wasting plastic.

S/M—or whatever the right letters were—offered benefits beyond direct pleasure and the sense of Muskrat service. It wonderfully distracted from the bottle and relieved him of the traditional demands that he had never been able to meet with Josephine. Now he just had to take it. Also, he reveled in the tender aftercare, a term he found in the online glossary he had finally consulted to catch up on what the heck was happening to him. There were even more terms in this world than in polyamory.

Once Graham had mastered the polycule's byzantine Google calendar, he found that his somewhat peripheral role left him time and space to be alone with himself, sober, in a room. All this time after his marriage to the more social Josephine had crumbled, he understood that he wasn't selfish, sad, or mean to want this. He needed it just because he did. Graham being Graham, alone with Graham.

During community studio time, he knocked off a spry white egret with a raised foot. The next morning at breakfast Athena hired him for piecework, crafting paddles and switches from scratch. It was his first paid labor since the *Beat*.

A supermajority at a special assembly allowed him to move into the ideal nook for his solitary moments and post-session healing: the studio apartment under the Muskrat's porch. On Friday nights he joined in the weekly assembly and voted on all matters after lengthy debates in which he increasingly played a decisive role. His judgment was respected. His root beers, which he gulped in lieu of the red wine that had become a tradition on assembly nights, were misinterpreted as a firm statement on the importance of sobriety in direct democracy.

He didn't win every initiative. His proposal to rechristen the Muskrat Colony as the clearly more beautiful-sounding Peacefield—after the Adams-family homestead—flopped. He carved a sign for his room instead.

All this time, he kept the Pennacook pad. He may have feared being burned by the Muskrat, as he'd been by Josephine, and tossed out homeless in Maynard. He periodically popped into his old rooms. They and his remaining things were tidy but seemed smaller, as if receding.

In early spring, Auntie Lil "passed in her sleep, painlessly, of old age." This was what they told Jeremy Wiggins and put in the obit, though who really knew. Her will designated Graham as Jeremy's lawful guardian, or even parent—if they wished. Why not go all the way? they quickly agreed. Graham adopted Jeremy as his son and they amended his name to Jeremy Quincy Adams Bundt.

One night early in their new family's history, they were popping cocktail wieners in Peacefield—they had managed to cram bunk-beds into the studio—when Jeremy said, "I don't want to eat this every night."

"Every man has his limits," Graham said, smiling inwardly. He had already stocked up on the easy good stuff: apples, bananas, and cucumbers, plus multivitamins, low-sodium vegetable juice, and those salad bags. He was in the market for an Italian cookbook.

They wouldn't share a roof for long. Bounty Bag's hovering probes (upside-down tin salad bowls with dangling cables) eventually circled back to Pennacook. An assistant manager from Chelmsford, Store #32, monitoring the probes' progress remotely from his virtual cockpit in the store's crow's nest, found Jeremy adrift in long-term unemployment. It was a slow, cool, late-summer day. Jeremy had accompanied Graham to the *Beat* for companionship. Through the window the probe's red eye spied him playing *Minesweeper* (1989), a frustrating "classic" that Graham had pushed. The Chelmsford manager checked his files: here was an untapped resource. He pressed the red button and, speaking through the squawk-box, offered Jeremy a senior-sacker position on the spot. Jeremy flung open the window.

"What's that you say?"

"Welcome aboard," the probe said, assuming he had accepted. (The mics were not yet up to snuff on these probes.)

That same afternoon an emissary arrived at the *Beat* carrying Jeremy's maroon tie. After a brief and clarifying exchange, the tie was accepted. While Graham had him, he flagged for the emissary an old grievance against the company: Bounty Bag's snub when he tried to work there after high school and they barred him for flatfoot—the very reason he'd decamped to Woonsocket.

"Flatfoot? What are we, the Green Berets?" He checked his tablet. "Ah."

"What?"

"Your mama nixed it. Said an Adams will sack groceries over my dead body."

To ease Jeremy's commute, he moved out of Peacefield and into Graham's old digs. A rare and mysterious new bus line, perhaps Bounty Bag's doing, departed in the fog of morning from Pennacook Depot on its way to Chelmsford, then trundled back at day's end. Graham visited every day after work to cook them dinner, pack Jeremy's lunch for the next day, and maybe catch a cartoon classic on the old projector.

For all major holidays, and many made-up-seeming Muskrat ones, Jeremy joined Graham in Maynard to celebrate. Even on the Fourth, Old Glory was not to be raised without significant consternation and strife, something Graham never understood.

Graham was no inventor. But one afternoon, as he watched Jeremy struggle to mount and steady the Avalancher, his hard-tailed mountain bike, he hit on a business idea that seemed such a useful and humane extension of the balance bike as to qualify for Adams-level plaudits. He wouldn't sell balance bikes generally. He'd market them instead as an adult bike for people like Jeremy who, because of a disability, couldn't ride the pedaled bike. He restructured as a non-profit and started tweaking the website.

The thought had briefly crossed his mind before. This was shortly after Josephine left him. Jeremy had sneered at his dirty old line of Bundterbikes, which looked so frumpy next to the

Avalancher (truly awesome in its way). Discouraged, Graham had dismissed the idea as utterly uncool and worthless, about what he thought of himself at that time. But now he relaunched the concept with a new force and a focus on a sleeker design that amped up the fun factor. Sensing his excitement, Athena made room in her workshop for Graham to build a prototype. With assembly approval, she even dipped into the Muskrat budget for a non-sexual saw for Graham to use for the wooden frame. It turned out that a cosmetic refresh—matte-black paint job, a couple of chrome attachments, and a constellation of lightning-bolt stickers—was all it took to win Jeremy's heart.

An afternoon balance-bike through Maynard Center revealed the banks were up to their old tricks again, hawking trap-door rates. Graham rode by. He was content to go it alone now, perhaps because, in a larger sense, he wasn't.

Autumn

November 4, 2032

Dear Diary:

As you know, I didn't meet my deadline. Senior Week came and went, as did the rest of June, July, and August. But autumn has been fruitful! While dabbling in my next project (a *roman-à-clef* based on the Bounty Bag supermarket protests of 2013), I've gradually come to realize that the "Spring Break" interludes—along with these diary entries—do belong in *Zodiac Pets*. They add a retrospective dimension without which it is hard to understand who I was as a kid or the aspiring grown-up she became.

I've decided to just dump them in chronologically. No more edits, no false smoothing. Final one is next.

WLZ.
Quito, Ecuador

Postlude: Quito

We went directly from Commencement back to Pennacook, where, like a kid, I lived with my mom, in my old room, for ten weeks. Except it wasn't only Mom but also Mr. Susco. It had been a slow dance, but in the four years I was away, Mom had romanced him (and his droid-torso Annika) out of his dumpster and married him.

The match makes sense. Like Graham, both are dreamers. For all Mr. Susco's talk of how democracy isn't utopia—that "it isn't a plan, it's a way"—he sure gets misty about it. He had converted Mom to the ideal of participatory self-government, and that summer the two of them wasted no time cooking, reverting to Red Barons and other such frozen delicacies, so they could speed off to their next "assembly," their catch-all term, used only half in jest, for any meeting whatsoever, even of the Pennacook Tic-Tac-Toers. I'd wish them the best and as soon as they were gone, I would ring up dear Lena in Grafton Hill.

I didn't know if we were together or not. We had gotten back together and broken up so many times and I had thought—known—we had broken up the last time we had discussed the perennial topic. But then on the phone she said she was glad we were still together. It felt like a reprieve, and I let it pass, hoping she wouldn't forget that and later tell me she was happy we had broken up. Early summer, we corresponded only like that, via text and phone. She was an hour's drive away, and we both had access to our parents' cars, but in that strange after-college time small distances seemed vast and between the familiar parental walls one felt the need to petition for one's freedoms. The broad world had redrawn its curtain.

Lena was preparing with increasing dread for Vietnam. She knew no one there and was quietly terrified of another breakdown, this time

285

on her own. I was lukewarm on grad school and in late June received a response to a long-forgotten fellowship application to work with the orphans from Venezuela and Columbia, in Quito, Ecuador. They not only had a slot for me. They'd had a last-minute cancellation and could offer a position to my partner, too. An escape plan formed.

"Do you want to?" I asked in a phone call.

"Am I?"

"What."

"Your partner."

"For sure."

"I'll consider it."

I had decided we would not part. Not only "not yet" but possibly never—if she'd have me. My reasons for wanting to leave her—they, more than Jesus, had driven our repeated breakups—didn't make sense anymore. I had told myself and Lena that I would leave her because she could never be happy, that cribbed line of Josephine's. But while we were apart, I had done another one of my self-scans and determined that I, of all people, am equipped to handle Lena's sadness.

You may think I'm replaying a script. I failed to save my dad, and here's my chance to relive that again: by burying my future in this new doomed person. No. It doesn't bother me at all. There are people like me who not only can stand it but whom it simply doesn't harm. Some of us even see it as a bargain, for everything we get from our Lenas. (I'm with the nineteenth century in thinking melancholy is often joined to wisdom and humor.) Besides, if people like me, who can handle the unhappy, reject them, too, what will happen to them? Where will they go? At the risk of writing a movie poster: Love isn't a plan. It's a way.

In July we met at Splash World in Agawam, our first date since college.

"Happiness is shallow and undefined, don't you think?" I said out of the blue. It was standard-issue college-dorm bull but no less true for that.

"What?" Lena asked. She was eating one of her favorite treats, fried dough with tomato sauce, from the snack stand.

"There are more important things."

"Mm."

She gave her answer in the parking lot. The orphans of Ho Chi Minh City would have to find another tutor (we were assured there was a line): Lena agreed to join me in Ecuador.

Quito is bold. It's not so much in the mountains as in the volcanoes, a crown of *momento mori* that suits us well as we settle down to our sober math and English-grammar duties. We are on a narrow colonial street, steps from Plaza de la Independencia and the presidential palace, which I can see now through our shutters as I write this. Most mornings are summery, with an equatorial brightness. In the afternoons, there are cooling thunderstorms, and in the evenings a fog rolls in and enshrouds the palms. Down the street, there's a fading mural of the quintessential old man of Quito, a dapper gentleman in black suit, hat and glasses, off to the café for his coffee and papers. I see more of the compact old women, some in Indigenous clothes (derbies, shawls, stockings, and flats), others city workers in belted uniforms with vests. They are quiet and busy. If their path meets a crowd on the plaza, of the tourists or the protestors with their drums and their whistles, they do not commune, unless they are peddling, or go around but pass through.

The other women in our lives are the nuns at Santa Lucía, the Catholic-billionaire-funded orphanage that granted us the fellowship. The sisters had eagerly greeted us just past customs at Mariscal Sucre but quickly came to worry precisely how Lena and I were partners. There was an uncertain and precarious moment by the curb. Then sometime during the bus ride into Old Town, they settled in favor of a misunderstanding that served everyone's interest. We were business partners, they informed us: a teaching team. They commenced their doting, which continues to this day.

On the table beside me is a book entitled *Ecuador: Land of Enchantment*. It is a children's book from the English Lending Library. I had consulted a similar one in elementary school in Bedford Corners, for my country project. A children's book is ideal when you want to learn hard surface facts about a place and then experience and interpret it yourself. *Land of Enchantment* is shorn of travel-guide hucksterism yet strikes a hopeful chord that isn't provably wrong and is certainly a more fruitful starting point than froth. Injustice is recast as one of the country's several collective "challenges." A very recent history of revolt is "fast-paced politics." The book predisposed me to root for Ecuador, and I do.

Our first week, we had an experience that sealed my bond with Lena while also removing the corrosive taint of pity. We had flown to Coca, for a bus to a canoe to a walk into the Amazon rainforest. The billionaire requires that all teachers take this enriching trip. The first day was the cultural part and of greater interest to me. Two women from the P. community told us about their mostly still Indigenous way of life and then they fried plantains and let us shoot blow-darts at a plastic monkey. Down by the canoes, I had a brief exchange with one of the women that recalled the seemingly mythological writings that Mr. Susco had shared from forced prodigy William James Sidis.

"How does the community make decisions?" I asked.

Through slow translation, the woman said they elected a president and vice president who served one year. They did not make decisions. They came up with proposals. Then the whole community met and voted. You could vote when you became an adult at twelve.

"Is this an old way of making decisions?"

"Very old."

"Was it before or after the Spanish?"

"I don't know. It's old."

"Vice president," for one, didn't sound like an ancient Indigenous word. On the other hand, I didn't recall the sixteenth-century Spanish being big on democracy the last time I'd met them, in my high-school World Civilizations textbook. Maybe something of this democracy did go back that far or further, even predated the perfect democracy of the Pennacook that Sidis had depicted.

The exchange excited me more than I would have expected. If direct democracy happened once you knew we could do it, and if it failed it might come back like any other truth. But if you found it in many times and places—Ecuador, Athens, Iceland, New England; Tlaxcalla, the Pennacook, and the Muscogee Creek; the Muskrat and the Bari Corporation—it seemed not only a prospect but consistent with our nature, well in range. And if we can do that on the small or medium scale, why can't we still pull off a more representative democracy (sort of the part-time version) as countries? If anything, it should be easier to save, if we care to.

I e-mailed Mr. Susco. He wasn't surprised. He re-sent the excerpts from *The Tribes and the States* and circled back to his hypothesis that our wobbling national democracy, if not Pennacook's shoddy local one, "may yet draw on its reserve energy and once more be the world's best example."

I don't know about that. The signs aren't good. Yet I hope in this rewrite I have corrected for the defects I noted at the outset. Here in *Zodiac Pets*, with its hinged-together structure of my story, both then and now, and Graham's, I have perhaps evoked something closer to what I believe in. Rather than the perfect or the shattered, the cracked and tattered whole: all that a country or person can be. I am reminded of something that our greatest and most suicidal president said. For a free people, political existence—like life—is a choice. In its bumbling way, Pennacook made the right one. For all his love, my father could not.

The rest of our rainforest trip dwelled on nature. The billionaire's concept—demand—was simple. We were to draw closer to nature and, after some time suspended among its hazards, love it. This would charge us to fight for conservation. I confess to a detachment that teeters on bad faith in this business. I love nature in the abstract. I know it's innocent, I know we need and harm it. But this isn't love. I don't know nature, really. Until a fellow student in a poetry class embarrassingly corrected me on the point, I wasn't even clear, at nineteen, on the difference between nature and the country (farms). Worse than not knowing nature, I fear it, "red in tooth and claw," and mistrust its unforgiving ways. Our guide paused in his paddling to laud the clever big monkeys who dashed low when hawks came so the smaller monkeys, a "buffer," would get picked off instead, but I sided with the little dumb ones. On the night walk, I was unmoved by the lovely and ingenious spider wrapping its prey, which you could still see twitching.

People, there were piranha, banana spiders, and bullet ants in that rainforest. It seemed to me that if it had a message for our species, it wasn't "love us" but the more administrable "stay away" (to quote one more song from Dad's playlists).

On our way to dinner the last night, I slid my hand on the arm-rail like my mother always told me not to do because of germs. I cannot provide a precise germ count but I do know that I brushed from the arm-rail and unfortunately disrupted exactly one otherwise somnolent, eight-inch tarantula. It flopped on my canvas sneaker, and I froze. People talk of the uncanny valley, how a robot might look very much like a real person but there's just something missing from those eyes. This tarantula was the opposite. Though it looked like a caricature, a stuffed Halloween toy meant to be visible from the sidewalk when hung from thin string, it roiled with life.

I could not breathe and my head throbbed. Had it already bitten and paralyzed me? Would I forevermore stand there on the lodge's boardwalk, or at best be helicoptered out in this stance, back to Mom and Mr. Susco in Pennacook?

I willed my eyes to rise and meet Lena's.

Her grin was wide and triumphant. She reached her shoe over and brushed the tarantula off my sneaker and then, in a second and bolder (because unnecessary) swipe, clear off the boardwalk and back into the muck.

She slapped my back and shoved me.

"I'm starving, Wen. Let's eat."

"The food is great."

It was true but also an incantation. Many of us at the lodge had been saying it to cope, to make it to the exits. I took a step toward the open-air restaurant. At the inner tables, there would be very few bugs to contend with and human light and warmth would reign.

THE END

Acknowledgments

I am most grateful to my family—in particular, Jasmine and our children, Rose and Woody—and for the fine work and friendship of the New Salem Books team: Dan Visel, Dan O. Williams, and Hillary Read. I also thank the early readers of some or all of this: Rose Chen Giroux, Frank Giroux, Mark Travassos, Andrew Palid, Lawrence Pisto, David Zukowski, David Marder, and Morgia Holmes; Stewart O'Nan, Beth Uznis Johnson, and Robert Kerbeck; the Vermont Studio Center (staff, fellow residents, and visiting author Crystal Wilkinson); and the scholars and writers who informed Mr. Susco's lessons and Wendy's thoughts on democracy, including Richard D. Parker, Michael Sandel, Jedediah Purdy, Morris Fiorina, Daniela Cammack, Lane Fargher, Richard Blanton, David Graeber, David Wengrow, Paul Cartledge, David McCullough, William Ian Miller, Donald Kagan, Bernard Knox, and William James Sidis.

About the Author

Eric Giroux wrote the novel *Ring On Deli*, which won the National Indie Excellence Award for Comedy and a *Readers' Favorite* award. His fiction writing has received support from Vermont Studio Center and Millay Arts. A graduate of Harvard College and Harvard Law School, he is a senior counsel for the U.S. Securities and Exchange Commission and lives near Boston with his family.

ATTENTION ALL SHOPPERS!

Enjoy *Zodiac Pets*?
Return to Pennacook for Another Visit with
Eric Giroux's *Ring On Deli*—A Novel about
Supermarkets and Democracy

When the Bounty Bag supermarkets erupt with
worker protests, deli-clerk Ray is forced to take a side.

WINNER,
National Indie Excellence Award for Comedy

**Available wherever books are sold and at
newsalembooks.com. Ring on!**

Printed in the USA
CPSIA information can be obtained
at www.ICGtesting.com
JSHW022304160624
64937JS00006B/9